Another Fine Mess

Fiction: Action and Adventure, Political Intrigue, Alternative History, Romance, Mystery, Thriller, Historical Fiction, Military Fiction, Science Fiction, Naval Battles

Judgment In Time Series

Book I: Judgment In Time
Book II: Imagine A New World
Book III: Another Fine Mess
Book IV: Another Side of Armageddon
Book V: Beyond Extinction
Book VI: Judgment of the Gods

New People Publishing
www.NewPeoplePublishing.com

Editor: Robert Allen Fisher
Cover Art and Full Page Illustrations: Jennifer Cole
Production Design and Illustrations: Tom Hultgren

ISBN-13: 978-0-9835020-4-3
Advance Edition: Trade Paperback

Printed in the United States of America by:
Lightning Source

10 9 8 7 6 5 4 3 2 1

About the Author

Kevin Klesert, a successful independent businessman, has experienced firsthand how small businesses all over the country carried a disproportionate amount of the burden to meet their legal obligations. The steady erosion of Main Street USA under mountains of onerous regulations, licenses, taxes, and fees from Federal, State, and Local Governments have all but destroyed their ability to succeed and turn a reasonable profit.

His intense study of historical trends brought to him the correlation between the downfall of dominant societies of the past and the current struggle to maintain the most noble and ambitious political experiment in human history, the United States of America. He discovered the seeds of ruin were planted within the very generation that launched the United States to world preeminence.

Kevin Klesert's desire to shed light on this dire situation through the means of a thrilling adventure has produced a story worthy of the fight against these negative forces. The ideas for the Judgment In Time Series percolated in his adventurous imagination while he raised his four children and ran an award-winning design and construction company. A 3rd generation native of Southern California, Kevin Klesert imbues his writing with his passion for history, adventure, and fantasy.

Table of Contents

Characters

Enterprise Task Force Main Characters

Rear Admiral UH Retired Sean Phillips – Former Commanding Officer, Enterprise Task Force

Captain Anthony Knox – Taíno God Yúcahu & later Tactical Adjunct to Admiral Sean Phillips

Rear Admiral UH Retired Alicia Calhoun – Former Secretary of Defense

Captain Renée Aslan – Former Naval Attaché to Alicia Calhoun

Captain Carl Eddington – Commanding Officer, battleship USS Missouri

Dr. Rebecca Cutler Eddington, PhD – Comstock Technologies Lead Specter Engineer

Enterprise Task Force Support Characters

Captain Daniel Osaka – Commanding Officer, carrier USS Enterprise

Captain Mark Daily – attack submarine USS Seawolf

Captain *Dash* Nelson – Air Wing Commander [CAG], USS Enterprise

Captain Tobias Harris – Deputy Air Wing Commander [DCAG]

Commander Logan Barrish – destroyer USS Decatur

Commander Andy Gable – cargo ship USNS Amelia Earhart

Lt. Commander Maria Brizuela – fleet oiler USNS Patuxent

Lt. Gloria Layworth – Bridge Communications Officer, USS Enterprise

Commander Michael *Thorny* Thornton – Task Force SEAL Commander

Commander Wesley Brenner – Executive Officer USS Seawolf

Captain Henry Jackson – cruiser USS Shiloh

Captain Randy Stone – Seahawk Pilot on USS Shiloh

Senior Civilian Officer Bradley Franks – fleet oiler USNS Patuxent

Dr. Forrest Phelps, PhD – Comstock Technologies Computer Specialist

Yacahuey – Interpreter for Taíno God Yúcahu, Captain Anthony Knox

Supernatural Characters

Darius – Carl Eddington, Aaron's Father, Sean Anthony's Father

Durius – Aaron's Mother, Ex-wife to Darius

Cromulus – Jesus

Advanced Entity Impersonating Benjamin Franklin

Advanced Entity Impersonating Various David Bowie Personas

Characters Continued

Additional Ship Captains

Captain Gordon Lincoln – cruiser USS Princeton

Captain Frederick Johnson – cruiser USS Chancellorsville

Captain Marlowe Turner – attack submarine USS Hampton

Commander Jonathan James – attack Submarine USS Indiana

Commander Regis Goddard – destroyer USS John Paul Jones

Commander Bob Bremerton – destroyer USS Winston S Churchill

Commander Melissa Wu – cargo ship USNS Cesar Chavez

Lt. Commander James Peck – fleet oiler USNS Laramie

2018 Reality Main Characters

Sean Anthony Eddington – Advanced Entity, Son of Carl and Rebecca

Phoenix – Black Hat Hacker

Adonis – Black Hat Hacker

President Susan Harrison

Aaron Fletcher – Advanced Entity, Chief of Staff to President Harrison

2018 Reality Support Characters

Admiral Dennis Flattery – Director of National Intelligence

General Addison – Commanding Officer, US Strategic Command

General Favors – Air Force Chief of Staff

General Leigh – Commanding Officer, US Northern Command

Pope Leo XVI

Sergei Romanov – Russian Prime Minister

Original 2018 Enterprise Task Force

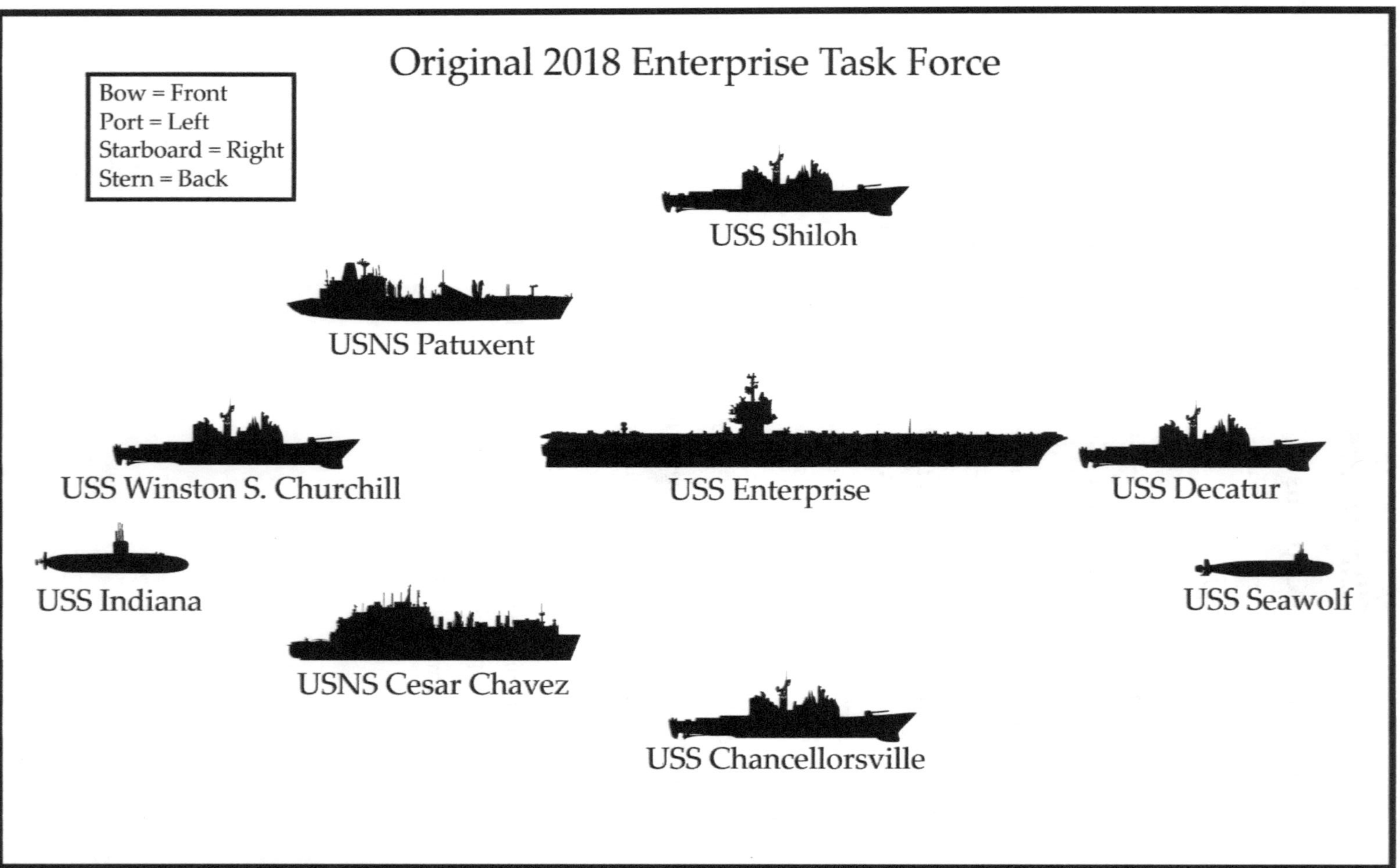

Part I
Another Fine Mess

Taíno Symbol for Angry Sun God

Dr. Rebecca Cutler Eddington had just left the office of the Senate Majority Leader and was about to ask her attaché if they had time for lunch when she noticed the look of surprise on the young woman's face. "What is it?"

"Look at your legs!"

When Rebecca looked down, the unmistakable green mist was working its way past her knees. "Oh sh…" was all her assistant heard before Rebecca vanished. It took the Capitol Police five minutes to revive the aide, and another hour to get anything coherent out of her.

"…it!" As the green mist faded, Rebecca realized she now stood on the bridge of the battleship USS Missouri. She slowly turned her head when the sound of footsteps on the metal deck behind her broke the silence. "Welcome home, honey."

Her joy at hearing her husband, Captain Carl Eddington, suddenly turned to fear. "Please tell me we're still in 1951." Then, in a panic, she scanned the bridge and asked, "Where's Captain Knox?"

Before Carl could tell her Tony had vanished off the bridge moments before her arrival, she rushed to the window just as the green mist rose above the bow of the Missouri. She glared back at her husband. "What about our son?"

"Don't worry about Sean Anthony, he's fine." Carl walked over and wrapped his arms around her. "You're not going to like what happens next, so let me get that out of the way first. As much as I would like to prepare you for what is coming, unfortunately, I cannot. Just know that you are the love of my life and we will be back together as a family if everything goes the way I planned it." Carl then gave her a quick kiss and broke their embrace.

"What are you talking about? Where are you going, and more importantly, where exactly am I going if not with you?"

The green mist had made its way to the front window, which brought Rebecca back into her husband's arms. He grabbed her shoulders to get her full attention. "Everything should work out fine. Don't worry about me, and don't worry about our son.

At that moment, Carl began to fade as Rebecca frantically tried to keep her arms around him, only to fall right through his disappearing image.

As he faded from view Rebecca heard, "All will be made clear in due time. Don't wait up for me."

Dr. Rebecca Cutler Eddington had every reason to be upset. Her first experience with the green mist was back in 2014 while onboard the USS Missouri monitoring the cloaking device known as Specter. During the experiment, an intense interaction between a powerful storm and Specter, the entire Enterprise Task Force suddenly found itself in the Pacific Ocean 2500 miles SE of Hawaii on 3 December 1941 with all of its technology and advanced knowledge.

After defeating the Axis powers in 1942, Task Force Commander Admiral Sean Phillips, Secretary of Defense Alicia Calhoun, and four ships of the Enterprise Task Force returned to the 2014 reality.

Left in charge of the now 6-ship Missouri Task Force, the Admiral's Chief of Staff, Captain Anthony Knox, entrusted Dr. Rebecca Cutler and Commander Carl Eddington to handle diplomacy. Their cautious release of advanced technologies to the world for development allowed progress to move forward seamlessly. Anyone responsible enough to live productive lives now had the opportunity.

For the first time in human history, the world and its myriad of inhabitants struck a sensible balance between exploiting the planet's natural resources and their standard of living. Solar power ruled, and not a single species of animal or plant faced extinction. It appeared the mad rush to Armageddon would have to wait – for now.

For all the positive strides to bring humanity into balance with their environment there was still enough evil left in the world that required the need for national defense. With the use of their superior technology and benign leadership, the world made great strides to give the individual nations room to explore their own methods of self-government. Unfortunately however, there were still despots who controlled over twenty-five percent of the world's population. Six times international coalitions of ships and troops, supported by the Missouri Task Force, interceded to end these misadventures. These conflicts ended within weeks, not years, with all outside forces withdrawn and without any attempts at nation building.

Greed and corruption had not ended, but society as a whole felt empowered as a community and made those who chose to glorify greed stand out. Greed and religious fundamentalism were out and a return to *true* family values was in. The concept of ideal relationships rapidly evolved to include every form of union. Live and let live became the mantra as America finally achieved the promise as the melting pot of the world.

This did not mean that everyone received a free ride. This new world understanding placed a greater burden on prospective parents to have the means to provide food, shelter, and a full time commitment to educate their children. Increased parental engagement for all students and smaller classrooms taught by teachers given the respect and resources to offer a wider range of education, led to the most well-adjusted generation in history.

This is the world Carl and Rebecca Eddington's son presided over.

Sean Anthony Eddington smiled as he looked out on the thousands of eager faces of his congregation. He thought back over the journey that brought him to this place in December of 1971. Back in 1951 when he was 6 years old, his parents had suddenly disappeared as mysteriously as they had appeared. After a year, it became clear that his parents and the US Navy task force from the future would not be coming back. From that moment on, the spotlight of celebrity followed him wherever he went.

Now a young man, he shined brightly under these lights. As one of the most charismatic kids this side of a young Shirley Temple, he used his talents to draw enraptured crowds to listen to his visions of a more enlightened world.

By the time he reached the age of 25, worldwide membership in his megachurch Heaven on Earth surpassed the Roman Catholics. His message was as elegant as it was simple, "Why do you need to bother your God with pleadings for blessings when the Creator has supplied a planet's worth of them?" With that simple message he ushered in environmental policies that forced his acolytes to recognize what most religions ignored; you cannot express your love for the Creator while raping the paradise it created.

This is not to say everyone bought into his revolutionary ideals. It was after the fifth attempt on his life that a growing number of followers came to believe Sean Anthony Eddington was a prophet or the second coming of Christ. That he did nothing to dispel these rumors rankled many from the established religions. All of this led to this moment.

"As I stand in front of you today, I must say how impressed I am with how much we have grown together over the years.

"There are still decades of work ahead to finish cleaning up the mess our forefathers left behind in their headlong rush to exploit the environment and each other. However, I can clearly see I am no longer needed here."

This brought a roar of disapproval from the congregation at the thought of losing their beloved leader. A chant of "Hell no, you can't go" began in the front rows, and like a wave rolled toward the back as more joined in. Within thirty seconds, the chant became so loud passersby heard the roar from a block away.

As the energy to the congregation reached its crescendo, a green mist slowly developed around Sean's shoes and crept up his legs. Those in the front rows with the clearest view stopped chanting, now more curious about what their prophet would do next. The rest of the audience noticed as the mist moved up around Sean Anthony's body. The chanting rolled back like a wave in reverse. When the mist reached the smiling apostle's chest, a stunned silence took hold. After the mist completely enveloped him, it exploded in a blinding green flash, much like a beautiful 4th of July fireworks show.

This energy surge overloaded the building's electrical circuit breakers to leave the entire arena in darkness. No one in the audience spoke or moved for the five minutes it took to get the lights back on. The vacant pulpit brought chaos. Their prophet had ascended.

⬩⬥⬩

Hidden in the bushes, a young boy crouched quietly watching two beautiful Red Macaws perform their mating dance. He had tracked them for the last half hour in the hope the pair would lead him to the rest of their flock. This was the next test of many given by his tribal elders as part of his transformation into manhood. His tribe had learned hundreds of years ago that the best way to survive in their environment was to understand how it worked. This is why little had changed in their way of life for over five centuries; they truly lived in harmony with the universe.

Suddenly there was a loud, cracking boom, accompanied by a bright green flash that startled the boy and sent the Macaws off screaming in protest. It took a minute for his eyes to clear and another to get control of his rapidly beating heart. When he did, he looked back to the clearing to see a strangely dressed man standing in the middle who uttered words the youth could not understand. However, the boy could tell the stranger was not happy.

"God damn it, now where the hell am I?"

Both Captain Anthony Knox and the young boy then heard a rather jovial voice that came from all around them. "You wanted action – action you'll get."

As the muscles in the lower half of the boy's body tightened in preparation, this seemed like a good time to beat a hasty retreat. However, his brain refused to implement the necessary actions to carry out the act. Too stunned to move, the young boy watched as the strangely dressed, light-skinned man's reaction ran contrary to his own. The stranger calmly stood there motionless in the middle of the meadow shaking his head.

Another flash of green light signaled the arrival of a second strangely dressed man, who now stood directly in front of the first. Oddly, the addition of the second stranger made the situation seem less threatening to the boy whose flight instinct shifted into a teenager's reckless curiosity.

Dressed in an 18th Century plum colored silk outfit that accented his plumpness, the second stranger stood about five feet nine inches tall. The bald crown of his head, long, stringy grey hair that fell halfway down his back and the wire-rimmed bifocals identified this Renaissance man as a character right out of America's history.

With a goblet of wine raised in salute in his left hand, Benjamin Franklin offered his right hand to Tony. "Greetings fellow traveler."

Tony ignored the offered hand while his mood whipsawed from irritation, to astonishment, to irritation, and finally to sarcasm. "Benjamin Franklin? What's next, Joan of Arc riding in on a Harley?"

"If that would make this any easier for you, I could make it happen."

Because Franklin stated this with such lightness, Tony believed she was about to appear.

"Will you look at that, didn't spill a drop. Wonderful," Franklin joked while continuing his charm offensive on Tony. "Now that would have been a shame if you considered King Louis offered this fine Bordeaux just before I was summoned here. Would you like a taste?"

Tony chose to ignore the apparition, instead taking a moment to observe his new environment. Dense vegetation surrounded the small clearing where they stood, and the thick humidity made it difficult to draw a deep breath, which suggested they were in a tropical region. As Tony spun around to get a clear view, he could see mountains surrounded them in all directions. When satisfied there wasn't anything threatening for the moment, he turned to confront the smiling Franklin. "Where am I?"

Franklin mimicked Tony's actions by slowly turning around with his hand over his eyes in the well-worn sign for scouting the surroundings. He then leaned in close to share what he discovered. "It appears we are standing in the middle of a clearing surrounded by mountains, and we both seem to be overdressed considering the oppressive heat." He then leaned closer and whispered as if a fellow conspirator. "By the way, we are not alone."

Tony drew his side arm and slowly scanned the jungle. When Tony's gaze reached his hiding place, the boy bolted and quickly disappeared into the dense vegetation.

Tony's brief glimpse of the half-naked youth only added another piece to the mystery. "So I'm in the subtropics with a drunken Benjamin Franklin, and the inhabitants wander around half naked. Great."

Franklin put his hand on Tony's shoulder. "You really should try the wine before I go."

Tony grabbed the offered glass and drained the contents. "What do you mean – 'Before you go?'"

"My apologies, but I was in the middle of a brilliant discussion at the court of the French King Louis XVI in regards to the inalienable rights of man." He smiled and seemed to get lost in the memory before he continued. "Pardon my rudeness; I almost forgot why I was here."

Once again, he leaned in close to Tony. "You are in the year of our Lord 1490 on the island you know as Cuba, and if you want to get off on the right foot, you better catch up with that young man."

Tony's reaction was not what Franklin expected. With a shrug to the absurdity of his situation, Tony turned his back and began to walk away.

"Where are you going? Are you not in the least bit curious as to why you are here?"

Without turning around, Tony answered, "I'm not interested in playing whatever game it is you have in mind, so find yourself another monkey to toss shit at."

"Even if that means you will miss your chance to see Miss Aslan again?"

This stopped Tony's forward movement, but only briefly. Then with fists clenched, he continued without comment.

Franklin looked at his now empty glass and sighed, "Looks like it's time to return to the party."

"Besides," Franklin thought, "Tony isn't going anywhere."

On Monday 7 May 2018, a bobtail cargo van carefully picked its way through the maze of heavy traffic in downtown San Francisco. The radical slopes of the city streets made the driver even more nervous than he already was. Two years of planning were about to play out in the most morally corrupt city in the United States, according to the Christian Fundamentalists who had hijacked the nation's political discourse.

The man driving the van was proud to be the one picked for such a biblical responsibility. Lost in thought, he fingered the large gold cross that hung from his neck. The base commander at Fort Campbell, Kentucky had personally picked him for the mission six months ago when the 24-year-old Corporal's pious fanaticism stood out from all the others. An intelligence specialist had discovered on the soldier's computer links to numerous sites bashing the gay rights movement.

Two blocks ahead lay his destination, the corner of Sodom and Gomorrah, Market St. and Castro. "Good," he thought. "Ten minutes ahead of schedule."

Driving south on Market, he made a left onto Castro and began to look for the miracle of miracles of driving in the crowded city, a parking space. As luck, or fate, would have it, the miracle showed itself 100 feet past the intersection, right in front of an outdoor café. From the looks of it, perfect in every way in the fanatic's warped thinking, as it was full of mortal sinners. He reached for the cell phone off the passenger seat and hit redial. "I have reached the target."

"Both God and your country bless you for the selfless act of courage you are about to perform, Captain." General Addison, the commander of the nation's nuclear arsenal [US Strategic Command] thought it rather humorous that the patsy they picked ate all of this shit up. Captain for a day, and then vaporized.

"God is great, Sir. I am proud to be the instrument of his glory."

"Yes, Captain. Time to fulfill your destiny" The General found it impossible to hide his disdain for the simpleton's psychotic beliefs.

The fanatic hung up, reached into the glove box, flipped the toggle switch that activated a timer on the dash, and began to pray.

For a Monday in the City by the Bay it was fairly crowded with tourists taking in the sites on an unusually comfortable sunny day. Unknown to any of them, the timer counted down to the opening gambit in a race toward a new world order.

When the timer reached ten seconds, the fanatic did the sign of the cross across his chest, jumped out of the cab, and screamed for all to hear, "The day of reckoning has arrived. Time for all of you sinners to burn in Hell!" In this section of the city, it wasn't all that unusual for someone to make such a pronouncement. Not a single person lost a step or took notice when the maniac looked back at the timer on the dash and counted down, "Three, two, one..."

When the timer reached zero, a small electrical current sped its way to the 300-pound warhead in the cargo bay. A nanosecond later, Albert Einstein's equation came to life in a blinding, white flash. The initial nuclear blast immediately vaporized everything within twenty square blocks. As the detonation spread outward, downtown, the Golden Gate Bridge, and the 38th Pier blew apart into billions of radiated pieces.

The blast atomized or burned beyond recognition every living thing within one square mile of the epicenter. The blast did not discriminate between the children in classrooms, the stockbrokers in downtown high rises, the firefighters waxing their engines, nor the attractive transsexual strolling along the Embarcadero.

News of the cataclysmic terrorist attack spread around the world almost as fast as the blast itself. First by tweet, followed quickly by the lurid 24-hour news merchants who threw up video feeds captured in some cases by phones that chronicled the maelstrom before melting along with the hands holding them. This horror show would play out live before a stunned world thousands of times from a thousand different angles over the coming days.

General Addison leaned back with a smile best described as wickedly ecstatic as he listened to the static on the cell phone. "We are ready to move, Sir."

The civilian seated across from him stretched his arms. "Very well General, give the order. Though the urban warfare games provided us the cover to preposition our forces in or around all the targeted urban centers, make sure General Leigh is on schedule. I want to hear the country is buttoned up tight by tomorrow morning."

General Addison felt a need to add, "I have to confess I am concerned about how the troops are going to react to their new orders. When is the President going before the cameras?"

"Don't worry General. This isn't two towers in New York. It was an entire city and most of its population. The troops will obey because that is what you have trained them to do. Besides, polling numbers suggest that over eighty-five percent of the soldiers you are worried about voted for the President's platform."

The shadowy figure who gave the General his orders sat behind the plainest of desks, especially for the highest-ranking member of the President's staff. He derived his pleasures from the subliminal things in life. Aaron Fletcher, Chief of Staff to President Susan Harrison, the first woman President of the United States, had planned this moment for years.

He picked up the secure phone from the desk and pushed the button with the blinking light. "Yes, Madam President. You have contacted the Cabinet. Good. Make sure they understand their only role is to support of your orders."

Though he knew the President wished for more time to soak in the moment, Aaron understood the shocked public needed to see their savior in action as soon as possible. "Yes Ma'am, the reporters are in the press room."

***

After Franklin left, it took Tony only minutes to clear the meadow and reach the edge of the tropical jungle that surrounded him. Before he got to the business of determining his location, he took a quick glance back to verify he was alone After a deep breath, he headed up the only path that held promise.

Tony concluded that animals had traveled this route for years based on the deep ruts worn into the center. "Better not be mountain goats," he joked out loud. With recent experiences as his guide, he drew his Model 1911 Smith and Wesson semiautomatic pistol upon entering the brush. "Better safe than sorry," he mumbled.

Two hours later and drenched in sweat from the tropical heat, Tony found himself half the way up to the summit and severely in need of water. He had gained enough altitude to see the valley below ringed with mountains, the one he climbed rose a good one thousand feet above the others.

While he climbed, Franklin's words about the love he lost, Captain Renée Aslan, pounded in his brain. "She is dead, so how could I possibly see her? Dead is dead, and why am I trying to convince myself of the obvious? Maybe it is because none of this makes sense. Benjamin Franklin, 1490, and nobody else anywhere to be seen? This is nuts."

Hundreds of conflicting thoughts and emotions raced through his mind as hour after laborious hour he ascended the steep incline. Though his legs felt like setting concrete, he continued to force one in front of the other. The occasional sound of rushing water led him to believe the source would cross the path around the next turn.

Stripped half-naked and so dehydrated he could no longer produce sweat, Tony came to the realization the time had come to rethink his plan before the lack of water crippled him. Unfortunately the dense undergrowth that rose like a wall all around the path prevented him from leaving the trail to seek out the source of the lifesaving water.

Finally the stress became too much. "Son of a bitch!" Tony vented his rage by grabbing up every stone he could lay his hands on and blindly pelted the forest before exhaustion drove him to his knees.

"One minute I am seated peacefully in the middle of a war exercise in 2014, the next minute I am in 1941 three days before Pearl Harbor. I lose the love of my life, all of my friends are God knows where, and now it's just me in some theatrical rendition of South Pacific."

Though the rage still burned hot, Tony could see a glimmer of humor, however dark. "At least whoever put me here didn't drop me in the middle of the Spanish Inquisition tied to a stake." The humor quickly passed as his thoughts returned to Franklin's parting words about Renée. "What if she wasn't dead? Hell, at this point I can't be sure of my own mortality. Here I am dying of thirst and talking to myself – again."

In desperation, he sprang to his feet and with an energy he didn't possess decided to push through the unforgiving foliage. After twenty minutes and now hopelessly mired in the tangled jungle, his situation only worsened. Tony's vision began to spin as he crashed face first to the ground. That was the last thing he remembered before he opened his eyes to see a set of feet.

A voice came from above the sprawled out Tony. "I could have saved you all this trouble."

Tony sighed deeply before he slowly turned his head to see Franklin seated above him on a small boulder, a goblet of wine in his hand.

Franklin faced another large boulder draped with a tablecloth and smiled while motioning for Tony to join him. "You know, if you took a good look at your current situation, you might want to at least humor me by listening to my proposal. After all the effort to bring you into this paradise was a rather risky one, monumentally so in fact."

Franklin looked down on Tony from eyes above the set of bifocal glasses, as he picked up a goblet and handed it to him. "The people who inhabit this island paradise are a very noble breed, and we believe you will be exactly what they require."

Tony slowly got to his feet and noticed that next to the bottle of wine was a full spread of cheeses, bread, and more importantly, a bottle of 30 Year Old McCallan Scotch. Without a word, Tony put down the goblet and took a healthy pull from the bottle of Scotch. He put it back on the boulder and in resignation asked Franklin. "You're not going to leave me alone are you?"

"My dear boy, I would just as soon cease to exist than leave you to the fates. You have a treacherous path ahead, and if you were to fail in your quest, it could speed up the end of all human endeavors. You do not want to be the one responsible for such an act of finality, do you?" Franklin exaggerated the last point to drive the guilt home.

"The lives of millions of beautiful people will end, along with the paradise they spent hundreds of years living in harmony with, if you refuse this golden opportunity." Then Franklin's smile disappeared. "You are here to make sure this does not happen."

"What the hell," Tony thought as he grabbed a piece of bread, topped it with a generous slice of the cheese, and finished it off in two quick bites. After another healthy pull from the bottle, he scratched his forehead. "I don't know, don't care, and don't want or need anything from what I can only surmise is another soul-sucking asshole who only wants to ram something else up my ass."

The sudden, sharp pain from the wounds he suffered in the underbrush stopped him short. "Though I have to admit this particular brand of Hell never entered my mind." Tony shook his head as he stood up and walked over to the stream he had spent the last three agonizing hours trying to find. "I suppose you managed some way to keep this away from me." He bent down, took a deep drink, and then began to clean his wounds.

With his back still to Franklin, Tony probed. "So why Benjamin Franklin and not some god from Mount Olympus? One would think if the gods wanted something of me, they would have sent a minion of Zeus instead of a mere mortal such as you. No way I could refuse a god's demand who could turn me to dust if I refused, that is unless the task was to slay a fire-breathing dragon. Better dust than dinner."

Tony laughed at the image of trying to scratch an itch covered in layers of medieval armor while a dragon exhaled fire all around him. "How exactly did they take a leak, a special trapdoor?"

Franklin sighed. "And I thought John Adams was a prig. It was the Middle Ages my dear boy, they wet themselves, and if you only had a dragon to slay, none of this would be necessary."

A grin almost broke across Tony's face, which he quickly hid. "So are you a god, or a minion of Satan? Better yet, am I going to wake up back on the Missouri before leaving San Diego in January 2014, and everything since then has been one hell of a dream? Wait, better yet, I have a brain cloud."

Once again, Franklin ignored Tony's obscure sarcasm while reaching behind the boulder he sat on to pick up a beautifully decorated duffle bag that he tossed effortlessly at Tony's feet. "As I was not the one who packed it, I can only guess you will find everything you need in there."

After Tony walked back from the stream and used the tablecloth to wipe himself down, he took a seat on the boulder that held the Scotch. "All right, I'll bite." After unzipping the bag, he reached in and pulled out a rolled up sheet of parchment. He quickly unrolled it and in a mocking tone wise cracked, "How did you know I wanted this? A map of the Caribbean, and, oh look, it's the navigation map of Christopher Columbus's first voyage of discovery."

Tony placed both his head and hands into the bag and rattled around mimicking a magician about to pull something out of a hat. Then mocking shock, he asked the now bemused Franklin, "Where's the boat? What good is a navigation chart without a boat?"

Franklin smiled, cocked his head slightly, and in the pose most people associate with the man, peered over the top of his bifocals. "That's because one of the reasons you are here is to build a small fleet of them."

Without anger, and more a statement of fact, Tony countered, "Like hell I will."

As before, Franklin casually continued as if Tony had not replied. "Now the boy who you saw earlier in the clearing is important. We need you to prepare for your formal introduction which will happen in the next few minutes." Franklin picked up the bag and began to search it. He pulled out a ruffled shirt, silk trousers, stockings, and an outlandish hat complete with plumage you would associate with a royal portrait from the Middle Ages, all of which he presented to Tony. "And seeing as I am passing you off as a representative of his people's god, you will need to make a good first impression."

"Not going to happen, Benji." Tony took the offered clothes and stuffed them back into the bag before he took another hit off the bottle. "Besides, I make it against my religion to go around impersonating anyone's god in the off chance they do exist and decide to throw lightning bolts my way for doing so. I have a better idea, *seeing as* you appear more than capable, why don't you take the job?"

Franklin smiled and could not resist baiting his companion. "Against union rules." Then in an offhand manner, he changed course. "By the way, what makes you think you are not a god?"

Franklin's abrupt segue took a moment to sink in. "Really? Are you going to go there? Because if I were a god, the first thing I would do is make you disappear." While he tried to sort out what this game was about, Tony hit the bottle one more time.

Franklin smiled at what he saw. "Never mind that for now, because I need you to meet Yacahuey, the son of the chief of the tribe in this area."

On cue a 13-year-old young boy crashed through the underbrush.

The surprise of his appearance caused Tony to draw his pistol. "Who the hell…"

Franklin rushed to stand between Tony and the boy. "Not a threat, Captain." Franklin slowly reached over to gently force Tony's gun hand down before he stood to one side so Tony could get a good look at the youth.

The boy had black shoulder length hair and wore little more than a loincloth. Tony could see by the panic in the terrified boy's eyes and the way he crashed into the clearing that something or someone else controlled his actions. "What are you doing to him? Let him go."

Franklin ignored Tony and spoke directly to the boy. "You have nothing to fear, Yacahuey."

This sparked a reaction from the boy. "Are you Yúcahu?"

Franklin turned and pointed to a surprised Tony.

That they were conversing in English, a language that should be foreign to the boy, and that Franklin's words immediately calmed Yacahuey, Tony realized there was definitely something more to Franklin than just a farcical Founding Father. Tony concluded it would be a good idea to play along for now, but only so far. "English? Really?"

Franklin shrugged his shoulders. "What makes you think we are not speaking in the Taíno dialect? Could you please attempt to be a little more godlike for the boy's sake?"

Tony immediately forgot about playing along. "I can't dictate one ounce of control over my own pathetic existence, and you want me to convince a child that I am his god? Seems to me you should have brought someone from the Catholic Church for the role. They eat this kind of shit up." Only what exited his mouth sounded more like some Gregorian chant.

A thoroughly bemused Franklin drained his wine glass and with a twinkle in his eye playfully pleaded with Tony. "Could you please work with me? Trust me; it will be much easier on all of us if you cooperate. After all, there is all of humanity at stake."

By the puzzled expression on Yacahuey's face during this exchange, it was clear he thought his god spoke in a strange way. However, who was he to question their actions. "Who are you?" was all the troubled youth could get out.

Tony glared at Franklin for a moment. Then ruling against his nature he decided until he discovered what this apparition wanted from him, he needed to keep his emotions in check. "God it is." This time, his words were in crystal clear English. "So what now? Isn't this the part where your magic staff appears out of thin air and the secrets of the universe open up to me?"

"First things first," Franklin replied as he walked up to Yacahuey and in a voice so low Tony couldn't hear, said something that made Yacahuey very excited. The boy then walked over to the food-laden boulder and began to eat.

A curious Tony asked, "What did you say?"

"Well, as you can see I offered him some of our delicious food." Then, with a twinkle in his eyes and a bit of drama for effect, he added, "And that he has been chosen by the gods to serve your every need." Franklin then reacted as if he forgot something important. "Oh, and I might have thrown a few images into his brain about powers he could obtain by doing so."

Before Tony could object, Franklin continued. "By the way, you should know a few things to get off on the right track. I advise you not to ask any questions when you meet the other members of his tribe. As their god Yúcahu, you would not fare well if they knew you do not have all the answers. Further, I am sure you are aware that two years from now Christopher Columbus will arrive. However, you may not know that over the two years following his arrival, he will massacre over ninety percent of the Taíno society, including Yacahuey."

Before Tony could blink, Franklin disappeared in a puff of green mist that left him alone with the boy who was jumpy again by the sudden departure.

"God, I hate it when he does that." He grabbed the bottle of Scotch and raised it to his lips, but put it back down when he noticed the confused and frightened look in the young native's eyes. "I'm such a schmuck."

He took a seat on the rock vacated by Franklin, and motioned the confused and tentative boy to do likewise. "What the hell," Tony thought, "I might as well let him believe I am a god." After several moments of uncomfortable silence, Tony had an idea about how he could take advantage of his first words as a god. He did his best to adjust to the foreign language that came out of his mouth. "Tell me your story."

Yacahuey had no idea what to tell his god who already knew everything about him. Looking down at the ground, he worried his god was testing his faith. Therefore, doing his best to maintain humility, he began. "My family is one of respect among all the people, while I have many years to walk before..."

Tony interrupted. "First off, look me in the eye when we talk. You should not fear me or feel that it offends me for you to look at me." Then reading the boy's obvious confusion he clarified. "Of course I know everything, but I want to hear it from one of my greatest of creations."

Tony could see Yacahuey's mood immediately change with a burst of pride, and over the next two hours, Tony barely got a word in. He thought if only a portion of what he heard was true, he had landed in the middle of paradise. His anger that Franklin forced it upon him, drifted away as his curiosity about such an enlightened people grew.

At 6:00 PM, President Susan Harrison briskly walked into the White House Press Briefing Room and stood behind the podium facing what passed for journalists in the second decade of the

21st Century. "Not half a brain among them," she thought as she glanced around the room.

At five feet six inches tall with salt and pepper hair that accented an air of feminine virility, Susan Harrison had fire and brimstoned her way to prominence. The former Alabama governor and granddaughter of Alabama Governor Frank M. Dixon became the Republican answer to the Democrats nominating a woman for president in 2016. She won the election as the country shifted further to the right. Some cynics say it was because of the perfectly timed terrorist attack that killed fifty Americans at the US embassy in France, and they would be right.

For a nation supposedly dedicated to Life, Liberty, and the pursuit of Happiness, the lunatics now ran the asylum. With the field cleared of all intelligent discourse, the time for the final solution had arrived.

The perfect situation landed in the President's lap when the last of the rational electorate mounted one last gasp with a week of protests that drew over one million to the Washington Mall. Thugs from one of the many state sanctioned security agencies fanned out into the crowds, and once in place began to beat up the protesters. Of course, the co-opted media completely demonized the violent, radical left by proclaiming they had instigated the brawl against the peaceful, America-loving patriots. This perpetrated the lie that the left was a threat to national security.

With the 30-year march of the South to take over control of the nation now complete, she couldn't have picked a better time to level the most liberal of the nation's cities. President Susan Harrison's moment had arrived.

"Good evening, I will be brief. As you all know, one hour ago at 5:00 PM Eastern Standard time, a nuclear device exploded in the heart of San Francisco, California. Initial assessments have established the blast had a 25-kiloton yield, which is slightly larger than the one dropped on Hiroshima, Japan in August of 1945. Early reports and satellite images confirmed the blast radius destroyed much of the city's core, and the death toll will be in the tens of thousands."

"Pause to let the message sink in, while looking properly indignant," scrolled in parenthesis across the teleprompter in front of her.

"We have concluded at this time that this was not an airborne attack, more likely a device that was either assembled locally or transported into the city."

Before she continued, the President took another teleprompter directed moment to let the import sink in on the hundreds of millions of viewers from around the world who hung on her every word. Then her demeanor turned deadly serious as she leaned toward the cameras. "To those of you who fought against this administration's measures to keep this nation safe from the terrorists who wish to destroy our way of life, you now know how misguided your efforts were. Determined to believe your fairytale fantasy of bringing those who strap on suicide vests to the peace table for a round of Kumbaya, the reality is you must shoulder the blame for such criminal ignorance.

After another pause for effect, she straightened up and threw her shoulders back before delivering the knock-out blow. "Martial law is now in place throughout the nation, with every branch of the United States military fully mobilized. As I speak, both the California National Guard, and all federal military bases have mobilized to aid the victims of this, the nation's worst terrorist attack.

"I have also ordered Secretary of Homeland Security Bob March to shut down all national, state, and local transportation systems including air, sea, and rail until further notice. With the threat of further attacks a serious concern, all content supplied by satellite including radio, television, and the internet are now in the hands of federal authorities. For the immediate future, at least until the level of culpability is discerned, the internet and all of its civilian applications will go dark."

"Now show a mother's love to her children," the teleprompter read. President Harrison leaned back as her body relaxed. "This government cannot take the chance that these forms of communications are enabling the terrorists. Chatter picked up over the last week suggests this was a domestic attack carried out by fringe elements intent on overthrowing this nation's constitutional authority. Because the threat appears likely to be a home grown internal one, I have informed Congress that habeas corpus is suspended until further notice per Article I, Section 9 of the Constitution."

Like monkeys in a lab, whose bell had rung announcing dinner, every hand in the room shot up as the reporters hurled forty questions at the President at once. President Susan Harrison waited patiently for the uproar to subside, and continued when it did. "Your reporting on this news conference will be released only after vetting from members of my staff. For those of you here who report by blog, I am sorry, but your stories will have to wait.

"Our government is responsible for the safety of its citizens, and I will do whatever it takes to fulfill my constitutional duty to root out every last one of those responsible for this despicable atrocity." Without taking a single question, she turned and strode out of the room, which left the reporters to do what they do best: speculate, misrepresent, mislead, and pontificate.

◆◆◆

Four hours after Benjamin Franklin's abrupt exit, Tony was dealing with how to react to this latest hallucination and what to do about the restless boy. That wasn't the only problem, as Tony didn't have any source to feed himself, and he knew he couldn't simply hang out in the wilderness waiting for the Franklin character to show up.

"Besides, I'll be damned if I have to depend on a guy who lives on wine to take care of me," Tony yelled out loud.

"Why would anyone have to take care of you Yúcahu?"

Tony cursed to himself. Though he did not want to be mistaken for a god, he figured it would be better to be a god than gutted for being a demon. "Let's go meet the folks, shall we?"

A split second after uttering these words of resignation, the two found themselves standing at the edge of a small village. Yacahuey's eyes went wide, and before Tony could react, the boy ran out of control toward the village yelling loudly, "Yúcahu is here, Yúcahu is here!"

"Just great," Tony muttered. "I hope you know what you're doing kid." As a precaution, Tony drew his side arm and chambered a round before putting it back in its holster. He then removed the bottle of Scotch from the duffle bag and took a stiff drink.

Tony took a moment on the outskirts of the village to get a sense of its size. In a circular pattern, he could see rows of round thatched huts, each big enough to accommodate twenty to thirty people. Based on the number of buildings, the village population probably surpassed 300 individuals. With a slight breeze blowing in off the ocean, the torches that lit up the village cast shadows on the buildings that made the scene appear otherworldly. Tony observed the humble village surrounded by a paradise right out of his childhood dreams; a paradise that Jacques Cousteau and National Geographic had nurtured in him for as long as he had a memory.

"Of course it would look like something out of a Disney movie." Despite his cynicism, the scene in front of him brought out the fantasies of his childhood, though that same cynicism warned Tony never to stop looking for the next threat. "I'm sure the guy running this show is going to love it when he finds out I'm supposed to take over."

He observed shadows subtlety shifting along the furthest fringes. As his eyes adjusted to the images, figures began to take shape.

Silently they worked their way toward him. Tony's hand went to his hip to assure himself, when suddenly Yacahuey rushed out of the shadows. "You must come and prove that you are Yúcahu."

Yacahuey impatiently tugged on his hand to follow. Without any other options, Tony reluctantly prepared to face the people he was pretending to be the god of, without understanding the slightest bit about their culture.

Before Tony could say a word, Yacahuey burst into his fantastic story, though for whatever the reason, the language became foreign to Tony again. "Hey kid."

The boy rushed over to Tony. "You want to say something?"

Clearly English. "Just checking."

Yacahuey waved for him to follow. As he walked toward the gathering group, Tony was surprised to see them bow down. Though the sight was disconcerting, it beat the hell out of the alternative. "So far, so good," he thought.

Suddenly the villagers began to part and in the distance Tony could see a small group of elaborately adorned individuals approaching. Yacahuey noticed them as well, and ran to greet them. Once again, in rapid-fire fashion, he repeated his story. After a moment to listen to their response, he ran back to Tony.

Tony motioned to calm Yacahuey. "Dial it down kid. You're going to fry your little body if you keep this up."

Flustered and confused by Tony's words, Yacahuey decided to ignore them and pointed to the two who stood out from the rest. "This is my mother and father, and they want to know why I believe you are Yúcahu."

"Here we go," Tony thought. He didn't have the slightest idea what their god represented, so he figured if there was any violence associated with the kid's parents, he might become tonight's offering.

As he made his first tentative steps toward his fate, a sudden bright green flash followed by an incredibly loud explosion froze the assemblage. The pressure from the blast sent everyone but Tony and Yacahuey tumbling backward, and as the smoke cleared, Tony's eyes took in a sky full of the brightest colors he had ever seen. When the entire picture became clear it took every ounce of discipline Tony could muster not to burst out in laughter. It was Tony in full native regalia. "Kudos Franklin, now that's funny," he mumbled under his breath.

His next surprise came shortly after the shocked audience recovered from the pyrotechnics when Yacahuey introduced his mother as the village Cacica [female chief]. Her thick black hair that shimmered in the dancing light, dark penetrating eyes, and a body built of wiry muscles described one of the most beautiful women Tony had ever seen. If Tony had to guess her age, he would say twenty, except for the 13-year-old kid by his side.

She whispered to her son, who relayed her question. "She wants to know if you are here to punish or reward us."

"I am here to save you," was Tony's blunt response.

Before Yacahuey could translate, a knife came whistling through the air, aimed directly at Tony's chest. Without time to duck out of the way, Tony tensed for the blow, however, just as it struck his chest, the knife bounced backward in the direction it came from. Then, as if guided by some unknown hand, the blade flew directly at one of the elaborately dressed nobles. It was his turn to frantically maneuver to escape, but to no avail as it headed straight for his throat. Instead of slicing through his neck, miraculously the knifepoint stopped in midair an inch from its target before falling to the ground harmlessly.

This elicited a wave of disbelief through the crowd, who in unison turned to Tony and fell to the ground in supplication. Though once again embarrassed, Tony motioned Yacahuey to him. "First things first; there will be no more kneeling. Get everybody off the ground. Second, who is the guy over there who threw the knife at me?" Though his heart was beating like a hummingbird, Tony maintained the same calm exterior he had developed from his years of commanding impressionable sailors.

Third, but unspoken was to Franklin. "Since you are going to hang around and pull off your bag of tricks, why don't you go all in and play the role yourself?"

"It doesn't work that way," came through loud and clear in his head. "By the way you are supposed to know the guy, and that the knife was coming. Remember, gods don't need to ask questions."

Before Tony could protest the intrusion, Yacahuey's mother yelled, "Bohique!" while pointing to the assailant.

Compelled to explain Yacahuey offered, "Bohique is the village spiritual leader and healer."

"Just great, the guy that is supposed to be the conduit to their god wants me dead," Tony thought, as he worked to figure out what his next move would be. Finally Tony sternly demanded with more confidence than he felt, "Bring him to me."

Four men grabbed the shaken holy man and dumped him at Tony's feet. "Tell him that his punishment will be to give his spiritual authority to you." Tony pointed directly at Yacahuey.

"Me!" Yacahuey had no intention of becoming a holy man.

This demotion brought Bohique into a violent rage. He jumped up yelling as he jabbed his finger at Tony, who could only wonder what profanities the rant contained. As members of the tribe tried to control the former spiritual leader, the third miracle of the evening occurred. In mid-rant, the man simply disappeared, leaving only a small puff of green mist where he had stood.

Without skipping a beat, Tony put his hands on Yacahuey's shoulders and announced for the second time, "You are the voice to my people."

The child still wanted to reject the idea, but since he could be the next one to disappear into the green mist, he hung his head in despair and announced his god's command.

The rest of the evening went in a flash, as first he received the honor to sit on the Dujo [Ceremonial Chieftain Chair] that Tony quickly learned acted as a throne.

Three hours later, with the wild celebration winding down, the beautiful Cacica spoke to her son.

"My mother wants to know if she should arrange a *liani* for you."

Before Tony could worry about what a *liani* was, green mist enveloped him. When it cleared, he found himself seated in a comfortable reclining chair in the middle of a well-appointed room set in a 21st Century ranch style home.

"A *liani* is a wife. She thought it would please you." Franklin sat across from Tony in front of a fireplace where a small fire burned, of course with the ever-present glass of wine in one hand, and now a pipe in the other.

"What a wonderful idea. While we're at it, why don't you send me to the 1950s and you could hook me up with Marilyn Monroe. Why stop there. Cleopatra, Mata Hari, what about Dorothy from the Wizard of Oz?"

"A simple thank you would have sufficed. You needn't be so truculent."

Satisfied he had made his point, Tony nonchalantly looked the room over. "Are we playing contemporary suburbia now? Where are Claire and Phil Dunphy?"

Once again, Franklin ignored Tony's sarcasm. "I thought it would help us both if you had a touch of your old life to relax in." Franklin walked into the adjoining room as he continued. "We are sitting deep in the jungle, about ten miles southeast of the village."

Tony jumped out of the chair and followed. "Though I know I am sounding like a broken record, why the hell don't you play their god instead of me? It seems to me you have the tools to do a much better job than me."

"Alas, it is not my decision to make dear boy. You like your new digs?"

"Digs? What's next? Are you going to start riffing a rap?" Tony stopped short when he saw the pictures on the fireplace mantle. Among pictures of the ships Tony commanded, were pictures of Sean, Alicia, and Renée in happier times, though the effect on him right now was anything but happy. "Is this your idea of a sick joke?"

"Not at all. I thought they would help bring you a sense of normalcy. You can make any changes you wish. You will find all of your favorite foods, and there is an entertainment system in the playroom where you can find all of your favorite music, movies, and television shows. You will also find a shop where you can build the weapons you will need to manufacture. I have also given you a fully stocked bar, but I would prefer you moderate when in contact with the Taíno."

"So if you thought of everything, where is the Jacuzzi?"

Without looking up, Franklin pointed with his pipe. "Next to the Koi pond out back."

Tony walked over to the bar, picked up a bottle of Jack Daniels Single Barrel, filled a tumbler, and sat back down. "So what do you mean when you say I have a chance to see Renée again, or will I start speaking in gibberish again for asking?"

"I said there was an opportunity to return the lovely lady to you. I didn't, nor will I say now what that opportunity entails." Franklin ran his thumb and index finger across his closed lips and stated, "Sealed. Now can we get to the business at hand? We need to work out how to prepare for the arrival of Columbus." Franklin paused for effect before he continued. "Unless of course you want to let these wonderful people down."

"You do realize that you have used this tired bit every time I get pissed off. How about instead of what you want, I try something different to break up the monotony like teach the women how to dress like Miley Cyrus and create the first vacuous celebrity for celebrity sake fad. Can't you see them all shaking their asses at you on the beach?" Tony turned around and wiggled his butt to drive the vision home.

"Thank you for that horrible visual. On the other hand…"

Tony didn't need to hear the rest. "God I hope you're still not here when I wake up," Tony said as he walked out of the room shaking his head.

From behind the closed door, Franklin heard him mumble, "We'll continue tomorrow, just don't make it too early."

"I always get what I want dear boy," Franklin whispered.

"I heard that asshole."

A week later, after Tony had worked out the designs, he instructed Yacahuey to send word to the surrounding villages. "I need long boats, ship builders, weavers, and warriors to gather at the bay [currently Levisa Bay, Cuba] directly north of your village."

The plan was to modify fifteen longboats with higher sides, cannon ports, masts, and black sails. Tony would design and build the cannon and small arms in the shop at the house. Franklin would later have them materialize at the shipyard on the bay.

The attack plan was simplicity itself. The Taíno would quickly make short work of the Europeans, as they stood off pounding the mostly unarmed Caravels with their cannon. The object was to kill without quarter every invader before they got anywhere close to land. Franklin had made it clear that any physical contact could transfer to the Taíno the small pox the Europeans carried.

On the morning of May 8, 2018, Rear Admiral Sean Phillips USN, Retired and former US Secretary of Defense, Rear Admiral Alicia Calhoun Phillips USN, Retired were in the front room of their suite at a small Bed & Breakfast in Cambria on the central coast of California. The joy of a relaxing champagne breakfast while on their honeymoon ended when they heard the emergency broadcasts proclaiming martial law had come to the streets of America.

Sean took a sip and calmly asked his new bride, "How long do you think it will take before they come for us?"

Alicia smiled for a moment, but could not hide her fear that circumstances would soon tear the newlyweds apart from each other. "I'm surprised we weren't the first ones on their list."

"Coup d'état 101, my dear. Control the media first, while you have emissaries burning the phone lines to ensure the rest of the world they are in control, and don't even think about messing with us. At the same time, our *beloved leader* has to make sure the thousands of officers in all branches of the military will follow the orders of the cowards at the top. You can be sure the ones who have been thoroughly vetted are surrounding Washington right now."

Alicia was not in the mood to hear from the book of emergency contingencies. "So, would it do us any good to disappear? I've had visions of hiding out with a militia survivalist group living off the land in Idaho."

"I guess for the sake of putting up a fight, we should."

Before either one of them could say another word, out of the corner of their eyes that familiar green mist appeared along the baseboard of all four walls.

"You've got to be kidding me," was all they could say before…

Since their return from 1942 to 2014, scientists and technicians combed over every aspect of the four ships of the Enterprise Task Force that had returned. A turf war between the powers at Homeland Security and the Navy only ended when the President decided the Navy would maintain the ships as a group. To avoid the spread of rampant speculation throughout the fleet about their trip to 1941 and into 1942, the President had decided it was better to keep the crews together on their ships. Almost all the officers and sailors, who were part of the trip into what scientists acknowledged as an alternate reality, remained aboard. Ironically, they spent their only liberty in Guantanamo Bay, Cuba, the location of the base they would have established if not for their sudden return to 2014.

The Navy repaired the battle damaged Decatur, Chancellorsville, and Enterprise, while Comstock Technologies installed a new second-generation Specter cloaking system on each of the ships of the task force. Technicians had completed diagnostic tests at Norfolk Naval Base and the task force had taken on supplies in preparation for a long sea trial when the bomb exploded in San Francisco.

There were many in the Navy going through some serious soul searching as to whether to obey the draconian orders or not. Any thinking man of conscience would know a coup was well under way. Everyone with the Enterprise Task Force knew without a doubt, which way the *hand-picked-by-Washington* Admiral in command and his Chief of Staff felt.

As part of the President's declaration of martial law, the US Navy sent orders to surface Commanders to enforce quarantines in United States territorial waters. Heading out into the Atlantic, the Enterprise Task Force gathered speed to carry out the disturbing orders. From the bridge of the Enterprise, Captain Daniel Osaka could see the Decatur on station in front, the Shiloh to port, and the Chancellorsville to starboard. Captain Daily of the Seawolf had reported in an hour earlier from his position a mile ahead of the task force.

Lt. Layworth [Lt. Gloria Layworth, Bridge Communications Officer, USS Enterprise] called out, "CIC [Combat Information Center] reports the Seawolf picked up six contacts twenty miles to the east; one contact submerged."

"General Quarters," Admiral Feller ordered.

"Aye Aye Admiral, General Quarters," Lt. Layworth responded.

Captain Osaka picked up a set of binoculars and trained them on the contacts. Moments later, he had trouble controlling his breathing when the unmistakable shape of the grand WWII battleship USS Missouri BB-63 appeared out of a rainsquall.

"Admiral, I think you better take a look at this."

When there wasn't a response, Osaka turned around to see Sean and Alicia standing where Admiral Feller should have been, dressed in bathrobes, each with a glass of champagne in their hands. Osaka looked around for Admiral Feller, only he was no longer there. He then understood, and with a big smile, Captain Osaka saluted. "Welcome back Admiral, Madam Secretary."

"Admiral is on the bridge!" the Officer of the Watch joyfully sang out.

Admiral Sean Phillips was the first to react to their latest experience with the time and location shifting green mist. He directed his comment on this latest trip to his wife. "You would think whoever is pulling the strings would have at least given us time to get dressed."

"It could have been worse," Alicia replied. "Be thankful we were not in the middle of something even more embarrassing."

"Fortunately for us, the President's decree put us off," Sean replied with a wink before addressing Osaka. "Good to see you again, Daniel. Oh, and a *Captain* too, I see. What are your orders, Sir?"

Somewhat embarrassed, Osaka returned to his military discipline. "In addition to the Enterprise, Chancellorsville, Decatur, and Seawolf, the task force is fully complemented with a new cruiser, destroyer, attack submarine, two supply ships, and a full air wing. We left port early this morning fully supplied for the long haul. And in case you are wondering, Sir, Captain Folger retired.

"With Admiral Feller gone," Osaka continued, "I am sure the mystical powers that be will have your wardrobe fully stocked in the Admirals Quarters in case you would like to dress for the occasion. However, before you go I have some exciting news. The Missouri, John Paul Jones, Princeton, Hampton, and the two supply ships are dead ahead and closing."

Alicia rolled her eyes. "And I suppose Winston is bringing up the rear in a row boat."

"Actually Ma'am," Osaka interjected with a grin, "our new destroyer, the USS Winston S. Churchill, *is* bringing up the rear."

"Thank you Daniel," Sean acknowledged struggling to maintain a straight face. Excited that he might see Tony again for the first time in four years, Admiral Phillips asked the bridge radio operator to contact the bridge of the Missouri.

On the Missouri, with both the task force CO [Commanding Officer], Captain Anthony Knox, and the ship CO, Captain Carl Eddington, no longer aboard, the experienced crew on the bridge knew exactly who was in charge. The XO [Executive Officer] turned to Rebecca. "I am *sure* this call is for you."

"Who is it?" she asked.

Without a word, the smiling XO handed her the phone.

Sean could barely control his emotions. "Tony?"

"I don't believe it, it's Admiral Sean Phillips. Truthfully, I thought I would never hear your voice again. By the way where is here?"

"You're back home in the year 2018 Rebecca. Are you in command of the Missouri? Where did Tony and Carl go?"

"They both disappeared off the ship right before we showed up here." Rebecca made sure her voice didn't portray her concern over her husband's disappearance.

Sean on the other hand didn't bother hiding his disappointment. "Disappeared? What do you mean disappeared? Disappeared as in gone overboard or like poof to new location disappeared?" It didn't make sense to Sean that of all the people who were part of the original task force left in 1942 that Tony would be the one who didn't make it back.

"Of course they didn't go overboard silly. I am so sorry Sean, but I don't have any more information about Tony, or Carl. I hoped they would be with you."

"Why would you think that? We haven't seen them since we were separated, and that was over four years ago."

This news rattled Rebecca. "Four years? We have been in the 1942 reality for nine. Anyway, so where are you guys headed?" While on the surface Rebecca maintained her usual cool, inside her mind raced as she considered the implications of this latest twist of fate.

"Hell if I know, Rebecca. Alicia and I were at a Bed & Breakfast in Cambria, California only a few minutes ago."

Upon hearing Rebecca's name, Alicia grabbed the phone from a surprised Sean. "Instead of trying to make any sense of what's going on now over ship to ship, why don't you come aboard the Enterprise so we can compare notes?"

"See you in a flash," Rebecca replied, still struggling with her emotions. She was eager to see her friends, but extremely pissed off that Carl had gone only he knows where.

Alicia hung up the phone, and whispered to Sean. "We don't know jack shit about our current trip down the rabbit hole, but I'm sure glad Rebecca showed up for the ride. Let's go get dressed."

"Good idea."

After a trip down one level from the bridge, and twenty feet to port, they reached a familiar door.

"I feel like I should carry you over the threshold," Sean whispered in her ear.

She slapped his hand away when he tried. "Don't be silly. Shall we see what changes the former occupant made to our quarters?"

Alicia grabbed his hand and pulled Sean through the door.

In the Admirals Quarters, as Captain Osaka had surmised, Sean and Alicia found everything they needed, and not a trace of Admiral Feller. They quickly dressed and headed back to the bridge.

"Admiral," Osaka reported, "considering it appears we are about to embark on another ride and Admiral Feller and his Chief of Staff are missing, I took it upon myself to order the Missouri Task Force ships to take up their original positions in our formation. I thought it wise to put the time shift experienced commanders and crews in the lead. Further, I informed Dr. Cutler to bring Dr. Phelps along with her since Specter is all new here."

"Good thinking, Captain. I am sure the new ship Captains and crew are wondering what is going on as well," Sean acknowledged.

Alicia turned and stared out through the front window. Her thoughts turned to their long-lost friends, Captain Anthony Knox and Captain Renée Aslan, the friend she lost to redneck assassins while they were still in 1942. "Why isn't Tony on the Missouri?" she asked to no one in particular.

Sean walked over to her and wrapped his arms around her. "I'm sure he is somewhere raising hell trying to bend the will of everyone around him."

"You can be sure about that," she agreed.

Sean's reassuring words were much closer to the truth than he could imagine.

As the two halves of the original Enterprise Task Force formed up, Specter's electromagnetic generators on all ships began to spin into action without commands from those monitoring them. Once again, the familiar green mist crept up the hulls of the ships, and in a blinding flash of light, they were on the move again.

◆

The Taíno were skilled blue water sailors long before Tony popped in eighteen months ago in 1490. Although the construction of the long boats was completed, training the crews for war lagged behind Tony's self-imposed deadline. After two months of abject failure and frustration, he was ready to give up. One particularly bad day included an overloaded cannon that exploded when fired, killing one of the men, and injuring five others. That evening his frustration boiled over, and he was in the process of trashing his home when Franklin arrived.

"As entertaining as it is to watch you take your anger out on this beautiful home, I do believe we would be better served if you discovered a less aggressive approach in how to train our passive friends."

This only prompted Tony to use the 12-gauge shotgun Franklin had given him on his last birthday to destroy the 98" wall-mounted flat screen display, before turning to face the ever-jolly Franklin. "You just don't get it. As insane as it is to state, these people do not possess the necessary DNA to go out of their way to murder other people. They are clueless about the greed and avarice that rules in the name of the so called civilized world's God, and that the people from that world are coming to kill or enslave them."

Tony paced back and forth across the living room. "Believe me, if alien invaders sailed across the ocean to kill everyone I loved, and the only thing available was a rowboat armed with a cap gun, I would row it out to defend my own. How have they managed to stay alive for so long? Besides, I believe part of the problem is they think with their god on the ground nothing bad could possibly happen. They merely shrugged their shoulders when the cannon blew their friend to bloody pieces, as if this is what I wanted, so everything is cool. You have an answer for that?"

"You asked how it is they cannot see what is right in front of them." To Tony's disgust, Franklin miraculously put the monitor back in one piece, and an odd-looking flightless bird walked across the screen. "Take the Dodo bird as an example. Perfectly happy and content, living generation after generation without a care in the world, and along comes a couple of rats, hitchhiking their way across the ocean in the hold of a ship. Well, these rats and a few of their cousins decided to jump ship on Dodo Island, where they discovered a tasty little morsel in the form of Dodo eggs. Then voilà, no more Dodo birds, because they never had to face a predator higher up the food chain, and could not adapt in time. This is the same reason the Taíno went extinct as a society, and why you are here to stop the rats from coming ashore."

Tony looked at Franklin in stunned silence for a moment. "That is the lamest analogy I ever heard."

A fire erupted in the fireplace as Franklin snapped his fingers. He sat down on the couch that faced the fireplace and lit his pipe. "You liked the story of the Dodo when you were a child, as memory serves me."

"You have an answer for everything don't you?" In resignation, Tony plopped down next to Franklin.

"I do have an answer for almost everything. Gather the people together tomorrow morning, and I think the right motivation will arrive in the nick of time." Franklin put his half-finished wine glass on the table. "In the meantime, let us watch some more of that show Leverage. I love that girl Parker."

"I'd rather put a bullet in my head." Disgusted, Tony got up and stormed out of the house.

Franklin shrugged. "Suit yourself."

True to his word, the next day Franklin schooled the Taíno in the ways of the wicked world. Gathered on the sand looking out over the bay, and unsure what to do next, Tony was about to summon Yacahuey to translate, when a large image filled the sky. Unfortunately, this time it would not be a fireworks show to awe the audience. Instead, images depicting the first year after Columbus landed on their shores played on for twenty minutes in gruesome detain. Tony could see the shock on their faces as tens of thousands were tortured to death, died of disease, or crushed under the burden of slavery. It did not take any time at all when it ended to convince them of the need to learn the ways of war.

While he watched their genocide, Tony was apprehensive. He knew none of those who were to be involved in the coming battle had the slightest idea of how to go about harming another human being. "Are we saving the Taíno," he wondered, "or destroying the very aspect of their culture that makes them unique, their capacity to live in harmony?" The hard truth was after 500 years of innocence, the images had begun the process of destroying something incredibly rare.

When the sky scenes faded away, the men rushed out to their war boats for training exercises. Silence and determination replaced their usual easygoing pace and conversations.

❦

When President Harrison returned to the Oval Office from the press conference, Aaron was there, seated on a couch. "That ought to do it," he observed. "Nice job."

"For the first time in years, I can breathe. Twenty years of planning, and finally the day has come where we can fix everything that is destroying this great country without the bother of phony consensus." The seventh generation of southern autocrats honestly believed she was merely an instrument to restore the principles the Founding Fathers wrote into the Constitution.

As was the emotional makeup of the 45th President, this euphoria quickly dissipated when the implications of what they had unleashed hit home with a rising sense of panic. "Are you sure no one can track the material? Where is the Vice President? Why isn't he here?"

"Settle down Susan. I have accounted for everyone and everything. Anyone who could possibly expose what you have done have been neutralized, or are about to be." Aaron stated this as if eliminating other human beings was as natural as using a spoon with your soup.

He had to get her under control. Though Susan Harrison became the face of the new America, she was not his first choice. The very passion she possessed that helped to get her elected had the equal ability to send her spiraling into paranoia. "Take a break. We need you rested and alert over the next couple of weeks, so have a drink and relax. If you need anything, I will be in my office coordinating our troop movements with the General."

"Thank you Aaron. Sound advice as usual."

As she reached for the phone to share her concerns with her doctor, who always prepared the perfect cocktail injection to balance her out, Aaron made his way out of the room.

"I will be so happy when I no longer need her around," he thought as he entered his office and closed the door, leaving behind the two new Secret Service agents assigned to protect him. In fact, the beefed up White House security had three special forces teams positioned throughout the grounds.

By the next morning, everything was still going to plan. With martial law now in effect across the nation, units of the United States Northern Command [NORTHCOM] had locked down the major cities along both the East and West Coasts of the country.

The Commander in Chief had complete authority and would do everything in her power to see that the right of habeas corpus became only a distant memory. With the use of the military might to cower the population, the government of the United States of America now resided in the category of the third world, a banana republic.

At DEFCON 4, United States ambassadors around the world warned any government foolish enough to believe the United States was vulnerable that any perceived threat could precipitate a nuclear response. With the world's only superpower turned inward, violence around the world escalated as threatened despots let their dogs loose. Third world countries around the globe began a wholesale roundup of their political challengers. In another nod to the severity of the crisis facing a world that spent the last two decades on the brink of chaos, the destruction of San Francisco pushed it into the abyss. All around the world, thousands of dissidents simply disappeared as foreign governments followed the lead of the wounded giant.

In the extreme cases in China, Russia, and throughout the Middle East shallow mass graves buried their outspoken critics. The old school approach of crisis government returned with a vengeance. The Great Experiment in government was officially over, despots ruled the day, and if you didn't get with the program, a shallow grave was guaranteed to you.

Alone in his office Aaron Fletcher had difficulty holding back the satisfaction he felt. The ongoing War on Terrorism, now in its 17th year since 9/11 had made all of this possible. Aaron smiled, thinking about what a valuable tool The Patriot Act was to put the veneer of legality on the President's actions, and his behind the scenes role in it. The rulings of the Supreme Court over the last twenty years had sacrificed the ideals of individual liberty for the supposed common good of the republic, meaning corporate bottom lines. Since Congress had lost its purpose, there was no one left to challenge her draconian escalation.

Leaning back in his chair with his hands behind his head and his feet on his desk, he thought, "What's the use of having trillions of dollars of high-tech killing machines, if you can't take them out for a spin once in a while?" Chills of excitement ran up and down his body, as he contemplated his next move.

Unfortunately, for most overly ambitious psychopaths, this is usually when the floor drops out. For the President's Chief of Staff the first such crack appeared with a phone call from the President's Secretary requesting his appearance in the Oval Office. When he arrived, Aaron recognized the President's mental state had not changed, so he quickly shut the door behind him. He knew what she needed, but he didn't have the time, or the inclination for such carnal remedies.

The President's mental state dropped further when she saw the look on his face meant he would was not there to comfort her. She quickly recovered and tried to get herself together. "If he can't give me a few minutes of private time, the hell with him," she thought.

Aaron ignored the tension in the room. "Leigh giving us trouble again, Madam President?"

General Nathaniel Leigh commanded NORTHCOM, and though extremely loyal, Harrison questioned his stomach for confronting unarmed civilians with M1 Abrams battle tanks and Predator drones.

The manic President took great glee in reporting something her sociopathic Chief of Staff didn't already know. "Nope, it's the Navy. The Enterprise Task Force reported that the missing ships from 2014 had appeared and formed up with them. Before Naval Command could respond, the entire combined task force, including the missing ships, disappeared."

Though Aaron knew the answer, he had to be sure. "When you say disappeared, do you mean flash gone or cloaked Specter gone?"

"A repeat of 2014, Aaron. Their last report to Naval Command was of a green mist rising around the ships, then no contact."

The Chief of Staff was livid and more at himself than the President. "How could I have not seen this coming, or better yet who was…" He stopped short and changed gears. "What about the attack subs?"

This was more than the President's fragile mind could handle. "I am telling you that an entire cloaked United States naval task force can pop up God knows where or when, and all you can ask is 'Where are the submarines?' Who the hell cares when an entire carrier strike force is unaccounted for?"

Aaron's first reaction was to strangle the crazy bitch, but pragmatism prevailed. In a calm voice he definitely didn't feel, Aaron counseled, "It's not a problem. If there were anyone trying to subvert our plans, I certainly would know. Besides, they are no threat to us if they are stuck somewhere else in time and space. Based on the after action report of their last adventure through time, nothing that occurred there affected anything here. They probably have more to worry about than we do."

This was one of the rare moments where President Harrison witnessed the master of deception clearly outclassed by outside forces. "I was always a little curious if you had a hand in what happened in 2014, and now I know. You had nothing to do with it, which means there is obviously something greater than *you*."

The President had delivered a kidney punch to her Chief of Staff. It was one thing for Aaron to have to deal with his adversary's opening response to his power play, and quite another to have this imbecile mock him. Struggling to keep from tearing her apart limb by limb, he responded through gritted teeth. "Let me remind you that all it takes is one phone call to have you imprisoned and then on trial for the murder of tens of thousands of men, women, and children."

Aaron walked around the desk and stood menacingly right next to Harrison. "Or you can be the face that leads the world into decades of stability that will place you with the likes of Washington and Lincoln." Then invading her personal space further, he concluded with menace, "So don't fuck with me."

President Susan Harrison literally fell into her chair speechless as Aaron stormed out of the room. He didn't believe in coincidences, so he had work to do to find out exactly where those ships went, and how to respond.

* * *

Franklin made his first appearance in six months interrupting Tony's early morning walk. "They will arrive in three days," he informed him.

Tony's stride didn't change. "Right when you told me six months ago."

"Having any doubts about what you have to do?" Franklin looked closely for Tony's reaction.

"Let's see, the death of maybe a hundred Taíno warriors to save millions. I can live with that." As much as he never admitted to it, over the last two years Tony had fallen in love with the Taíno people he now called family. Though he kept up the illusion of a benevolent god, he had grown into the role, and nothing would stop him from saving their way of life. He knew he was on the right side of the angels regardless of his European heritage.

"You do have to admit I have given you the chance over the last two years to heal your injured spirit. Care to share a drink to your success?" As always, when Franklin played this game, a bottle of Scotch would appear in Tony's hand, and a goblet of wine in Franklin's hand. As they clicked glass, Franklin could not pass up ribbing him on another issue. "I cannot understand why you stay away from all of those beautiful women."

"That's because I am not a lecherous old man like you. So now that the day is almost here, are you finally going to tell me where all of this leads to?"

"Where is the fun in knowing your future? Even I don't know how this is going to play out. What I can tell you is that everything you think you know is probably wrong." Franklin stopped to sip from his wine glass before continuing. "I do know, however, that once you make your move on Columbus and his ships, you are not going to have time to think about the future, because you will be the one creating it."

Franklin's cryptic statement left Tony perplexed. "What do you mean by that?"

"Sorry, not at liberty to say."

"As usual, you're a fountain of contrary news."

"Glad not to disappoint you. Have another drink."

Franklin's words were on Tony's mind later that morning as

Yacahuey, using Tony's words, addressed the men and women who would crew the ships. Yacahuey had matured so much in the last two years that Tony was sure the teenager had figured out his god was merely flesh and blood.

Yacahuey motioned to those present for silence, and began to speak. "We must destroy these invaders before they can get anywhere near us." Pointing to Tony, he continued, "Yúcahu warns of all our deaths if any one of these demons from across the great ocean with their evil magic came into physical contact with us."

When an image formed in the sky, the Taíno became restive, anticipating another round of gruesome pictures from their god on his magic screen. They were not wrong, for over the next half hour they sat in stunned silence as they watched once again all they loved massacred by the Spanish conquerors. Overall, it was much more graphic and brutal. As he watched the hostility and rage build up among his people, it became the worst half hour Tony had ever endured in his life.

"You son of a bitch," Tony muttered.

"Would you rather see history repeat itself?" Franklin rebuked, this time without his usual humor.

Tony nodded to Yacahuey, who again addressed the assemblage. "We have two days of sailing to reach the islands to the northeast where we will camp. That night we will sail out to meet the devil ships and destroy them."

To that, the Taíno let out a terrifying, raging howl so contrary to their usual demeanor it made Tony cringe. The time had arrived to face the Europeans.

"When the Taíno sight Columbus, I will have you appear on the deck of your flagship, the Renée Aslan," Franklin announced.

Tony nixed that idea. "Always with the bullshit. If I leave them on their own, they will more than likely forget everything and paddle away as fast as they can at the first sign of trouble. Without their leader, there isn't any way the sailors and warriors could think clearly after being whipped into a fury by the threat of their annihilation."

At this point, Tony finally won his first argument with Franklin when he reluctantly agreed to let him accompany the flotilla out of the bay. "Just make sure you don't get yourself killed. I would hate to have wasted the last two years for nothing."

"You're all heart."

An hour later, the fifteen ships that made up the armada sailed out of the bay. It took two days to reach the north shore of what is now Samana Cays in The Bahamas. Here they joined their Taíno cousins from the neighboring islands, who worked much smaller craft. Their role would be to serve as scouts and decoys. Records that Franklin brought to Tony's attention, declared Columbus had sighted land at 2:00 AM on 12 October 1492. The night attack was set to begin in the early morning prior to first dawn while the Nina, Pinta, and Santa Maria were still fifty miles offshore.

With the news that the Enterprise Task Force was loose in time once again, Aaron Fletcher had to act. He picked up the phone to call the Secretary of Navy, but before he could get an outside line, there was a knock on the door. He put the phone down and sat down in his chair expecting it to be his aid. "Enter, Timothy."

There wasn't any response so he repeated, "Damn it Timothy, I don't have time for this." Once again, there was another knock on the door.

This time the agitated Chief of Staff jumped out of his chair, eager to vent some of his current anger on someone. However, when he jerked the door open, all he saw were the two Secret Service agents standing halfway down the hall. "Who was just knocking on my door?"

"Sir, there hasn't been anyone in the hall since you entered your office."

Aaron closed the door more agitated than before. Still facing the door, he didn't notice the green mist that was forming around one of the chairs behind him. When he finally turned around a young man sat in his chair, relaxed with his legs crossed, and wagging his index finger back and forth – shame, shame it spoke.

Aaron smiled at the intruder. "I was wondering when you were going to get involved. Comfortable?" He tried to open the door, but quickly discovered as he tried to turn the knob that it was fire to his touch. Aaron looked down at his smoldering hand. "Cute. Is this where we start to throw lightning bolts, and rain fire and brimstone around each other's heads?" He showed Sean Anthony Eddington that his hand had healed.

Closely watching the man, Sean Anthony calmly responded, "Nobody will come to your rescue when this is over and I have crushed you. You know, for someone who finds it so easy to murder thousands of innocents without remorse, my bet is it won't be that difficult to defeat you."

Without warning, Aaron threw his hands in Sean Anthony's direction, releasing a bolt of energy that should have blown him to pieces. Instead, the attack harmlessly bounced off some kind of force field, which sent Aaron flying across the room in the other direction.

Sean Anthony took great pleasure in the look on his enemy's face as he flew into the wall. "It appears that you still have much to learn grasshopper." He then calmly motioned for the humiliated Chief of Staff to take the seat opposite him. "As much fun as it would be to enjoin you in a personal battle royal, we both know nothing will be resolved in that manner. It is past time that a final decision is reached, one in which one of us is simply not going to get what they want."

Aaron picked himself up, and brushed smooth his suit. He smiled at the thought of the two enjoined in a life or death struggle, however, that would set back the plans he already had in motion. "And I presume it is your father who is up to his old tricks again. It seems rather bold of Carl to entrust someone as inexperienced as you to challenge me. So when did he send them this time?"

Sean Anthony ignored Aaron's question, and put his feet up on the simple desk. "You know what I enjoy the most about my job, Aaron?" He could not resist prolonging the Chief of Staff's frustration and rage. "I love to get into the middle of a tortured mind like yours and stir up all that poison to find the true insanity. However, don't worry, I am not here to fight you, only kick you around a bit. Seriously, have a drink and relax. I will let you know when it's going to hurt."

A tumbler of Aaron's favorite Vodka appeared in his hand, from which, contrary to the wariness he felt, he calmly took a drink. "Nice touch, though I did expect someone with a little more authority than you, considering the chaos I unleashed. I thought a little bomb going off in the middle of one of the United States' biggest cities would probably be cause for taking a closer look. Did your daddy send you to cover his ass for his earlier impetuous actions in 2014?"

Sean Anthony ignored the dig. "Here is what is going to happen. Events beyond your pathetic understanding are unfolding throughout time and space that will render your horrific abuses irrelevant. Unfortunately, when you detonated that bomb, you put things on a faster track, so I am here to slow you down a bit. Capish?"

"You can try, but I doubt you are up to it."

The man was so predictable. "You know all of those twisted little S & M adventures you liked to practice on the many under age, defenseless altar boys your aids used to bring around? Instead of those wonderfully creative torture sessions, how about a role in the Persian King's harem as eunuch, oh let's say 11th Century Constantinople?"

This prompted laughter from Aaron. "And you think you're the one who is going to put me there? Besides, how else do you explain my presence here? A breach of an immutable law perpetrated by dear old dad has allowed me the room to mix things up a bit, and maybe even bring an end to this misguided experiment. By the way, where is the old fart? I know someone who would simply enjoy a sit-down with him."

"Well, you have painted a clear picture of your intentions, so let me enlighten you about mine." Sean Anthony stood up, and walked over to Aaron as he continued speaking. "The beauty of my job is that you have done most of my work for me. Unfortunately for you, you have laid the groundwork for your failure, as well as the failure of any others who wish to come to your aid when things do begin to unravel."

Aaron rose to the challenge. "This isn't 1942 where one battle group from 2014 upset the world order. In those primitive times, the pieces were in place for an easy victory. Patriotism and unity were much easier to use against people who lacked the sophistication and information to question their leaders. Rally round the flag and all.

"In today's world, the only thing people want is protection from the bogeyman, and the governments of the world use this fear to domesticate their populations like a bunch of kick dogs. Now, after seventy-five years of this shadow game, their leaders can whip their populations into a frenzy every time they ring the dinner bell, and that blast in San Francisco was one hell of a big bell. Right now, only a few survivalists hiding out in the mountains would dare to challenge their constitutionally elected leaders in a time of national emergency.

"And when I..." Aaron stopped short, leaned back against the wall, and smiled. "I think that is more than enough for today. As I see it you only have one option, and I don't think you and Carl would contemplate such a final solution."

Sean Anthony had his own thoughts on the subject. However,

it was time to get to work. "It has been a hoot brother. Give my regards to mom." With that, he disappeared into the same green mist he arrived in.

⸎

As Sean's eyes cleared from the flash that sent them on another quest, the sight that came into focus jolted him straight back to 1973. With shocking red hair, cropped short on top, but shoulder length in the back, a bright red and blue lightning bolt across his face, and wearing only a pair of sequined briefs stood David Bowie as Aladdin Sane.

"I'll be buggered. Look at me, tossed about time and space and still can't get rid of this bloody persona."

Sean and Alicia stared at each other and in spite of their uncertain situation, in unison burst out laughing at the insanity playing out in front of them.

An offended Bowie sarcastically retorted, "I'm glad my sorry state of affairs amuses you."

Sean was first to get under control. "At least you're thirty-five years younger than the last time I saw you perform."

"A lot of good that did. You still have me dressed in the 70s. Why is it so hard for you people to get over it? Either of you got a fag?" He then wandered over to the forward window and stared out at the ocean, apparently losing interest in them.

Alicia took the moment to whisper in Sean's ear "What did he mean that you have him dressed in the 70s?" She glanced back to see Bowie still occupied with the ocean view and grabbed Sean's arm hard. "Where is the bridge crew? And shouldn't we see what's going on around the rest of the ship?"

Sean shrugged his shoulders. "We're retired, remember." However, after a look of disbelief from Alicia that Sean knew portended of a stream of pragmatic reasons why he was obligated to take action, he headed toward the bridge phone.

Before he could reach it, Bowie turned back to them and admonished, "We are years away from anything that can threaten your ships, Admiral Phillips." He then turned deadly serious, at least as serious as a man could get nearly naked and covered in makeup and glitter. "Once again you and your ships have been chosen for a very special mission, and the decisions you make will send ripples through what you know of your history. Bugger it up and you could be responsible for the demise of every living creature on this daft planet." His face relaxed into an easy grin. "Seriously, do either of you have a fag?"

"Out of all the insanity we have experienced to date, I'll have to admit your appearance is my new number one." Then it was Sean's turn to get serious. "What the hell are you anyway? I mean, between Alicia and I, we have read most of the theories of quantum physics, multiple realities, and extraterrestrial visitations, and I can't think of anything to explain what you represent."

He then turned to Alicia. "Can you?"

"Outside of this being one hell of a kick ass dream for you, Sean, with one of your musical heroes center stage, no I seriously can't think of a single thing." Alicia hesitated before continuing. "Can I find you something to cover yourself with?" Bowie's physical appearance definitely distracted Alicia.

"What I am is exactly what I appear to be. And thank you for the offer Alicia, but I'll be leaving now, so the need to protect your prudish morality will not be necessary."

Sean wanted answers. "Are you telling us you are leaving us without a clue about why, when, or where we are?"

With a nonchalant wave of his hand, Bowie affirmed Sean's question. "Of course I am. Who do you think I am? Nietzsche with all the answers? Freud to tell you why? Or, how about Marx, out to bring social equality to the masses? Jesus?" Bowie stopped and gave them both a good looking over. "Definitely not him. That whole hanging on a cross thing doesn't work for me. No, I am none of the above. What you see is what you created, but what I am is way above your pay grade. The only thing you need to know is you have less than a week to figure out your situation before it gets exciting."

He took a rolled up joint out of the band of his briefs, lit it, and took a hit before continuing. "You will figure the situation out soon enough that is as soon as you start acting like the Admirals you both are supposed to be. All else will be revealed as you navigate through your environment. Just remember, every decision you make could be momentous in their implications for things that will only become clear if you make the right decisions." He then let out a laugh reminiscent of the one that began his song *Andy Warhol* before he added, "By now you should be used to making life and death decisions in the middle of insanity."

Before either Sean or Alicia could demand any further explanations, the unknown entity masquerading as a David Bowie persona began to fade into a rising cloud of green mist. However, before he disappeared completely, he added sarcastically to Sean, "I wanted to flip a coin with Freddie Mercury to see who came, but I was overruled when reminded you are also a big fan of Iggy Pop. It's too bad really, Freddie would have loved the gig. He still loves to do his 70s thing."

Sean stared at where Bowie had stood; only now there was only the empty ocean in front of the Enterprise. "Where the hell did he go?"

"Where did who go Admiral?" Captain Osaka asked.

Taken completely by surprise, Sean jerked around to see the bridge of the Enterprise had its full complement of personnel back, dressed to the hilt in battle gear with the klaxons loudly sounding General Quarters.

"Are you all right, Sir?"

Sean struggled to focus. "I'm fine Captain Osaka." Sean grabbed a pair of binoculars and scanned the ocean. He easily picked out the Missouri in the same station keeping as their last deployment, with the John Paul Jones forward, the Princeton to Port, and the Chancellorsville to starboard. "Launch the F-35s and do a 250 mile sweep. You know the drill. Let's try to figure out where and when they sent us this time. Have the task force synchronize to the Enterprise CIC time until we get a better fix. And begin sextant readings."

"Yes Sir. The F-35s are already in the air, Admiral."

Captain Osaka was prepared with part of Sean's last order, and in his delight that Sean and Alicia had replaced his former Admiral, almost stumbled over himself to spit it out. "Captain Daily on the Seawolf has reported in, and I am trying to re-establish contact with the rest of the task force now. Because we deployed for an indeterminate time under extreme conditions, command loaded us to the ceiling with all the supplies they could think of. Regarding the Missouri Task Force, I can only imagine what they have brought back from the 1940s."

"Thank you Captain." Sean looked over at Alicia to see her nod that she was fine with letting him take control. Satisfied, he continued with his orders. "With Admiral Feller and his Chief of Staff missing, as the Captain of the Enterprise, you are now my interim Chief of Staff until I get my bearings."

"Aye Aye Admiral."

Do we have satellite communications?"

"No Sir."

"Then keep a Hawkeye [E-2D Advanced Hawkeye carrier-capable tactical airborne early warning and communications aircraft] in the air at all times until we have a better understanding of our situation."

"Of course, Sir. The Hawkeye is already deployed, Sir."

Sean realized he was still a bit out of sync with the way carrier ops work. "Right, Daniel, it has been a while."

"Understood, Sir."

Sean had one more order on his way out as the bridge came to attention. "When Dr. Cutler arrives, have her meet us in the Admirals Quarters."

Alicia stood in his way, shaking her head. She knew the bridge personnel needed something more from their new Admiral.

Sean noticed her concern, and after giving her a smile in acknowledgment, abruptly turned to face the bridge crew who were now standing at attention. "At ease. I see many familiar faces from our previous voyage into the unknown. However, for those of you who are new to the mind-numbing experience of leaving your time and space, you *will* acclimate to this new reality. Think of it as losing your virginity, because boys and girls, this is going to be as memorable, so focus on your jobs. Turn to those around you who are old hands at this for support. This isn't where you want to be, but if we don't respond to the standards expected of us by the oaths we took to the United States Navy, none of us will likely survive." With that final incentive delivered, he spun around and followed Alicia out the door.

"Admiral is off the bridge!"

After the Seahawk crew deposited Dr. Rebecca Cutler and Dr. Forrest Phelps onto the flight deck of the Enterprise, Dr. Cutler addressed Dr. Phelps. "Forrest, why don't you go down to the hangar deck to check out the 2nd generation Specter system while I head to the bridge to find out what is going on."

"Sounds good. See you later." Forrest waved as he trotted toward the elevator that was about to lower.

Minutes later, Rebecca stood in front of a smiling Captain Osaka. "Any idea of when and where we are?" she deadpanned as if nothing out of the ordinary had occurred.

He pointed her to the view out the bridge window. "All I can tell you for sure is, we have quite an armada surrounding us, and the

Admirals are now husband and wife."

Rebecca looked out to see the Missouri next to the Enterprise and surrounded by the other support ships. "What, get out of Dodge. Sean and Alicia are married?"

"Snatched right out of their honeymoon nest and delivered half naked to our bridge." Osaka's hand held radio chirped out a warning someone was trying to reach him. He motioned for Rebecca to give him a moment while he took care of the call. "Yes Sir, Dr. Cutler is with me. She just arrived. Yes Sir. I will send her to your quarters right away." As he hung up the phone, he relayed to Rebecca, "Both Admiral Phillips and Secretary Calhoun are waiting for you in the Admirals Quarters."

"Yeah, I got that when you said, I'll send her to your quarters."

Osaka realized he had missed the eclectic, high-strung scientist. It also gave him greater confidence in their future knowing she was around to handle the sci-fi aspects. It also didn't hurt matters that her brilliantly red hair highlighted one of the most gorgeous women he had ever seen.

"Looking at how much you have matured I would have guessed you were there longer than the four years since we returned to 2014."

Rebecca angrily poked Osaka in the chest with her finger. *"How much I have matured?"*

Osaka tried to back away from her well-deserved assault on him.

"What the hell is that supposed to mean? I see you have gained a few pounds, and I don't recall so many wrinkles around your eyes."

"My apologies, Dr. Cutler. What I meant to say was how the combination of grace and dignity has made you more beautiful than ever." To Osaka's relief the poking ended and he anxiously waited to see if his compliment mollified her.

Rebecca continued to glare at him before a sly grin appeared. She gave him a quick kiss on the cheek and a hug. "I'm just messing with you, Daniel."

She released him and started toward the door before she paused to get her bearings. "My God, It's been over nine years since I last saw Admiral Phillips and Secretary Calhoun."

⊷⬥⊶

Sean Anthony found himself in the part of Baltimore, MD off limits to the typical snow-white suburbanites of any large 21st Century city. Yet, as he parked, the dozens of eyes focused on his ostentatious BMW had no idea that it was they who would be wise to keep their distance. He casually exited the car and strolled up to a rapidly forming group of predators, directing his attention to the fiercest looking one. "Could you direct me to Adonis?"

After the laughter died down, this especially mean and nasty one pushed his massive bulk into Sean Anthony's chest, and wrapped one of his hands around his throat. "You have come to the wrong neighborhood whitey."

Just when those watching expected the beat down to commence, green paper began to flutter all around the group. One of the onlookers grabbed one out of the air and after a quick glance, shouted, "They're fucking one hundred dollar bills!"

This of course brought about the desired distraction, as Mean and Nasty forgot about Sean Anthony and joined the fracas. Fights for the airborne bills escalated until one of them pulled a piece. Before he could pull the trigger, the gun and all the bills went up in a green puff of mist. This act of magic froze the group, who then in unison turned their attention back to the intruder.

"I still need to find Adonis. Can any of you fine boys point him out to me?"

Mr. Mean and Nasty pulled his weapon and pointed it at Sean Anthony's head. "You've got some explaining to do."

Sean Anthony merely shook his head as the weapon went the way of the bills. "I was hoping to avoid any unpleasantries, yet here we are. So let me make it simple for all of you. Tell me which one of these apartments belongs to Adonis, and I guarantee you will all eventually benefit greatly for your assistance."

All eyes turned toward the building across the street.

"Which number?"

Ten mouths all came to life at once spitting out the number 325.

"Now was that so hard?

"Mr. Mean and Nasty, would you please accompany me." Then turning to the others, he asked, "I certainly would appreciate it if you looked after my car while I am gone. I promise to be back shortly."

However, they quickly dispersed after Sean Anthony crossed the street with his newfound friend. "I could use a guy like you. What's your name?"

"How the hell did you do that shit? You some kind of voodoo doctor or something?"

Sean Anthony didn't answer until they reached the front door of the building, and turned the doorknob. "Or something. Stick with me and you can find out, or, more than likely die in the process, Mr. Adonis."

This stopped Mean and Nasty short. "If you knew who I was, what was that about?"

"Maybe I wanted to make an impression."

After taking the elevator to the third floor in silence, Adonis approached a door in the middle of the corridor that was out of place relative to the surroundings. On the wall next to the door and totally out of place in this tenement building, was a high-tech keypad that Adonis shielded with one hand while he punched in an extensive code with the other. Once completed, a series of clicks emanated from behind the door that took a good thirty seconds. "One can't be too careful these days," Adonis cautioned as the door suddenly swung open by itself.

Sean Anthony looked inside the room and smiled. "This is

exactly what I was looking for." The room, filled with stacks of computers, extended at least 100 feet in either direction, taking up the entire length of the corridor.

"Welcome to my pad Voodoo Man."

As he stared at the massive array of servers in the hollowed out apartment, Sean Anthony asked Adonis, "Have you ever thought of doing some serious damage with all of this computing power? Or are you another greedy-ass technocrat, Mr. Mean and Nasty?"

"The name's Adonis, and what in the hell do you want from me?" The constant moniker Sean Anthony kept using was making Adonis edgy.

"I want you to help level the playing field. In case you haven't noticed, your government has gone off the rails. From what I have been able to ascertain, you are quite capable of helping me save your lovely little republic."

"And I want to do this why?" Adonis asked. "As I see it, all I have to do is sit back and watch you kill each other, and then pick up the pieces when it's all over. I got no skin in the game."

"I beg to disagree." Sean Anthony walked over to the closest monitor as it sprang to life. "Take a look."

"How did you…" What Adonis saw on the monitor surpassed his surprise at Sean Anthony's ability to control his computer. The video feed showed several rows of monitors in an unfamiliar room. What had caught his attention was the one with the video that displayed his shocked expression staring right back at him.

"Did you really believe that with their resources, you could fly under the radar? All of those other surveillance monitors are monitoring your other so-called Black Hat buddies and unless…"

Adonis wasn't listening as he noticed on another monitor, cameras that he had placed in strategic locations around the neighborhood had picked up the arrival of military vehicles. He watched in shock as fully armed troops climbed out and began to fan out and slowly work their way toward his location. Quickly reaching a level of panic that would dictate a quick decision on his fight or flight options, Adonis fought to try to figure out how they breached his firewalls. "Damn, a couple of hundred thousand dollars don't get you shit anymore. Damn, damn, and damn." Flight it is. He rushed to a closet and pushed a hidden button that caused one of the walls to slide back, exposing a space between the rooms.

Impatient to move on, Sean Anthony waved his hand and suddenly Adonis was back in the middle of the room.

"Stop messing with me. I've got to get out of here."

Sean calmly smiled as a flash of green mist exploded throughout the cavernous room. When the mist cleared, every piece of electronics in the apartment had disappeared. "Problem solved. Now can we get the hell out of here before those who were watching you give the go ahead because they lost their surveillance feed?"

The shocked look on Adonis's face at the loss of all of his precious data made the oversized man look like a small child who was just told Santa didn't exist.

Sean Anthony watched the wave of despair wash over him for a moment, before he added, "If it were me, I would find a way to use your tremendous skill set against them." Sean Anthony then paused for effect to let it sink in. "Or are you nothing more than the king of this little slice of ghetto?"

That hit the right nerve. Adonis's expression hardened, as he demanded, "Go where? How do you suppose we get around all of those Army dudes with guns?"

At that moment, a red phone on the desk in front of them rang. Adonis picked it up, and as the seconds ticked by, his expression went from anger to fear. "It looks like the man is rolling in with some heavy-ass shit." Before he could say another word, the sound of gunfire exploded in the streets immediately below.

Sean Anthony looked at his cellphone, saw the time counting down, and smiled. "An Apache attack helicopter is about to launch a Hellfire missile through the wall in roughly ten seconds. If you don't want to be splattered into little roach treats, I would suggest..."

"Get us the hell out of here!"

"Just the words I needed to hear." Sean Anthony smiled as they both disappeared in a puff of green mist, one second before a massive fireball engulfed the entire floor.

A split second later, Adonis found himself in a cavernous underground chamber. If the sheer size of the place didn't overwhelm him, then the light show that illuminated the state of the art technology that filled the room surely did.

Seated at numerous workstations, a multinational mixture of young adults worked away oblivious to his arrival.

Adonis took several deep breaths of air as if to soak it all in. "If I didn't know better, I would say all of this is Triple-A government grade cyber warfare technology."

Sean Anthony twirled around with his arms fully extended, as if he was about to launch into the air. "Welcome to heaven, Mr. Mean and Nasty. Come, let me introduce you to the people you will be working with to save the world. If you can all live up to your self-proclaimed genius status, you will become major players in recreating the paradise lost that is your birthright."

Sean Anthony shrugged as he noticed the blank expression on Adonis's face. "Or, if that doesn't trip your trigger, how about the idea of playing with the coolest technology in an all or nothing quest to destroy the Black Hats of government."

Still pissed off about the loss of his lair, this style of motivation put a smile back on his face. "I'm down with that."

Adonis slowly walked down the middle of a room at least a football field long and half again as wide. He stopped in front of a workstation where the boy at the keyboard looked to be no more than 12 years old.

The boy looked up. "Good to finally meet you in person, Mr.

Adonis."

All at once, the other geeks in the chamber stopped what they were doing, and turned to face the new arrival.

Adonis stared at Sean Anthony. "How did you get all of these dysfunctional ego maniacs to agree to physically meet in the same place?"

"The same way you came here. They were as busted as you were. As your encounter with the now completely militarized law enforcement has shown, the government has turned to a new page about how to eradicate the problems people such as you represent. Every person in this room was moments away from oblivion when they agreed to relocate."

"Why now?" Adonis aggressively questioned. "How can the world's most powerful military have orders to kill American citizens in their homes? It is one thing to watch your back in the hood, but quite another to have a Hellfire missile crash your crib."

Sean Anthony looked at Adonis as if he was nuts. "Aren't you the one that has ranted for years about the shadow government, and how the New World Order has replaced both capitalism and nationalism with a modern version of a Medieval Oligarchy?"

Sean Anthony put his arm around Adonis's shoulder, and faced him toward a massive ceiling to floor monitor that extended horizontally at least twenty feet. The screen came to life with an aerial live feed of an inner city neighborhood that burned as fiercely as Dresden, Germany in 1945. At least twenty tenement buildings were involved, yet there were no fire units on the scene.

"They killed everyone?" Adonis could not believe his whole life was going up in smoke. "Why would they kill everybody in my neighborhood? They wasn't doing nothing but trying to get by."

The video then rolled through many other scenes of urban and rural attacks with overwhelming force against civilian soft targets. Sean Anthony's voice turned steel hard as he steered Adonis away from the monitor. "These attacks started up within two hours of the nuclear detonation in San Francisco."

They had moved only slightly, when Adonis whipped around. "How did you get those pictures? That wasn't off some local news channel. That was military grade transmissions, real time! No one can hack into that."

"We can, and more." Sean Anthony took on the character of a used car salesman. "Here in this chamber, I have assembled the best hackers in the world and supplied them with the world's latest cutting-edge technology, some of which isn't in the government's hands yet. By the way, that is your station three rows down to the left."

Instead of rapture, Sean Anthony could see the hackles of distrust rise up.

"How do I know that you are not the government?" Adonis demanded. "Why should I trust someone that I don't think is human based on what you have done? Flash, bang, and I am out of the hood. Damn, I might as well be on another planet for all I know."

"Who is to say you are not?" Sean Anthony replied with a grin.

Adonis, above all else a survivor, had a bomb go off in his brain as he thought, "Who cares who the dude is? I am still alive, and the man has the cash to fill the room to the rafters with bling eons beyond what I could dream of. Besides, if things get too real, I'll jump out."

"What's in it for me?" A broad smile slowly broke out on his face.

Sean Anthony laughed. "Only the opportunity to become a god is all."

He then addressed the group as he walked. "I guess the only answer that matters is, if you all live up to your hype, you can write evil and corruption out of existence." Then Sean Anthony half-jokingly added, "Or die in the glorious attempt."

Three rows down on the right, he stopped at the empty

workstation. "Besides, Mr. Mean and Nasty, how many people do you know who can give you complete access to every vital computer program in the world? Go ahead and take her for a spin." Sean Anthony swiveled the chair to face the suddenly eager hulk of a man.

Before Adonis could agree, the four monitors that hung in the air all around the desk lit up with data from his old systems. "That is just cold man. Lead a brother to think you wiped out all of his life work." With an air of anticipation, Adonis plopped down in the chair and immediately began to rearrange the desk. "So what is it exactly that you think we can do? You got any Red Bull and Vodka around here?"

Sean Anthony moved past his request. "The downside, Mr. Mean and Nasty, is that we will have to break a few eggs to make this particular omelet. You think you can handle destroying the object of your worship if it came down to it?"

His suspicions quickly returned. "If it came down to what, Voodoo Man?"

⋘⋙

As Rebecca walked the short distance down to the Admirals Quarters, memories flooded her mind of the abrupt shift into the world of 1941. Then she remembered the day in the English Channel in 1942 when half of the Enterprise Task Force including Sean and Alicia had disappeared. She stood at the door for a moment to imagine the changes she had missed in the world of her birth.

Suddenly a stray thought froze Rebecca. "Who is to say that this is the same Enterprise I remember. Why can't this be another version of the same thing, only with an evil Sean and Alicia? If that is the case, why did Osaka appear normal? Come on, girl. Don't get crazy here."

With firm resolve, Rebecca reached out to knock on the door.

Before she could, the door flew open, startling her so bad she fell against the far wall of the corridor. Sean cracked up after he saw she was unhurt.

"I haven't seen you for nine years, and you find it funny to scare the shit out of me?"

Though she did her best to feign anger, Sean saw right through her mask. "Welcome back aboard the Enterprise, Dr. Cutler." Still chuckling, he reached out to shake her hand, forgetting about the young scientist's proclivity for big hugs.

She rushed into his arms and squeezed him so hard he could barely breathe. Seeing that she was not ready to let go, Sean pivoted back into the room where he watched a bemused Alicia taking it all in.

When Sean finally untangled himself, he grabbed both of Rebecca's shoulders to take a good look at her. "Look at you, all grown up."

"At least you were smart enough not to say *mature*." Then, ignoring Sean's look of confusion, Rebecca rushed over to throw her arms around Alicia, who unlike her husband had prepared for the onslaught.

"Déjà vu all over again," Rebecca said over Alicia's shoulder to Sean.

After Alicia managed to free herself from the hug, it took only seconds for Rebecca to segue to the business at hand. "When Carl disappeared from the bridge of the Missouri, and we immediately jumped into 2018, I was hoping maybe he would be here – and Tony of course."

"We haven't heard a thing. We arrived in our bathrobes, so the only thing we have had time to do is get into some clothes," Alicia responded as she gave the crazed scientist a good looking over. "My God, you *are* all grown up. Look at you, even more beautiful than ever." Alicia stepped back and took another long look, obviously puzzled.

"What's the matter, is there an alien on me, or what?"

Alicia smiled, and then assured her, "No, nothing creepy, crawly that I can see. It's just that you look so…, normal. What happened to the freak?" Alicia always enjoyed the latest 60s hippy-dippy outfit Rebecca normally wore during their earlier adventure. "Please tell me you didn't get rid of all of those beautiful clothes and accessories. To see you bouncing along the deck of the Missouri in a rainbow printed mini dress against the sea of military fatigues will remain one of my favorite memories until the day I die."

"Don't be deceived by the appearance. I had to do your diplomatic job when you guys split. You have to remember it was the 1940s, and as I was a woman doing a man's job, the rest would have blown their little minds. Besides all the biggie's wives hated me without it anyway. Let me tell you, what a bunch of whiny little bitches. I did think of breaking out the good stuff for when I met Einstein, but Carl wouldn't let me. Outside of the birth of little Sean Anthony *that* was the best day of my life so far." Rebecca quickly caught them up on her marriage and the subsequent birth of her son.

"You didn't. You didn't name him after me did you?" The news embarrassed Sean.

"Get over it," Alicia admonished Sean with a smile before returning to Rebecca. "Go on – your husband? Little Sean Anthony? Do tell."

Sean went over to where he hoped his predecessor kept the booze, but instead discovered it full as if left from their time in 2014. "I don't know about you, but Alicia and I need a drink; Admiral's prerogative and all. Want one?"

"Please." Rebecca continued her story while Sean poured. "I modeled my diplomacy after Alicia's masterful performance at the Palace of Versailles peace conference in France that prematurely ended WWII. You set the table, so all I had to do was serve dessert. Of course, it didn't hurt that our technology kept all of their little dicks in line. I finally learned why it is so important to let everyone know that you have the biggest one in the room."

Sean almost dropped the Jack Daniels Single Barrel he was pouring. "Obviously you have grown up in other ways as well. Big and little dicks – really?"

"Come on. It was the 1940s. Do you honestly believe anything else mattered back then? Hell, even after I married Carl, everyone was still convinced Eleanor and I had something going on." Rebecca winked seductively to show the two women had played up the rumor to the hilt for their own advantage and amusement.

After Sean handed out the tumblers to the girls, Rebecca took a quick sip, and motored on. "Anyway, we were there for almost ten years, and let me tell you, there is no way you would have recognized the world. No wars, everyone working to improve the environment, and best of all, a world of less than two and a half billion inhabitants, which let me tell you, made life so much more rewarding. Everyone had opportunities.

"Then out of nowhere, here I am with you, my son is still in 1951, and God knows where my husband and Tony disappeared to."

Rebecca didn't see any reason to bring up her conversation with Carl before he left. She needed to work that one out on her own for now. "Okay, now it's your turn. Give it up. What hell have you two been raising, and how did you finally get Sean to get his head out of his ass and do the right thing?"

"Hey, enough piling on. First, it's all the men of the 1940s, and now me? Neither of us was ready, until we both were."

Alicia came to Sean's rescue when Rebecca's sour look showed she didn't buy it. "I would have eaten him up and spit him out if it had happened earlier girl. Trust me it was an act of compassion that I waited."

As much as he enjoyed their reunion, Sean needed everyone to get on task. "Do you two want to be left alone for a while, so you can get ribbing me out of your systems, or can we get down to business?" To move things along, he gave a rapid-fire recollection of how violently the 21st Century had become, and ended with the destruction of San Francisco. By the time he finished, Rebecca was in tears.

"What are you crying about?" Sean could not see how the life that she had not interacted with upset her.

"Empathy would be my guess, *Tony*," Alicia admonished.

Sean grimaced at the dig. He thought about all the times Tony, the master at saying the wrong thing at the wrong time, stuck his foot in his mouth. Sean missed his best friend as he listened patiently while Alicia tried to cheer Rebecca up. Fortunately, fate intervened when a call from the bridge interrupted.

Sean rushed to answer, and after a quick response of, "We'll be right there," he put the phone down. "Any further reminiscing will have to wait. Osaka needs us on the bridge. Do you want to come along, or would you rather check out Specter? I'm pretty sure any upgrades they made are not up to your standards," Sean concluded with a wink to the scientist.

"Good idea. I'll catch up with you guys later." Rebecca had another reason to check out Specter. The sooner they got through this latest journey through time and space, the sooner she could reunite with her family. As the eternal optimist, she knew Carl would be along shortly, and more than likely accompanied by Tony. As the door closed behind her, her voice continued down the hall. "You will let me know when Carl turns up."

"Of course," Alicia replied, as she smiled and gave Sean a kiss.

"What was that for?"

"Nice save, getting her centered like that. You're *almost* forgiven for your lack of sensitivity."

He shook his head in mock confusion. "You never know why you get in trouble, and you never know how you got out of trouble. Is it a gift all women are born with, or do you all belong to a secret society of the mind?"

"I'll never tell." Alicia answered with a wink, as they headed to the bridge to receive Osaka's report.

When Sean and Alicia arrived on the bridge, Captain Osaka saluted with one hand while cradling the phone in the other. "No one has reported any problems from the jump. Everything is battle ready. Here is the list of ships and their Captains."

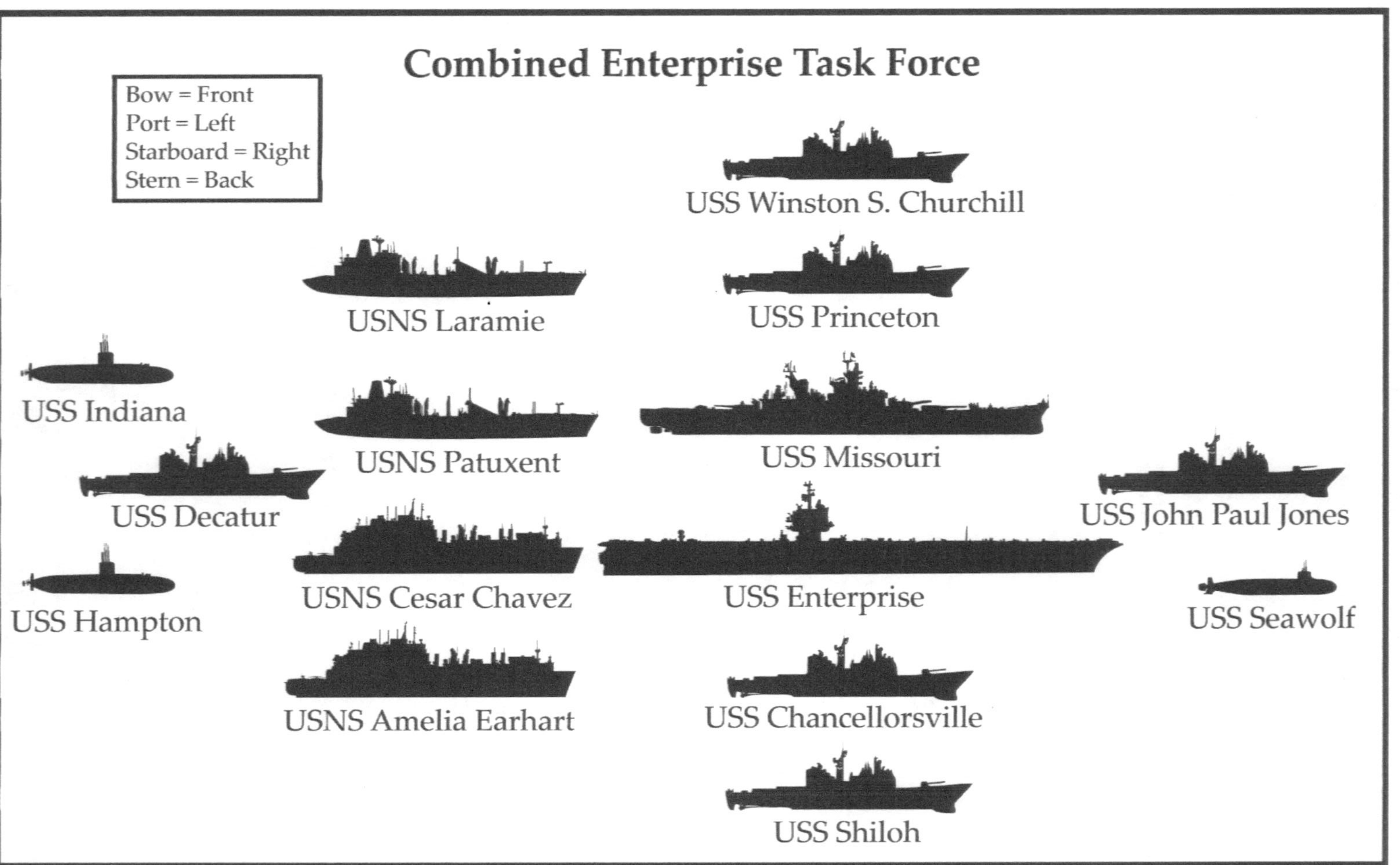
Combined Enterprise Task Force
Bow = Front
Port = Left
Starboard = Right
Stern = Back
USS Winston S. Churchill
USS Princeton
USS Missouri
USS Enterprise
USS John Paul Jones
USS Seawolf
USS Chancellorsville
USS Shiloh
USNS Laramie
USNS Patuxent
USNS Cesar Chavez
USNS Amelia Earhart
USS Indiana
USS Decatur
USS Hampton

Enterprise Task Force Captains & Their Ships

Missouri Task Force Segment left in the 1942 Reality

Captain Anthony Knox (missing) – Commander, Missouri Task Force

Captain Carl Eddington (missing) – battleship USS Missouri

Captain Gordon Lincoln – cruiser USS Princeton

Commander Regis Goddard – destroyer USS John Paul Jones

Captain Marlowe Turner – attack submarine USS Hampton

Commander Andy Gable – cargo ship USNS Amelia Earhart

Lt. Commander James Peck – fleet oiler USNS Laramie

Enterprise Task Force Segment that Returned to 2014

Captain Daniel Osaka – Commanding Officer, carrier USS Enterprise

Captain Frederick Johnson – cruiser USS Chancellorsville

Commander Logan Barrish – destroyer USS Decatur

Captain Mark Daily – attack submarine USS Seawolf

New Ships Added to the Enterprise Task Force in 2018

Captain Henry Jackson – cruiser USS Shiloh

Commander Bob Bremerton – destroyer USS Winston S Churchill

Commander Jonathan James – attack Submarine USS Indiana

Commander Melissa Wu – cargo ship USNS Cesar Chavez

Lt. Commander Maria Brizuela – fleet oiler USNS Patuxent

Senior Civilian Officer Bradley Franks – fleet oiler USNS Patuxent

Something bugged Alicia about this new hop. "How is it we didn't lose power like our first jump through time in 2014?"

"Thank you Captain," Sean replied as he looked over the printout.

Alicia looked over Sean's shoulder at the list and was surprised, and concerned at the size of their new battle group. "I count eight warships, four supply ships, and three attack subs. The task force has grown from 10 to 15 ships. Our responsibilities have grown by half again. Let's hope there aren't too many Safires or Brewsters among them."

Dr. Safire, the primary scientist responsible for Specter's development, went mad and tried to destroy the group when he accessed the program for the Harpoon missile batteries after they arrived in 1941. Captain Steven Brewster and his fellow Christian Fundamentalists attempted a mutiny in 1942 that cost him and dozens of others their lives.

"Too bad there wasn't an additional aircraft carrier," Sean stated to no one in particular.

"Has the Seawolf checked in?" he asked Osaka.

"Captain Daily, Captain Turner of the Hampton, and Commander James of the Indiana have all reported in," Captain Osaka reported.

"Well done, *Captain* Osaka," Sean acknowledged with a touch of amusement, as he joined Alicia. "Based on the humidity we are definitely on a tropical latitude. Hopefully, the search planes will locate recognizable land masses."

Almost as an afterthought, he turned to Osaka. "Reduce the task force speed to 10 knots to conserve our fuel supply and order the ship Captains to report to the Enterprise in one hour for a staff meeting. Admiral Calhoun and I will be in the Admirals Ready Room waiting for news from the search planes."

"Aye Aye Admiral."

After joining Dr. Forrest Phelps and running some diagnostic checks on Specter, a stunned Rebecca collapsed in her chair. "You did this? I can't believe the complexity of the modifications you made Forrest. And how did they get from the Missouri to the Enterprise?"

"I had help."

"Don't be so modest. The simplicity in how the systems communicate with one another is sheer genius. If I didn't know any better I would say the only way to improve it would be to bring it to life. The more I look through the coding, the more it feels like I have seen it somewhere else. Seriously, how did you get all the separate operating systems synchronized?"

"To tell you the truth while we were on the latest cruise and you were in Washington, I began to have the weirdest dreams." Abruptly Forrest became uncomfortable with where he was going and changed the subject. "I'm sorry for not asking how you are doing. Here you've lost your husband and child, and I haven't taken a moment to ask how you're holding up."

"I'm a wreck, but I'll be fine as long as I can be of use. I just have to be patient until Sean and Alicia figure our way out."

Rebecca stopped to give Forrest a stern look. "Look at you, changing the subject. You are sweet for being concerned, but let's focus on the here and now. Finish your story. I need to know how you came up with all of these modifications. They are years ahead of anything I could imagine."

One thing Rebecca's years of experience dealing with politicians and bureaucrats had taught her was to disregard what they said, and focus on their body language. At the moment, Dr. Phelps's body screamed guilt. Besides, the Forrest she knew lacked the skills to evolve Specter's technology to this level. "Give it up."

To say that in a room of poker players Forrest would stand out like a stripper on a pole in St. Peter's Basilica was an understatement. He folded immediately. "It was like I was talking to another person whose back was to me all the time. Night after night it felt like I was in a quantum physics lecture where the professor taught a reality 100 years in the future."

Now fascinated, Rebecca interrupted. "Was it a man or a woman?"

"I didn't get a sense one way or another, so no, I don't think there was any sexual element to it. And the voice was too young to be mom or dad, so sorry, no Oedipus complex, Sigmund either."

She smiled. "Just checking, please continue."

"Anyway, after six straight nights of this I was no further along in understanding what this person was trying to teach me. The information didn't make any sense, and at the end of every night, the voice rose in anger and frustration. Finally, on the seventh night, after what felt like hours, when I was about to wake up the figure turned around and it happened."

Now thoroughly engrossed Rebecca pleaded, "What happened? Who was it?"

Forrest's face flushed, as he had hoped she would never ask.

Rebecca knew that now would be a good time to stroke his ego a bit. "Genius like this only comes around only a couple of times in a generation, Forest. What you did with the programming is more impressive than when Dr. Safire created the original code. You have nothing to be ashamed of, and if it is that personal to you, I won't tell a soul."

"Carl Eddington, your husband. Not knowing if the entity in my dreams was actually him, I didn't dare say anything to anyone until I was sure."

The abruptness in how he blurted out the name caught Rebecca completely off guard.

Forrest could see the pain in her face, so he hurried to finish. "When he turned around to face me, all the frustration was gone. Then he raised his left hand, and a powerful green beam erupted from his index finger and slammed into my head. When I woke up it was all there, the entire structure.

"It took me weeks to put all the pieces together. Just as I finally got it working, we jumped to 2018. When we joined the Enterprise Task Force, I connected to their Specter network, and it all came across to this system without my doing."

Forrest's words had dazed Rebecca, who now appeared to be miles away. Her body tensed, her eyes began to dart back and forth, while her face remained frozen, as the epiphany took shape in her fertile mind.

"What's wrong?" Nothing. "Say something," Forrest pleaded, torn between his concern for her wellbeing, and his survival.

Continuing to ignore Dr. Phelps, Rebecca rushed to the keyboard and began to furiously type in commands.

Adonis typed furiously on his keyboard, oblivious to all the others equally engaged at their workstations. Here he was in the middle of the most notorious hackers in the world, and no one to brag about it with. Cloudwalker, Komitose, Ariac the Slayer, Cleopatra, and Jade to name a few of the heavyweights. "How did Voodoo Man get all of these geniuses from around the world out of their government's grip, while leaving thousands of others to their brutal fate, and why us?" His thoughts quickly passed as his excitement grew over what they were about to set in motion. "No one will see this coming."

"If you perform as advertised, I can't see how they could."

Adonis didn't bother to ask how Sean Anthony knew what he was thinking. "I don't care who or what you are. Anyone with crazy ass skills like yours who could put all of this together has my vote for Ultimate Warrior of the Universe."

Adonis's fingers continued to fly across his keyboard as he talked. "I see where you are going man, but you can't possibly expect to win more than a tactical victory. You of all people should know the second the government stooges figure out what happened, they will see every one of our fingerprints all over the coding, and we're toast."

"You're not seeing the big picture, Mr. Mean & Nasty. That is the reason the government techies always managed to find members of your fraternity, no discipline. None of you have ever worked together on a grand plan. It was always about breaking through the toughest security protocols to access secrets that you could care less about, all so you could loudly announce to the world your genius. Instead, you should have learned how to be quiet, church mouse quiet."

Adonis's monitor began a slow scroll of images of young men and women locked in small jail cells. "As you can see, the loudest and most uncontrollable went into solitary confinement, or worse."

The pictures changed to show other youth dressed in office attire surrounded by similar technology. "Or sold their souls and became the guardians at the gate.

"Then there was your group. Loud enough to be tracked and quiet enough to be left in place so your data could be scooped up and turned against others."

The pictures changed again and now showed a spider web of connections back to a network Adonis immediately recognized that his hacker group had exposed. He now knew exactly how ignorant he and his crew were about their reality.

"Either way, you only knew what the government wanted you to know. The government completely fooled you into thinking the intelligence they dangled as bait told the whole story, so instead of exposing them, you led hundreds of like-minded souls to a brutal assault. All because of this one fatal flaw of arrogance, you proved to be every bit as complicit as those you rail against."

Adonis felt horrible enough about Sean Anthony's indictment of his part, but there was more. "Your work was also used by those who drank the Kool-Aid. Over half of those in your network were working you. They stroked your ego and acknowledged your hubris as gospel, so you couldn't smell the foul odor of their greed."

For the first time he could ever remember, someone had humbled Adonis. "If I am such damaged goods, why did you grab my ass to help you?"

Sean Anthony smiled. "Because I knew you didn't know any better. That you had skills useful to the top computer specialists in the government says much about what you could do if you had all the information. The same is true for everyone in this room.

"The American government has unlimited resources to bring consumer heaven to even the most ardent anarchist once they decide they are worth rehabilitating. Most chose to live in luxury, instead of spending the rest of their lives getting the shit beat out of them while they slowly starved to death in a secret prison in Kazakhstan. Unfortunately, I was powerless to do anything until recently; otherwise, many of those who you helped purge would now be with us as well.

"Anyway, either we get it right over the coming days or there will be nobody left to care. You can also be sure those same government techies are trolling the cloud looking for any remnants the assassins might have missed. The smug bastards are sure they had you all smoked, so they will never see what we have coming their way."

Sean Anthony could see Adonis needed some time to make the trip from humiliation to righteous indignation, so he addressed the group. "I think it's a good time to take you all out of your virtual worlds where your dead warriors come back to life, to the real world where any mistake is permanent. So, are you geeks ready to deliver a small appetizer to get the show started?"

He walked over to a young Asian girl dressed up as one of the many anime characters, and nodded his head in the positive.

She swung around and entered a set of commands. All at once, every monitor in the room shared the same picture. It was an aerial video in what looked like real time.

In a small, windowless shack somewhere in upstate New York,

a pimple-faced young Air Force Airman First Class focused on the monitor in front of him. The joystick in his hand controlled the latest generation Predator attack drone. His orders tasked him to locate and attack one of the many rural area militia groups that had surfaced across the country to challenge the martial law edict from the President.

To the faceless Airman about to murder scores of his fellow citizens, the moral implications were completely lacking, as was the case with most of his Millennial Generation. His interpersonal skills had atrophied long ago, as touch screens, ear buds, and monitors made the rest of the outside world disappear, along with his ability to empathize with his fellow human beings.

It was another day at the office being a winner on the winning side. That was until the Predator he controlled unexpectedly altered its preprogrammed course to the southeast.

"Not a problem," he thought as he disengaged the autopilot to gain manual control. Only after several failed attempts, nothing happened. Never having experienced a serious glitch before, he began to type in conflicting commands in a blind panic, while at the same time fumbling with his headset and console switches to reach his Commanding Officer. "Sir, I have lost telemetry on flight niner, seven, able. I am declaring an emergency along its new flight path."

Fortunately, the Commander was not yet worried because he had experienced drones malfunctioning before, including numerous crashes.

He calmly pulled up the drone's video feed to see if he should command the drone to self-destruct. "Do you have the new course plotted yet, Airman?"

"Yes Sir," he nervously reported. "Its current course will take it over Waterbury, Connecticut and then Wallingford. Its speed has increased to three hundred miles per hour. Should I wait until it is over the ocean to abort?"

As the Commander was about to order an over the ocean

downing, the picture on the drone's monitor changed to the cartoon with Bugs Bunny flying the bomber in WWII. "So you want to be a wise guy, eh? I told you what would happen if you got this little bunny pissed off." Bugs then stared with one bloodshot eye into the camera and concluded, "Bombs away sucka."

When the screen went black, the Commander scrambled to get interceptors in the air to chase down the renegade drone. Unfortunately, for all concerned, only minutes later the Predator launched its four Hellfire missiles into two of the most prominent estates in the Hamptons that belonged to American elite.

An F-35 pilot from the USS Enterprise reported in to the CIC. "Radar shows a land mass to the west."

The pilot banked to those coordinates and five minutes later, a series of islands began to dot the ocean. "I recognize where we are. I trained in these waters."

Another F-35 pilot flying to the south reported. "I am pretty sure I am approaching… Yes, I recognize it as the Windward Passage. I am cloaking to fly lower for a closer look." After ten minutes of silence, she reported from her new position. "I see small villages with thatched roofs, but nothing that resembles anything modern."

The pilot, a highly educated, sensible woman of 32, but new to the task force, continued to circle the island village amazed at how it could exist at all. "What have I got myself into?"

In the Admirals Ready Room, the curtain of green mist suddenly returned. "This is really getting old." This quick assessment of the situation was all Sean had time to express before trouble announced itself in the form of Bowie's second arrival. This time looking like he had just left Berlin in 1979.

"Sorry, am I interrupting anything important?" He looked incredibly stoned.

Alicia was not amused. "Are you like Beetle Juice, except we don't have to think about you and there you are like a bad date who can't take a hint?"

Bowie said nothing, yet his actions were those of one who stood listening to the sound of nails on a chalkboard. To minimize the noise, he reached into the worn leather jacket he wore and pulled out a vial of cocaine. "Anyone up for a snort? Who knows," he said, looking sternly at Alicia. "It might get your tight ass to unclench."

After a quick look at their horrified expressions, he proceeded to lay out two lines on the conference table. "Suit yourself, more for me." After a couple of quick toots, he threw back his head and blasted out in song. "We can be heroes, at least for one day."

"So do you want to be heroes?"

Alicia of course was the one to explode. "What the hell are you doing? My God, is this just a sick joke to you?"

Now with a look of total amusement, Bowie could not help himself. "Well, my dear lady, you are at least partly correct. You can assume that I am your god, because as far as I can see I am the only god you have ever known. Moreover, yes, in many ways this is a great big joke. Your only other option would be a tragedy. Though I have experienced this many times over, I am sure you both will agree that without a sense of humor, any thinking person would go stark raving mad. Which master do you choose to worship?" He then pulled out a fag and lit it.

These last comments forced Sean's brain into overdrive. "It seems like you know a lot about us, as if you have spent time observing our actions. Therefore, you would know that we are more than capable enough to chart our own course."

"What kind of idol would I be if I didn't understand the most basic of your motivations?"

Alicia bit. "So you profess to understand our motivations? If this were the case, then why don't you wave your magic fag, and take us to the end of this nightmare so everyone can go back to…"

"You mean back to face solitary confinement in one of President Harrison's new secret gulags, or hanging from the entrance of a football stadium while seagulls peck out your lifeless eyeballs? Sounds exciting. I thought you two had loftier goals, like, oh, I don't know, saving your world. According to those in the know, you did a good job of it last time, though I am not so forgiving with my judgment. If you make any of your last mistakes I'm afraid the fates will not be so kind this time." As he finished, Bowie began to cough violently, and pulled out a vial of pills, rapidly shaking three out and swallowing them.

Alicia took satisfaction from his obvious discomfort. "So what you are saying is because we have principles we are willing to sacrifice for that gives you the right to run us around like marionettes. Just because we fight for our principles, regardless of the limited chance of success, does not mean we will do whatever bullshit that pleases your overinflated ego."

This elicited another round of laughter from the drug torn entity. "Limited? More like infinitesimal impossibility. Okay, so maybe we don't share everything, but I wish you would take a more British attitude about our situation."

Alicia had enough. "How can you speak of *our* situation when you can disappear in a puff of mist anytime you want while we are stuck figuring out the depraved life or death situations you put us into!" Alicia was in full on rage mode. "Your *fun* cost us two of our closest friends along with hundreds of sailors the last time we were hijacked, and now here we go again. EHYY arvv yodv bhkgsd, eehy, aaanggg!" Suddenly, all she could produce was gibberish.

"Sorry about that, but you are making my headache unbearable. Really, I don't understand how you deal with it, Sean." However, before Sean could defend his wife, Bowie continued, "Let me assure you, this is the first time I have been a party to your little adventure. If it were me who set this in motion, believe me it would be much darker."

To accent this, the lights dimmed, the air became freezing cold, and a sudden dark wind swept through the room. "Trust me when I say, you should prefer your current course of action over any that I might imagine." The room immediately returned to its former atmosphere. "Anyway, you better make sure everyone is well rested, because tomorrow is a very big day for all of you." Without a chance for any rebuttal, Bowie disappeared in a flash.

Alicia looked as if her head was about to explode. "This is all your fault! Why couldn't you have been a fan of the Bee Gee's?"

"You're kidding, right?" Sean didn't have anything else to add in his defense.

She looked at him, like, duh. "We are definitely not going to tell anyone about these visits from Bowie or whatever that was. I don't think it would help to share this bit of new crazy with anyone else in this already too crazy situation."

Before Sean could agree, the phone rang.

"Admiral, the planes have sighted land. The reconnaissance reports combined with the sextant readings have fixed the task force position approximately two hundred miles east of The Bahamas, and it appears we are in pre-Columbian times."

"Thank you Captain Osaka." Sean thought for a moment before he continued. The quickest place to seek shelter was also one of the best natural harbors in the western Atlantic. The irony of setting course to this anchorage was also not lost on Sean. "Set course for Guantanamo Bay."

"Yes Sir," Osaka replied. "The senior commanders have all arrived aboard the Enterprise."

"Have them come to the Admirals Ready Room, and inform Dr. Cutler to join us."

"Will do, Admiral."

Sean then turned his attention to Alicia. "Though I made Osaka my temporary Chief of Staff, on second thought, I think it would be better if you held the position. Do you want to be by my side while I play God again?"

"What the hell, though the choice doesn't seem up to us," Alicia said with a degree of cynicism. "However, it's agreed on. Neither of us say anything about Bowie's visits, right?"

Sean shook his head at the absurdity of it all. "If we did, Dr. Safire and Captain Brewster's mutiny would probably look like a party compared to what would happen if their Admiral was taking council from a coked up cockerel."

⚜

The President's National Security Advisor rushed past President Harrison's secretary, Sarah Whineglaus, without a word into the Oval Office.

Seated behind the Theodore Roosevelt desk, President Susan Harrison was conversing with an agitated Aaron Fletcher, who sat in his usual position on the couch. "You have a list of the casualties?"

"Twenty-five confirmed dead, and another thirty-six injured, and six still unaccounted for, Madam President. Among the dead are seventeen high ranking foreign dignitaries, including the finance ministers of Denmark, France, the United Kingdom, and Germany. Apparently, there were two distinct targets, the members of the IMF [International Monetary Fund], and I am sorry to say, your home, Mr. Fletcher."

He glanced down for further information and frowned. "On top of all that, six other Predators were hacked, and turned their weapons back on their controllers."

Aaron shook his head and wondered how Sean Anthony had put together such an elaborate attack so quickly. He now knew where all the hackers had gone. "Excuse me, Madam President, but do you mind if I take the lead?"

"Not at all Aaron." She figured it was his mess to clean up, and in fact from here on out she would protect herself by letting her Chief of Staff deal with all the fallout.

Aaron looked up at the President as he thought, "Do you think

I can't see what you are doing? It is now only a matter of when and how I kill you, not if," he silently fumed.

"Thank you, Madam President." He then turned his attention back to the head of the NSA, who was on the phone. "Now, Dennis, do your geeks know where the attack originated yet, or do I need to remind you that no one is irreplaceable."

Admiral Dennis Flattery [Director of National Intelligence] knew from previous experiences that one did not report to the President's Chief of Staff unless a solution was at hand. By comparison, Aaron Fletcher made Nixon's Chief of Staff H. R. Haldeman look like a lap dog.

"My people are at a loss to explain who and more importantly, how our firewalls were breached, so for now all drones have been grounded. However, we have narrowed the location of the hackers down to a four-block area in West Virginia. The most likely location appears to be at the Greenbrier Hotel. Tactical teams have cordoned off the approaches and are now working their way through the area."

This prompted laughter from Aaron.

"What's so funny," the President wanted to know.

"First they blow up my home, and then we discover they are operating out of a Cold War bunker the Beltway elite built to crawl into before they destroyed the rest of the world. Order your troops to the Greenbrier, Dennis."

In the bunker at the Greenbrier, the hacker group reacted with elation to the success of their drone attacks, until the reality sunk in that they had just killed real people. The Rockefellers, Bloombergs, and Kochs, names that before were only real to them through the media, displayed on their monitors as very real, visibly bloody, and dead.

All of them, that is, except for Adonis. "Big picture, little picture, it's all the same to me. The more of these assholes we take out, the better I'll sleep at night."

Sean Anthony watched as the shelter went quiet. "Welcome to the battle ladies and gentlemen. Mr. Mean and Nasty is mostly correct in his justifications for lacking empathy for those we murdered today. Let me tell you what we gained. By taking out those who make policy for the IMF, we have disrupted the flow of money to the very oligarchs who have set their agenda to enslave the world for the next three generations. A good day's work if you ask me."

Sean Anthony didn't give them time to dwell on it. "Pack up folks. It is time we changed locations. A rolling stone gathers no moss and all of that." He watched as the group slowly gathered their stuff. "By the way, we are about to have a lot of angry people with big scary weapons blow a large hole in our door."

Their pace rapidly accelerated.

He watched as the hackers threw their gear into duffle bags, and marveled at what this small group had set into motion in such a short order. When everyone appeared ready, Sean Anthony snapped his fingers and they faded behind a curtain of green mist.

⟡

Unlike the first senior staff meeting when they transported into 1941, this time experience sped up the deliberations. After informing the new ship Captains who had not accompanied them on their previous adventure about their trip into WWII, Admiral Sean Phillips laid out their limited options. He knew he had the support of ship Captains Osaka, Daily, Johnson, Lincoln, Goddard, Barrish, Turner, Peck, Gable, and the carrier Air Wing Commander Captain *Dash* Nelson from their shared experience in the 1942 reality. If any of the others had a problem, this time Sean would not give them any choice but to obey his orders.

"Though we have twice as many supplies this time, our first order of business is to find a safe harbor to anchor the task force, which is the reason I altered our course to Cuba. We must conserve our limited resources because reports from our reconnaissance indicate there is little hope of resupply."

To add to the imminent sense of threat, Sean took a moment to look his commanders over before continuing. "We are on our own in this, and how we handle the next few weeks will determine who among us will come through it alive." The tone of Sean's voice and his demeanor conveyed the seriousness of their position and succeeded in filling the room with tension.

Satisfied he had made his point, Sean calmly relayed his orders. "As you all know, we are on course to cruise through the Windward Passage to shelter in Guantanamo Bay. With the exception of the nuclear powered Enterprise and submarines, one of our main considerations will be fuel. To that end, since we cannot afford her fuel needs, I have decided the Missouri will remain in port as the centerpiece of a temporary settlement ashore.

"Based on our last experience, once we clear a 250 mile perimeter around our task force, you will stand down from General Quarters, and we will reduce speed to conserve fuel. To those who were a part of our last displacement, I need each one of you to select strong leaders to transfer to those ships experiencing this for the first time. There is going to be scuttlebutt, so if we can reassure the sailors throughout the task force that we have some control over the situation, it will help lower the confusion and uncertainty. Any questions?"

Captain Henry Jackson of the Ticonderoga class cruiser USS Shiloh CG-67 was first to respond. "I don't know about any of the others who haven't served under you, but I don't care if you have experienced this insanity before. I don't see how you can be so cavalier with so many lives at stake. For all we know this could be some form of chemical warfare and we are all hallucinating."

This got a laugh from those who had experienced the early hours following the jump into 1941.

"You will learn quickly, Captain," Sean replied sternly. "Nevertheless, as we don't have the time to work you through your difficulties right now, you will follow my orders completely and without hesitation."

Fourth in command and second ranking officer by seniority, Captain Mark Daily of the nuclear powered attack submarine USS Seawolf SSN-21 calmly backed his Admiral. "Captain Jackson, we learned the hard way that argumentative debate aboard ships of war only leads to insubordination and in our case a deadly mutiny during our trip into the 1940s. Therefore, those of us who were there understand strict discipline throughout the ranks is essential."

As the other experienced ship Captains nodded in agreement, Captain Frederick Johnson of the Ticonderoga class cruiser USS Chancellorsville CG-62 added his opinion. "Captain Jackson, I was one of those who questioned our purpose and direction last time, and from our experience in the 1942 reality, I can assure you that following the orders of Admiral Phillips and Secretary Calhoun *is* our best chance of getting through this."

Sean had heard enough. "From now on, when I give an order, it will be carried out as if your life depends on it, because ladies and gentlemen it very well might be. Unfortunately, I can assure you all that whoever is pulling the strings will be quick to ensure their intentions in a manner most disadvantageous to us.

"Our responsibilities for now are to use every means at our disposal to see if there are any scientific advantages we can exploit." Sean pointed to Rebecca. "Dr. Cutler is in charge of this endeavor, and you will give her your full support whenever it is called for."

Unaccustomed to this *in-command* version of Sean, Rebecca meekly nodded in acknowledgment.

"Since Admiral Feller and his Chief of Staff were left behind, former Rear Admiral UH Alicia Calhoun Phillips has agreed to take on duties as my Chief of Staff and second in command. For clarity you are to address her as Admiral Calhoun." Then much to the chagrin of Captain Jackson, Sean added. "Cruiser Captains Lincoln and Johnson will share Alpha Whiskey [AWC – Air Warfare

Command] on 12 hour shifts. To Senior Civilian Officer Bradley Franks, Commanders Wu, Brizuela, and Peck, Commander Gable will be the senior supply commander. As CWC [Composite Warfare Commander] I, and Admiral Calhoun in my absence, will hold certain assets close."

Sean then turned his attention back to Captain Jackson. "We now sail in the most treacherous of waters Captain, and if we do not act in unison, ships will sink and sailors will die. I want it clear right now that I will not suffer insubordination from anyone down to the most junior rating in the task force."

The firmness of Sean's delivery had the desired effect; the chain of command was not open to debate. The meeting ended when no one else dared to ask any other questions.

"Captain Nelson and ship Captains Osaka, Daily, Goddard, Gable, Lincoln, and Johnson, please remain, you too Dr. Cutler. The rest of you are dismissed."

When the others had left, Sean turned first to Dr. Cutler. "Rebecca, I need you to come up to speed quickly on the Specter upgrades."

She was quick to respond. "I have discovered that except for the John Paul Jones, Princeton, Laramie, and Amelia Earhart of the Missouri group, each ship can now cruise independently and stay cloaked. I will look into what it will take to install the upgraded Specter on those ships. I have spent enough time to understand the networks are communicating at a level I did not expect. I will meet with all of those in the task force who are responsible for Specter on their respective ships so I can see how all the new pieces fit. I need all the help I can get to catch up with what have I missed."

"Thank you Dr. Cutler. Make the Princeton and John Paul Jones your priority. That will be all."

"See you guys around." Rebecca was about to hug both Sean and Alicia when she realized by his reaction that now would not be the time. Instead, she turned to spread her sunshine on the other ship Captains when Sean waved her off, to their disappointment. Rebecca had matured into quite the beautiful woman, and Sean instinctively felt it necessary to protect her, and them.

As soon as she left, Captain Daily asked Sean, "So what do you need from the rest of us?"

"From you specifically, Dean, I need you to acclimate our new sub driver as quickly as possible. For all we know, I may need to deploy one or more of our nuclear powered subs to far waters. We need to conserve the destroyers and cruisers time at sea. Anyway, I need you to determine if we can count on Commander James for independent operations."

"Yes Sir."

"Captain Lincoln and Commanders Goddard and Gable, you will do the same with the new cruiser, destroyer, and cargo ship Captains."

"Aye Aye Admiral," they responded in unison.

"Captain Nelson, I know we have more aircraft and personnel aboard this trip, so do the same throughout your air wing."

"Yes Sir."

"Captains Lincoln and Johnson, as Alpha Whiskey you will be responsible for our defenses, however, I will coordinate with Captain Nelson for certain air missions before orders flow through the system."

The two acknowledged their orders.

"Commander Gable, I want a complete inventory of our supplies, and I want you to coordinate with the XO on the Missouri to establish a settlement ashore.

"Any questions?" When silence greeted him, Sean dismissed them.

Once they were alone, Alicia queried her husband, "So what do you think lover?"

"I think we need a drink," Sean responded as he grabbed two

glasses from the bar.

"Seriously," Alicia probed as he poured.

"Okay, so here we are in the Caribbean basin, reconnaissance reports a few scattered small settlements, and in the way of modern technology, nothing. If I were to hazard a guess, the only thing that makes sense is they are pre-Columbian societies."

Sean handed Alicia her drink. "This must have something to do with European expansion into the New World. All of that aside, I can't imagine the need for our firepower against such primitive people, so there has to be more to the picture."

Alicia shook her head in the affirmative. "Then we are in agreement. That must be why you impressed upon Rebecca the importance of her coming up to speed with the second generation Specter. So what do you think we are going to run into tomorrow?"

Sean thought for a moment, and then smiled. "Almost anything would be better than another audience with Beetle Juice Bowie."

As evening approached, with the Enterprise Task Force headed southwest toward the Windward Passage, the radar operator on the starboard trailing Los Angeles class attack submarine USS Hampton SSN-767 reported in. "Sir, I am picking up multiple small contacts on the water seventy miles to the northwest, traveling east at 5 knots."

Captain Marlowe Turner relayed the information to the Enterprise CIC, who then immediately reported the news to Sean in the Admirals Quarters.

Sean quickly contacted Captain Nelson. "Send an F-35 to check out the contacts, with orders to stay cloaked. We are headed to the CIC."

Twenty minutes later the first report came in. "Fifteen contacts, wood built, rigged with large square black sails, and appear to be highly modified ocean-going canoes heading east, running in battle formation." On closer examination, *Dash* noticed something vaguely familiar about the canoes' construction. "One more thing. These canoes definitely have elements of 15th Century European architecture built into them."

The voice sounded too familiar to Sean, so he took to the mike. "Captain Nelson?"

"Yes Sir?"

"Couldn't stand to sit it out, could you?"

"No Sir. Born to fly a jet, not a desk, Sir."

"All right, extend your search along their projected course and see what they are hunting."

Sean then called out to the Operations Specialist in charge of cloaking the task force. "Engage Specter."

"Aye Aye Admiral, engage Specter."

Alicia knew Sean was worried. "What is it?"

"Pre-Columbian Caribbean and a fleet of altered native canoes rigged with black sails in attack formation heading into the dark of the night. Sounds like someone beat us here."

Another ten minutes passed before the F-35 reported another three contacts forty miles to the northwest. Captain *Dash* Nelson, as Air Wing Commander, normally would have tasked others for the mission, but considering the history that now sailed on the ocean directly below him, was glad he had not. He took great joy in reporting it. "Admiral, you are not going to believe who else is sharing our chunk of ocean with us."

Sean's response brought all conversation in the CIC to a sudden halt. "The Nina, Pinta, and Santa Maria."

Nelson was not surprised the Admiral already knew. That is why he was the Admiral. "Looks like someone down there is trying like hell to change another history, boss." Nelson had to laugh at the absurdity of the moment.

Sean wanted to laugh with Captain Nelson, but knew better. "Captain, a little more professionalism, please." Sean needed a moment to think. "Continue to orbit and stand by for further orders."

Then, with a nod to Alicia, they left the CIC for a private consultation.

Back in the Admirals Ready Room, Sean poured a shot of Jack Daniels Single Barrel as he posed the issue. "Here it is. Should we engage or stand down?"

"I suppose if we did intercede, we would be doing exactly what Mr. Bowie set us up for," Alicia replied. "What other reason can there be for why we are here?"

Sean took a drink from his tumbler and countered. "Or, he expects us to let history change. Either way, whoever is commanding those altered native craft has already changed history."

Alicia summoned her historical memories of the era. "Okay, let's think the problem through. Columbus sighted land at 2:00 AM on 12 October 1492, and based upon Captain Nelson's report of their position, this must be the evening of 11 October 1492. Slavery and the genocide of millions of the indigenous population followed his arrival. It boggles my mind that we still celebrate Columbus Day. That is like closing the banks for Hitler's birthday."

"Screw Bowie. I am for staying out of it and let's see what happens," Sean announced emphatically like a little boy who wanted to take his ball and go home.

"Regardless of what happens?" Alicia exclaimed. "What if they wipe out the Spanish?"

Sean attempted to lessen her worries. "As we have discovered from our past experiences, this reality has nothing to do with the reality we left behind, so why not? If you remember correctly, our world was in the middle of a complete breakdown when we left."

Alicia walked over and gave him a quick kiss. "And by us deciding the fates of others here, do you think we can guarantee a better world anywhere else? Ideas like that led Lenin to the Russian revolution, which led directly to Stalin and Hitler. I think you had better try to find us a different path lover. I don't want to go down in any reality's history books as a monster."

"I hate this existential claptrap." Sean was exasperated. "Can't we click our heels together three times and go back to drinking champagne in Cambia?"

"I wish," Alicia agreed, but after a moment to enjoy the thought, she returned her attention to this reality. "Look, in 1941, we stopped the attack on Pearl Harbor, stopped the slaughter of WWII, and worked toward changing the world for the better. Now we are in a similar position, but what bothers me this time is why weren't we tasked to take out Columbus' ships?"

Sean agreed. "Good question. If whoever is pulling our strings is trying to rewrite history to avoid the next five centuries of carnage, why would they put someone else here to do the same before us?"

They looked at each other and simultaneously exclaimed, "Tony!"

With a bit more confidence, Sean pondered their choices and came to a decision. "Let's see how it plays out."

"Agreed."

When they returned to the CIC, Sean had the radio operator contact Captain *Dash* Nelson. "Continue to observe and report. We will send you up some juice so you can extend your mission. And one other thing Captain, we have reason to believe the leader of the attack might be Captain Anthony Knox."

"Tony? Yep, that figures," *Dash* interrupted.

"*Captain Nelson*, do I need to remind you of Navy decorum, *again*?"

"No Sir, sorry Sir."

"If we are correct and you can confirm it is Tony, briefly uncloak and give him a salute to let him know we are here."

"Aye Aye Admiral."

Captain *Dash* Nelson chuckled as he thought forward to see the look on Tony's face when he found out the task force was bearing down on his little armada. "This could be fun." He then thought about the irony that not only was he the first to deliver an atomic weapon in 1942, dropped in the Russian wilderness as a show of force, but now he will also witness the cancelation of one of the landmark events in Western civilization history.

⎯⎯✦⎯⎯

Special Forces teams stormed the underground maze of the Greenbrier Hotel, only to find nary a soul in any of the dozens of rooms. Aaron strode through the massive blast doors of the National Historic Landmark in such a manner the exiting soldiers scattered out of his way. He surveyed the rows of computer terminals in the cavernous cafeteria hall and wondered why Sean Anthony had left them there.

"Everyone out now!" His shout echoed throughout the massive complex. Minutes later when he was alone, he placed a call to Admiral Dennis A. Flattery. "Get your people in here now and figure out if any of our other security networks have been hacked." After listening to the Admiral's response, Aaron continued his order. "Tell your techies if it looks too good to be true, then it is. No one is to connect a single piece of equipment to our networks. Also, make sure that you keep anyone who enters this complex in complete lockdown until I say otherwise. None of this gets out."

After he completed the call, he took one last look around to see one of the monitors halfway down row of computers come to life. As he approached it, big as life sat Sean Anthony in a Jacuzzi sipping a margarita through a straw. "Are you ready to give up?"

Aaron responded with laughter. "I control the levers of power across the entire world, which also means with a flick of my wrist I can blow everything into a pile of rubble. What do you have? A few self-important children bred to entitlement as if the gods had sired them. So you can still kick up a little dust, so what. I still hold all the cards."

"Well, Aaron, I guess this means you haven't any interest in what comes next. After all the work I put in to derail your egomaniacal trip, I would be hurt if you are not interested."

"What like corrupting missile defense, retasking important satellites, or flushing all the toilets in the world at once? Come on Sean Anthony, we both know what comes next. Do we really need to play it out?"

"You are the one, or at least the representative of the one who decided long ago to make a big deal out of nothing, or none of this would be necessary." A hand appeared in the video and replaced Sean Anthony's margarita with a fresh one. "Thank you hand."

Aaron was still not impressed. "Nothing I have done so far compares to what *your* dad did. You better than anyone else knows why I have the freedom to interact with these idiot humans, which means your dad can't change the rules simply because I influenced the humans to nuke San Francisco. However, I must say I am ecstatic that he did with his direct intervention, because now we can end the charade."

Sean Anthony used his free hand to make waves in the water. "There you go again, counting your scalps before the bodies are cold. To argue your point would be a complete waste of breath, though I still don't understand why you decided to interfere with life here on Earth, when you had so many other options to exercise your unique brand of chaos elsewhere. However, I suppose the whole idea of conflict by false gods has always been your favorite tool."

Aaron suddenly appeared in the Jacuzzi alongside Sean Anthony, with his own margarita in hand. "Unlike you and *your* father, I never saw the point of parceling out bits and pieces of what took us hundreds of thousands of years to become. On other worlds, life begins and life ends without any help from us, yet it is you who presumes to play creator on a world better suited for our enjoyment than billions of self-centered primates."

Sean Anthony smiled. "You didn't seem to mind the millions of years that came before. In fact, I recall your hand in the T. Rex and the Variraptor, whose predatory skills you so thoughtfully brought out of extinction to sprinkle throughout everything now living."

Aaron shot Sean Anthony a piercing glare. "The difference is no other creature in this planet's history ever took so much joy in the sport of killing than those you now try to save. Besides, how can you possibly compare your brittle little creations with those that were so massive you could feel their approach from miles away? What is truly laughable is that it took dad 60 million years to come up with this after 200 million years of perfection. He built a creature so foul it consumes everything in its path as their birthright, and then shits it out all over the place without regard to consequences.

"I'm obviously not the only one who understands this. It is only because interest in this planet has plummeted to the point of complete irrelevancy that father has the room to flaunt his disregard of the rules. Surpassing this arrogance, he has the balls to grant them the power to be able to spread this filth to other planets. Not going to happen."

Sean Anthony mockingly rolled his eyes. "So the chicken or the egg thing again. I say interest waned because of 200 million years of the same old same old while you pine for the good old days like the police officer who does not understand why he can't shoot a man because of the color of his skin. You claim it as inevitable, while I argue otherwise, so here we are. I truly believe you and those who support your interventions are simply afraid if we left them alone, they would evolve beyond our control to become something greater than us."

Sean Anthony snapped his fingers and the spitting image of Senator Elizabeth Warren appeared in a bikini, and with a smile handed him another margarita, then disappeared. "We have evolved other life forms to successfully outgrow the limits of this planet, but with their passion and intellect, humans have accomplished more in a thousandth of the time. They will be allowed to continue in spite of the horrific roadblocks you and your mother continually place in their path."

Aaron snapped his fingers and the image of a drug lord appeared with syringe in hand, which he calmly injected into Aaron's arm before he too disappeared. "This is boring me. You know how I get when you cover the same tired ground about right and wrong. I have a much better idea. Why don't you tell me where father sent your friends flying off to? You do know it got mom's attention, though she still worries about me knowing too much about her plans."

Sean Anthony slowly sunk beneath the water and remained under long enough that Aaron was about to leave in disgust. He sprang to the surface like a small child, drink still clutched in his hand. "Look at that, didn't spill a drop." He wiped the water out of his eyes and answered Aaron. "To tell you the truth, I'm not sure what dear old dad has in mind. Maybe he sent them someplace where he could get some food that wasn't grown in poisoned soil, genetically modified, or hosed down with glyphosate, and no one else was available."

Aaron ignored his sarcasm. "I would think that you would be more concerned, since your *mother*, one Dr. Rebecca Cutler happened to be aboard the Missouri, which appeared like a blast from the past right before they all disappeared. Who knows what could happen to her if there isn't anyone around to protect her." Aaron knew he scored with the threat, and his twisted smile gave it away.

Sean Anthony refused to bite. "Wherever she is, you can be sure she is working hard to successfully craft an outcome detrimental to yours.

"Anyway, it has been a hoot catching up and all, but I have more important matters to deal with." Sean Anthony picked up his cell phone and checked the time. "Besides, you should be receiving a call any minute from your boss, and I don't want to be around when you get it."

With a final yank on the tiger's tail, Sean Anthony concluded, "You really must learn to channel all of your daddy issues away from the slaughter of millions of those you deem less than you, into something a little more constructive. Seems to me that you have a sociopathic need to prove your worth, bordering on self-loathing."

"As opposed to you, the picture of perfection with your gleaming white teeth and nary a hair ever out of place? It isn't hard to see why it is so important for father to save life on this planet, after all, he modeled it in his image. Add to the burden to live up to father's expectations without losing yourself, and I perfectly understand your lack of perspective."

Aaron paused long enough to accept a refill from Charles Manson, who quickly came and went. "However, none of this changes the only fact that matters. I refuse to be stuck any longer on this little backwater planet surrounded by over-amped simians who live as if the universe revolves around them. In fact, it is simply a testament to our patience that we have waited this long to put an end to their stunningly obvious hubris."

"As usual, you give yourself too much credit Aaron. From the moment you resorted to turning Faux News and Rushbarf loose on the masses, only an idiot couldn't see where you were headed. Now the question you have to ask yourself is whose idea was it really? Is President Harrison your creation? I don't know, sometimes it can be hard to remember exactly why one does anything."

A towel appeared next to Sean Anthony, which he grabbed as he stepped out of the Jacuzzi. After a vigorous rubdown, he waved to Aaron in farewell. "I've got to go for now, but you really should learn how to show a little curiosity for once in your existence. You might surprise yourself and actually come up with an original idea." With a smile, Sean Anthony faded away.

Enraged, Aaron's mind filled with images of the hundreds of

methods he dreamed of eviscerating his rival, finally settling on a slow death tied to an anthill, this time with a new twist. "Yes, violating his human pet while he watches in helpless agony as thousands of hungry ants slowly rip him apart would be even better." An enticing thought to lighten his mood for the rest of the day.

Aaron had returned to his White House office, where he now sat with his feet up on the desk, and true to Sean Anthony's earlier prediction, the phone rang. After taking a moment to compose himself, he answered it. After listening for a moment in silence, Aaron's face began to turn red. He slammed the phone down and stormed out of the office, quickly walking to the Oval Office where a clearly agitated President Harrison waited. Aaron reigned in his anger to report with an attitude of indifference what he found in the bunker.

"We missed them. However, the geeks at the NSA are working through the encryption codes on the computers and servers they left behind. We will be able to find out what else they have been up to."

Aaron quickly noticed that President Susan Harrison wasn't showing the slightest interest in what he said. "Am I boring you?"

"Obviously you haven't been listening to the latest financial news, what with being so involved in trying to run your *New World Order*." For one of the few times in their relationship, Harrison felt she could be the one who dished out the ridicule.

"What in the hell are you talking about?"

President Harrison did her best to mimic Aaron's patronizing mannerisms. "If you have all of their equipment, then could you please explain to me how they managed to hack the New York Stock Exchange and wipe out over one trillion dollars of assets only an hour ago?"

Aaron put aside for a moment his desire to punch the smug look right off the President's face. Instead, he reached into his pocket as he thought, "How did they launch such a complex program so soon after the drone strikes?" Aaron fished out the small bottle of oxycodone, which he shook two pills out of, and handed to the President. "Take these before you say anything else that you will regret."

Without regard to President Harrison's power and fed up with the time it took to protect her from her stupidity, Aaron informed her, "I will be out of touch for a little while. Meanwhile, order that idiot Dennis to limit data exchanges through our satellite uplinks until we get control of the situation."

President Harrison hesitated before swallowing the offered drugs that fed her addiction, but only for a moment. "Where are you going?" All the earlier bravado had disappeared from her voice, replaced by the needy whine of a small child. "You can't leave me in the middle of a crisis without my permission."

Aaron walked over to where the President stood with a look of pure evil and schooled her on what was what. "First off you stupid whiny little bitch, don't you ever tell me what I can or cannot do. Second, if you want to keep breathing through that pretty mouth of yours, do not raise your voice to me ever again. Just because I occasionally let you suck on my cock, does not mean I will not hesitate to carve the tongue right out of your mouth. It wasn't that good anyway. Are we clear?"

The President was too stunned to speak. The man who she spent twenty-six years on the road to the White House with, a man whose ability to charm his way to the top of the food chain, had exposed his true self. President Harrison's world came crashing down with the realization she could do nothing about the psychopath who had exposed himself to be every bit the tyrant as Hitler.

Then to prove the complexity of his evil, Aaron reverted from his sociopathic aspect, and turned on the charm. "I need to reach out to some people who, let's say, you don't need to know about, plausible deniability and all, and let them know that we are still on track. I will be in touch when I return." Aaron pulled a piece of paper out of his pocket. On it were the names of every one of those Sean Anthony used to design his cyberattacks. "Don't worry Susan, I should have this sorted out in short order, and will return tomorrow."

After he left, Aaron took a moment to savor his mental rape of the President. With a sigh of contentment, he let the mist take him away, all the way to a private office in the Kremlin. "I need a little help Sergei."

From the crow's-nest of the Nina, the lookout shouted to those on the small ship's deck below "Land ahoy, 5 degrees off the starboard bow!"

Normally one would think a wild celebration would commence on the three waterlogged wooden ships after seventy plus days sailing into the unknown. However, this was the 11th false sighting in the last three weeks, so Captain Vincente Yanez Pinzon needed further validation before he ordered the helmsman to alter their course. Small hand held telescopes on the Nina, Pinta, and Santa Maria scanned the dark ocean ahead.

"Captain Pinzon, I think the lights are coming from objects on the water instead of land."

Captain Pinzon's only concern was to step on firm ground again. If there were boats in the water, that meant land might be near. "Change course to intercept," he ordered the helmsman.

As the three ships steered toward the lights, it quickly became apparent the unidentified guests changed course to keep their distance from the sluggish Spanish vessels. Barnacles that fouled the ship's bottoms and long trails of moss slowed them to a walking speed. It became clear after several course changes that the intruders were not going to let the Spanish galleons come any closer.

"I don't like the look of this." Now fearing an impending attack,

Columbus ordered the three ships to break out the weapons, and prepare to repel boarders. The crews rushed to dispense muskets, pistols, cutlasses, and mount swivel guns to the ships railings. The ships didn't carry any of the traditional cannon because with only a six foot draft any heavy weapons would have capsized the dangerously top heavy ships. Armed for a sea battle they were not.

With the 100 plus members of the expedition focused on what was going on in front of them, nobody dreamed that their ruin now lay in the darkness a mere mile astern.

On the bow of the Renée Aslan, Tony had his telescope focused on his prey. Everything appeared to be working perfectly, but he knew of too many times that was when things had the greatest chance to go wrong. With his Taíno fleet under strict orders not to make a sound, Tony motioned for the helmsman to alter course. Six long boats moved to the Pinta's starboard side, while the remaining eight split off to the Nina's port. He would fight the battle from 400 yards, out of reach of the Spaniard's pitiful arsenal of weapons. With sails black as night and oars muffled, they reached their desired positions undiscovered. When at last lookouts on the Pinta thought to look behind them, it was too late for the doomed Spaniards.

"Fire!" Tony screamed. All at once from both sides, cannons launched their 10-pound balls at the Spanish ships. With the Spaniards all forward watching the decoys, the first explosions only tore out large chunks of the ship's sides without many casualties. This all changed as the ships pulled even with each other. The second and third volleys blasted wooden shrapnel into the crews as they scrambled to their battle stations, shredding and dismembering them by the score.

It was all over in ten short minutes. Completely engulfed by fire, the Pinta rolled over and slid beneath the sea, followed in quick order by the Nina, and finally Columbus's ship, the Santa Maria. Columbus himself did not survive the third volley, as one of the cannonballs cleaved his head cleanly from his body.

Now the part of the attack Tony had dreaded for the last year, the slaughter of any of those who managed to survive the battle. He knew they could not risk the slightest chance of disease to come ashore.

As drilled into them by Tony to protect themselves, the Taíno kept their distance by using long spears to slaughter any survivors still in the water. After thirty minutes, the last of the pitiful cries for mercy ended.

As they broke off to head for home, one of Tony's Taíno crew screamed out, "Yúcahu, is that flying monster one of your servants?"

Surprised, Tony whipped around to see an uncloaked F-35 hovering 100 yards off the deck of his ship. His heart jumped into his throat when the plane gave him a wing dip acknowledgment.

"Yúcahu, why are you leaving us?"

"Damn it!" was all Tony had time to yell as the green mist worked its way up his body.

As the report came into the CIC confirming the total destruction of the Spanish ships and sailors, Alicia spotted the telltale wisp of green mist. With the regularity of this insanity, she warned Sean without a hint of excitement in her voice. "Here we go again."

In the blink of an eye, Sean and Alicia found themselves seated at a dining room table, in an average looking suburban home. Though the extensive spread of food was impressive, it was lost in who also sat at the table across from them. Though dressed only in enough clothing to cover his junk, and with salt and pepper colored hair down to his shoulders and a beard to match, in his gone native look it was still Tony.

Sean rose in excitement from the table and walked around the table to embrace his long lost friend. "Of course it had to be you on one of those canoes!"

Though Sean wanted to ask Tony a thousand questions at once, especially the one about his Robinson Crusoe appearance, the situation demanded otherwise. Instead, he gathered himself and calmly asked, "Why did you feel a need to wipe out Columbus?"

"Good to see you too." As he said this, Tony walked around the table to Alicia's seat and gave her a kiss on the forehead. "I'm glad to see you both in good health, and yes, I guess there is much for us to catch up on. Have you met Franklin yet?"

"Franklin who?" Alicia suspiciously asked. "We never met a Franklin, but we did have the displeasure of the company of an apparition presenting itself as David Bowie personas *way* too many times."

As if given their cue from the director, Benjamin Franklin appeared at one end of the table and David Bowie the opposite. The juxtaposition of these two iconic characters, especially with Bowie in his suave *Duke* incarnation with white suit, fedora, and all, left the other three speechless.

"Well Franklin, it appears we are off to a smashing beginning," Bowie stated, as he lifted his glass of wine in salute.

Franklin returned the salute with a smile, before he added, "That's easy for you to say. All you had to do was pop in at the last moment, while I've spent the last two years making sure Anthony did his part."

"Like you didn't enjoy all the drama," Bowie retorted. "Besides, what would be the point of having old diplomatic you with Sean and Alicia? You people would have talked each other to death before you could accomplish anything. And me with Captain Anthony, two divas together? We both know I would have killed him within the first hour."

While Sean and Alicia were content for the moment to enjoy the bizarre exchange, Tony was not. After spending two days on the ocean, and then attacking and destroying Columbus, he didn't need any of this. It didn't help that he felt dressed like a clown at the Met surrounded by tuxedo's.

"Who the hell are you supposed to be? I mean really, two years listening to Benji over there, and now a nutjob performing artist brings my friends and enough naval power to destroy this world ten times over. What's next, the Lone Ranger and Tonto riding in with Custer and the 7th Cavalry being chased by Soviet T-74 Battle Tanks?"

This elicited laughter from Franklin, who responded with his infamous charm. "You have to admit the last two years of your life were the most at peace you have ever been Captain Knox. How many people do you know who have had the honor to single-handedly save an entire culture?"

"Two years?" Sean ignored the insanity for a moment and leaned in to look directly at Tony. "According to Rebecca, you and Carl disappeared off the bridge of the Missouri earlier today while in 1951."

Tony glared at Franklin. "It figures. I can see where two years could seem like one long day when spent pretending to be a god." He then turned to the others. "Franklin convinced me that taking out Columbus would give these people a chance to prepare for the new world."

Alicia surveyed Tony in amusement. "I don't know about all of that, but you look ten years younger. Whether it was ten years or ten minutes, it's obvious that your time here has been good for you." Alicia then subtly shifted the conversation. "By the way, it isn't like I am not thrilled to see you again, but where exactly are we, and I mean literally where is this house currently situated, not where is it in time?"

Tony thought for a moment if he should share the part about Renée being the other reason for his actions, and concluded that now would not be the best time. Instead, he decided to tweak the lion's tail. "It's a little something our faux Founding Father here set up for me while I played God. You want to see the Jacuzzi Alicia?" He winked at her and motioned for them to follow as he stood up.

"Playing God?" It was Alicia's turn to laugh as she got up to follow Sean and Tony out of the room. Except when they went through the door, instead of the outdoor patio, they found themselves right back in the dining room.

Though Franklin's back was to them, he ominously warned Tony, "It's rude to walk out on your guests, Captain."

"It's not like I can hide anything from you, so what's the big deal?" This time Tony headed for the patio door, but before he could turn the handle, this time he found the three of them back in their seats.

Bowie leaned forward and glared at Tony. "Cheeky bastard. I can now see why he is yours."

Franklin smiled at the oil and water effect Tony and Bowie shared. "Come now David, we don't want to give our guests the wrong idea."

Franklin politely asked once again of Tony, "Mr. Knox, as I have repeatedly informed you, your reward for today's efforts would be something special. And now here you sit breaking bread and..." Franklin stopped to lift his wine glass in salute. "Drinking wine together again with your most trusted companions. And if that isn't special enough, we both know what will complete the picture." He slyly gave Tony a wink before he ominously proclaimed to those present, "Now the real work can get started."

Tony made a show of feigning boredom, before he once again stood up to leave the table. "I'd *really* like to show you guys the Jacuzzi."

Sean and Alicia looked at each other to see what they should do about the drama playing out between the two hardheaded men. With a nod, they stood up to follow Tony's lead. This time they hadn't taken a step, before a lightning bolt erupted in Bowie's hand, which he then hurled across the room, striking the wall behind Tony.

The three hit the deck as debris showered down all around them.

Franklin turned around and looked down on them while shaking his head. "I suppose I should have warned you, David has quite the temper when he feels put upon."

Before they could get to their feet and brush off the dust, the damaged wall reformed and the debris disappeared. "He is awfully hard on the environment when he gets this way. Please sit back down. We have much to negotiate now that you have saved the Taíno, who if I am not mistaken you should be curious about how they are doing after you so mysteriously disappeared."

When Tony did not reply immediately, Sean decided to risk further affronting Bowie. "So why did Tony destroy Columbus? And may I ask what my ships and crew have to do with that or pre-Columbian history?"

Franklin decided it would be better for all concerned if he answered for Bowie. "If it were within my power to explain the whys of your crazy little adventure, believe me I would love to Admiral Phillips. Unfortunately, all it would accomplish is to hurt all of your heads.

"Every one of your actions will have consequences, both here and back home. Trust me when I tell you that you don't want to know the true scope of those consequences. There are some very unpleasant people who have taken steps to elicit major changes to the landscape of your home reality over the coming weeks."

Sean mustered up all the defiance at his disposal. "So in effect, we are merely the fodder that you chose to act out your own conflict. What if we choose not to participate?"

Franklin smiled and cocked his head to peer at Sean over his bifocals. "Those who choose to be an active partner in these adventures with us not only get the joy of our company, but they also receive the opportunity to become something greater than merely mortal. Sound intriguing enough to all of you?"

Then Bowie added in a manner that implied he didn't care one way or another, "Or you can watch as I turn your ships and crews to dust."

Sean didn't doubt for a moment he could make it so with merely a thought. "So what do you want from us." He needed to buy them some time.

"At the moment, nothing. The Taíno who attacked Columbus will return safely to their homes, and you three go do what you would normally do as commanders of your people."

"You got a Gordian Knot I can untie? Seems it would be an easier task than what you want from us." Tony was back in full voice and unconcerned what further damage Bowie might deliver. "So all you want from us is to sit on our hands and wait for the next disaster to reveal itself?"

"Careful Anthony," Bowie warned. "Just because Franklin values your warrior spirit does not mean I will allow you to criticize our actions. You are so typical of your race and gender, quick to rage and slow to reason."

Bowie then pleaded with Franklin. "Can't you do something with this one?"

"With your history, you know better than anyone that you have to take the bad with the good. Look at how you over reacted when Daphne rejected you."

"I wasn't the one who turned her into a tree."

Franklin raised his eyes above his bifocals as if to admonish Bowie. "You ran that sweet thing into the ground before *he* intervened. Anyway, we are getting ahead of ourselves. The way I see it, the opposition will move rapidly now that we have thrown down the gauntlet. It has been a pleasure working with you Captain Anthony Knox."

Before they could ask anything else, the two disparate entities disappeared as Franklin's voice without form left a final comment. "I do wish you will enjoy the Jacuzzi one day soon, especially you Mrs. Calhoun Phillips."

"The guy's a pervert," Tony snarled, as the green mist swirled around them.

Before they could take another breath, Sean, Alicia, and Tony found themselves seated in the Admirals Ready Room aboard the Enterprise.

Alicia thought for a moment about her reaction to the sudden shift in location, or more properly put, her lack of reaction to transporting through space from one physical location to another. "Proves you can get used to anything."

"What was that?" Still dealing with his confusion over the rapid-fire turn of events, Sean could not pick out the one particular *anything* Alicia had referred to.

"Nothing important." Alicia tilted her head slightly as her eyes wandered off to another place. "What I wouldn't give to not have anything to do but serenely stare out at the ocean after a nice two hour sweat fest with my new husband."

Tony jumped in with his take on their situation. "Someone up there definitely has a sense of humor. You two, the brains of this outfit, get Sean's favorite artist from the 70s, and I, the reactive monkey, wind up with one of the greatest minds in history."

Tony went straight for the JD, but stopped abruptly. "Slow to reason? A diva? Who is he kidding? This coming from a guy who thought it would be a good idea to go up against an empire with a bunch of rusty muskets." Tony grabbed some glasses and handed them out before he retrieved the bottle of Jack Daniels Single Barrel.

After Tony had poured them all a liberal amount, Sean gave a toast. "Here's to being thankful they are not Iggy Pop and Jack Kerouac or we would never get anything done."

Tony didn't agree. "I'm just saying any of them would be more fun than Franklin."

"Jealous?" Sean enjoyed the moment of distraction.

"You saw what they are capable of. It's like the age of enlightenment meets the terminator on steroids." Tony was not happy that his understanding of the situation had to change so abruptly with the sudden appearance of the Enterprise Task Force and its own sponsor. "If I am so slow to reason, then explain to me how I managed to convince an entire culture that I am their god. Slow to reason? Screw Bowie. What did he ever do, besides seduce the best of his generation to question their sexuality? Wait a minute, I get it."

Sean did not want to travel down that messy road. "So Alicia, what do you really think about our all-powerful hosts?"

Her eyes focused on him, yet Sean could see his words failed to penetrate her thoughts. "So if given the choice, which personality would you choose to torment you?" Still nothing. "You know I would enjoy this more if a naked Goldie Hawn in her prime..." Still nothing. "Alicia? Earth to *Alicia*." Sean couldn't remember any time Alicia had zoned out so completely, so he reached over and grabbed her arm. "What is going on?"

Sean's insistence finally punctured Alicia's idyllic musings. With a smile, she reassured him. "Fret not lover, I just needed a moment. These little surprises can really upset one's perspective. So what do you have in mind?"

Tony looked at Sean as if Alicia had lost her mind. "Maybe you should have Sickbay check her out. Either that or summon a preacher to see if we need an exorcism." Tony crossed his fingers in the shape of a crucifix, and thrust it at Alicia.

"Are you sure you're all right?" Sean asked to make sure.

"I will be as soon as I get another drink."

After Tony refilled her tumbler, Alicia rejoined the conversation. "Okay, I get it. We are stuck with superior beings posing as personalities we can relate to." Alicia drove her fantasy from her mind and focused on the situation. "Goldie Hawn? Really?"

Once again, without context, Sean merely shook his head and informed Tony what he needed from him. "If you don't mind, will you head to the bridge, and after Osaka recovers from seeing you, call the CIC with the coordinates for the location of the Taíno village that launched the attack?"

Then to Alicia he added, "I want to get cloaked F-35s over them and park the Hampton on their front door. Also, I need to know how long until we reach Guantanamo. We need to get a foothold on shore as soon as possible. I'll be in the CIC."

"Will do," Alicia replied, as she reached for the phone.

Tony hesitated.

"Problem?"

"I need to be with my people. I'm sure they are confused by my sudden disappearance immediately after the battle. They probably think I abandoned them."

"Not yet you don't. It would be a bad idea to separate until we find out why some joker decided they needed to send our task force with so much firepower against the equivalent of cavemen with rocks." Sean also needed more information about how Tony had spent the previous two years, and how it related to the attack on Columbus. However, he wanted Tony to offer more on his own. "No need to be pushy, yet," Sean reasoned to himself.

"Besides, don't you think if your buddy Franklin wanted you there, you would be instead of here? Why don't we let things play out for now?" Instinctively Sean also knew it would be dangerous to give Tony time to devise his own course of action. He could not afford to be working at cross-purposes with his refound friend.

Tony wanted to argue against Sean's logic, but he couldn't find fault. "I hope you know what you are doing," was all Tony could offer, still worried about Yacahuey's safety. "It doesn't do us a lot a good to know there is a potential enemy out there right now with us clueless about what it is, other than they will act quickly."

"So let's figure out what *it* is, and what possible reason *it* would want to destroy us in 1492." Alicia went past the liquor cabinet and over to the kitchenette. "My guess is it's going to be a long night. I'll make us some coffee."

Tony got up and paced the room. "It seems obvious to me the only target would be the Taíno. Why else would you show up exactly when we attacked Columbus?"

"You know the worst mistake we could make is to focus on a single variable," Sean argued. "Think back to the first month after we landed in 1941, and how many options we looked at, but discovering sometimes too late that we didn't have any choices to begin with. It isn't as if any of us know what we are doing, Tony. The only thing I can promise is this time we will maintain strict command and control over the task force. The best chance we have to protect your friends is to use our training to the best of our abilities." Sean looked closely at Tony to see if his message had sunk in.

However, the longer he looked, the more absurd Tony's appearance mirrored the insane nature of their situation. In the excitement, everyone had ignored Tony's less than military appearance, which Sean now compared to his childhood memories of Robinson Crusoe. Sean laughed at the thought. "If you head to the bridge looking like that, some Marine might throw you overboard. You better stay here to shower and shave, and I will have a uniform sent to you."

Tony was not amused. "Okay, but if it's all right with you, I'll keep the long hair for now. A god doesn't get haircuts, and I *will* return to check on the Taíno, Franklin, or no Franklin." Tony delivered this in his *nothing will stop me if it comes to that, so you better not be in the way* voice.

"Agreed." Sean then quickly thought of the means to keep his friend nearby. "I think it would be wise to give you a position of authority in the command structure. You know idle minds and all."

"What exactly do you have in mind." Tony wasn't sure he liked the sound of what Sean was offering.

"No sense in shaking up the current command structure with Alicia as my Chief of Staff, so how about acting as my adjunct?"

Tony looked at Sean as if to say, *duh.* "Fine with me, as long as you keep in mind my main concern is to ensure my people are not caught in the middle of whatever this is. After two years of planning, I executed one tyrant, so I am not going to let another one come along and screw it all up. Considering the way things worked out in 1942, I'll make sure there won't be a repeat of that disaster."

Sean couldn't blame Tony for his cynicism. Of all the losses they experienced in 1942, Tony's was the most personal. "We will deal with all of that after we get settled in Guantanamo. For now it would be helpful if you showed Alicia the coordinates for the Taíno so she can inform the CIC."

They pulled up a map of Cuba on the computer and Tony pointed to the location of the Taíno settlements, which Alicia relayed to the CIC.

Suddenly it occurred to Sean that other than her two calls to the CIC, Alicia had been unusually quiet. "If you're sure everything is all right Alicia, it would be helpful for you to get with Rebecca to determine the extent of our capabilities with the upgraded version of Specter."

The sound of her name once again snapped Alicia back into the conversation. "I'm on it." Happy to take action, any action, she eagerly grabbed her coat, gave Sean a quick kiss, and headed to the door. "When the door opens, I will walk onto a beach in Cambria, California in 2018," she fantasized. She eagerly turned the handle and quickly pulled the door open to see an empty corridor instead. "Damn."

Sean grabbed the cup of the coffee Alicia had poured on his way out. "I'm headed to the CIC."

Left alone Tony muttered, "Once again, situation normal, all fucked up."

The End of Part I

Part II
Coming To Terms

Taíno Symbol for Coqui (Frog)

Forrest was so deep in thought while staring at one of Specter's power schematics that he failed to notice Rebecca enter the room.

"Still trying to fathom the unfathomable?"

Like a teenager caught by his mother who entered his bedroom without knocking, Forrest jumped so bad that he sent the coffee mug on his desk crashing to the floor. "Dr. Cutler, I didn't hear…" The vision in front of Forrest stopped him short. "Your clothes, you changed your clothes. I mean, of course you changed your clothes. However, I didn't expect those…"

Rebecca smiled at his flustered state and interrupted. "Calm down, you're going to have a heart attack." She walked up to him and when well within his personal space demanded, "You like? Apparently, the powers that brought us all together again remembered to add a few clothing items from my past."

The Rebecca who stood in front of Forrest had tossed her diplomatic attire aside, and posed as if she was the famous rock groupie Marianne Faithfull circa 1972. Resplendent in a sheer maroon colored silk blouse that flowed around her breasts like a gentle wave, she slowly sashayed around the poor distraught Forrest. If this wasn't enough to send his blood rushing, the blouse was complimented with shocking yellow hot pants that left even less to his fertile imagination. The ensemble finished off with black laced up knee boots, and you had the ultimate backstage pass package who now reached out to send electrical charges pulsating through Forrest's rapidly expanding manhood.

Rebecca gently pushed the shocked scientist backward into his chair. "Close your mouth. You're going to attract flies." Rebecca continued her seductress dance, while slowly turning to face the monitor. She ran her tongue across her lips in a slow circular motion, and leaned close. "You know where to go to get some of this when you get tired of acting like a ghost, don't you?"

The image on the monitor didn't change, nor was there an automated response. Then as Rebecca started to turn away, a ghostly apparition with a ghastly smile plastered on its face floated across the screen and slowly faded away. Rebecca was satisfied she had validated her suspicions.

Because the shape of her well-defined shocking yellow ass was only inches from his face, Forrest could not react without further embarrassment when Rebecca stepped back from the monitor.

"He wasn't this excited when I was lying next to him in bed naked," Rebecca thought, as she fought the urge to break out in hysterical laughter over his predicament.

Fortunately, Alicia arrived in time to spare Forrest from what was going to be Rebecca's second act. "Holy shit, girl! It is so good to see you all the way back."

Alicia quickly walked across the room and motioned for Rebecca to spin around, which she did, albeit in the pose of a girl wrapping herself around an imaginary dancer's pole.

"Turn up the A/C in here, I'm burning up." Alicia could not hold it in, and within seconds, both women were out of control.

Rebecca couldn't resist one last dig toward the monitor. "All of this isn't getting any younger tiger."

Alicia had calmed down and shot Rebecca a, *what the hell was that about*, look.

With her back to Specter's monitor and Forrest, Rebecca put her finger to her lips, and waved Alicia to the door. Once outside Rebecca began to laugh so hard she had to use the ship's bulkhead to support herself.

Alicia stared at her as if her friend had lost her mind. Fortunately, her calmness allowed Rebecca the time to regain her senses.

Rebecca threw her arms around her friend after her hysterics had abated. "I am so glad you are back. You will never believe what I had to do when you left us all of those years ago. My God, I had to be you. I don't know how you did it. Kissy, kissy, how do you do, blah, blah, blah. Your job sucks. You do know I married Captain Eddington and had a son. I don't know where either of them are right now, but I do know with us all together again, it shouldn't take too long to figure out."

Thoroughly amused, Alicia thought, "So much for manic under control." It was if they hadn't gone through all of this earlier. "When was the last time you got some sleep? Why don't we go back inside and get you some coffee."

Inside the room Alicia poured their coffee while Rebecca paused to calculate how long she had gone without sleep.

Seeing another rush of energy building up in her, Alicia took a step back to brace herself for the next barrage, and thought, "4...3...2..."

"Let's see. If you factor in that I was just in 1951, then in 2018, and now in 1492, it would be difficult to say exactly when I last slept. Anyway, with you and the Admiral married, what could be better than to have our task force parents lead us on another journey into the abyss of the unknown? We have so much catching up to do. Did you know we helped put the first solar panels up in 1951, oh, and one of the most progressive countries in the world turned out to be of all places, Russia? Can you believe it? The best part of all, is almost all the subcultures that had been creating internal strife are now mostly self-governed, except of course in the Middle East. Hell, even God herself couldn't put those pieces together."

Forrest risked body and soul to help bring this mass of energy under control when he stepped between the two women, and offered his hand to Alicia. "It's good to see you again, ma'am."

Grateful for the save, she winked her thanks. "It's good to see you too, Dr. Phelps, though if you ever refer to me as ma'am again, I swear I will hurt you."

Forrest's intervention gave Alicia her chance to get a word in, so she walked over to the control panel to get some separation from Rebecca. "I can't wait to catch up on your part of the craziness; however, we need to know what we have to work with. You know how it is with all of this time shifting. For all we know there could be something from Planet 9 just over the horizon."

Rebecca high-fived Alicia. "Buckaroo Banzai. Nice reference girly, girl." Fortunately, this was enough to refocus Rebecca's attention. "According to everything I think I understand about the nature of science, I would have to conclude that over the last several weeks while on the Missouri in 1951, Dr. Phelps was in contact with beings of a far superior skill set. By the way, what he learned overnight would take my entire life to figure out, if I was lucky, or if Archimedes genius suddenly blossomed fifty generations later in my cranial cavity."

Alicia took a second to parse the disjointed statements before responding. "Am I to understand you found brilliance in the Specter upgrades that you believe Dr. Phelps shouldn't be...?" Suddenly uncomfortable, Alicia turned to Forrest. "Sorry, no offense meant, but not intellectually up to the challenge to have accomplished?"

Forrest calmly admitted, as he took a seat in the nearest chair, "None taken. It isn't as if I had any control over what happened."

Unmindful of bruising Forrest's ego, Rebecca explained, "Specter has developed a distinctly human personality. Now I know Forrest has absolutely no training in artificial intelligence, never mind that what we have here is a quantum leap over anything I am aware of. So the question remains, where did these upgrades that he developed while on the Missouri come from, if not from some higher intelligence?"

Rebecca looked at Alicia as if she could supply the answer.

Of course, Alicia had no idea. "And that would mean what Rebecca? Forrest?"

"Specter is alive," Rebeca and Forrest whispered in unison.

"Alive? What do mean, alive?" Alicia wondered if the two scientists had become delusional. "You know I could use a little sleep myself. Why don't we revisit this idea after a few hours of shut eye?"

Rebecca ignored Alicia's suggestion and continued her mad speculation. "Not get up and walk out of the room Japanese robotics alive, or I would like a glass of wine alive, but more of a Hal 2000 series from Space Odyssey alive."

Forrest did not like the sound of that. "Didn't he kill everyone?"

A wide-eyed Rebecca wildly shook her head in the affirmative.

Alicia could only sigh as Rebecca pointed to the large plasma monitor and asked in an overly authoritative manner, "Tell me again, only let's see if you can come up with an alternative option that is a little more in the technological realm of things."

To Alicia's amazement, a smooth young male voice, foreign to all present, replied instead. "Tell you what again? Should I tell you about the diagnostic I ran, or did I like what you are wearing? You must be more specific as I am asked billions of questions a second and it would be virtually impossible to speculate on which one you seek an answer to."

The clarity of the computer-generated voice astonished Alicia. If she didn't know better, she would have assumed it was a living, breathing human on the other end of a cell phone. "You asked the computer if it liked what you are wearing."

Rebecca ignored the sarcasm and explained. "As I was going through the new coding Forest programmed into Specter, I noticed fluctuations in the energy output. The fluctuations were minor and did not exceed operating parameters, but it made me curious enough to find out what caused them. What gave the game up was the rhythm of the changes, as if there was intelligence to it. I routed that excess energy to an advanced audio program I created, and voilà, say hello to Presper."

"Presper? You've changed Specter's name?" Alicia asked, wondering what would come next on this most bizarre of days.

"J Presper Eckert, the designer of Univac, the first computer built in the United States in 1951. I thought the legacy fitting."

"Okay, so it talks. Excuse my ignorance, but are there not thousands of programs that spit out dialect? What makes Specter any different?" Alicia imagined that she had asked Bill Nye The Science Guy that question, and felt a headache coming on.

"What would you think if I were to tell you that Presper knew the minute Admiral Phillips, Captain Knox, and you arrived back on board, and more importantly where you had come from?"

Okay, Alicia had to admit that was impressive. "How is that possible?"

Rebecca bounced up and down in excitement as she signaled Alicia to follow her.

Alicia noticed that Forrest still looked shell shocked, so she threw him a bone. "Why don't you keep Presper company while Alicia and I catch up on what you two have been up to?"

Grateful to be excused, Forrest didn't argue.

Before they could reach the door, Presper spoke out again. "If I were a woman on a warship, I would change into something more functional. After all, you are surrounded by thousands of men whose hormonal controls are minimal at best."

Without turning back, Rebecca assured Presper, "Not to worry,

I made my point. Trouble is, I may forget once and awhile if I don't get what I want."

As the door closed behind them, Alicia warned, "That is if we have months."

Rebecca led Alicia up to the flight deck, and when they arrived, explained what she had discovered. "It turns out Forrest became the vehicle for an unknown entity to get inside Specter's operating system. The further I went into his coding process the more obvious most of the technology was beyond poor Forrest's abilities, or mine for that matter. This early on, I can't say if it shares our interests or not."

"Well, it told you about the house in Cuba, and Tony." Alicia went on to detail all of their bizarre encounters with the self-proclaimed gods."

"Do you think Presper is one of them?"

"At this point Rebecca, I am beginning to think we are in the middle of a god conference, and we are no more than pawns in a game they concocted." Obviously, Sean needed this new information, so Alicia came to the point of her visit. "Sorry to cut the reunion short, but I came to find out about the new Specter capabilities. Can you quickly fill me in on anything different in how it now works that you might believe to be essential?"

"Sure. Most importantly, with the exception of the John Paul Jones, Princeton, Missouri, Laramie, and Amelia Earhart, all the ships can operate independently while cloaked. I accessed the manifests of each ship to determine that we do have the parts available to add to and modify the first generation Specter electromagnetic generators. I believe we can upgrade the warships for independent cloaking in about a week, and add the necessary generators and command consoles to the cargo ships immediately afterward. Of course, this is assuming some halfway decent technicians came along for the ride. If I have to oversee the whole show, triple the time."

Alicia didn't need Sean's input to give Rebecca her orders on such obvious choices. "Upgrade the Princeton and John Paul Jones within the next few days if you can. The Missouri will remain in port as a centerpiece for the onshore settlement. Can you modify her cloaking to encompass the settlement as well?"

"With the new technology, yes we can."

"Good. Princeton, John Paul Jones, Missouri, Laramie, and Amelia Earhart, in that order. Anything else?"

Rebecca squeezed her eyes tight to feign deep thoughts, and then shook her head yes. "I'm sure there is, but nothing earth-shattering, or you know I would remember."

"Seriously, I don't know what we would do without you. In less than a day you have done more than most could accomplish in a lifetime." As she said this, Alicia, began a slow withdrawal to avoid Rebecca's goodbye bear hug, but misjudged her reaction time. Two minutes of thank you, miss you, and hugs later, Alicia finally broke away to head for the carrier's island.

As she made her way to the Admirals Ready Room, Alicia began to analyze what they knew so far. "With all of this omnipresent power arrayed around us, how can we hope to exercise any kind of free will? Free will? Are you kidding woman? We haven't had any free will since the moment we popped out of our mother's womb."

Alicia paused to collect her thoughts. "Now I know how mice feel before the trap springs shut. Hell, what makes me think any of the loved ones around me are really who I assume them to be." Alicia's mind began to race at all the possibilities based on her lifetime of experiences. Every oddity turned into a conspiracy, and the alternative theories of Erich von Däniken and Oliver Stone took on new meaning.

Alicia vigorously rubbed her eyes to clear her mind. "Slow down girl," she warned herself. "Until Bugs Bunny, Isaac Asimov, and Mark Twain show up to tell me we are all *Rolling on a River* toward a massive waterfall, all is good."

She laughed at the memory of the dreams that repeated in several variations after she had read the complete works of both authors in a marathon at 11 years old. Alicia's final thoughts as she reached her destination were equally vexing. "I never did figure out how Bugs Bunny fit in."

As Tony rinsed off the last of the shaving cream, he stared into the mirror with his former life now staring back at him. Without the beard, and wearing his old khaki naval uniform, the resurrection of Captain Anthony Knox was almost physically complete. "If Yacahuey could see me now. All I need to complete the picture is Captain Nemo's Nautilus and a giant squid."

A voice from behind the door joined his conversation. "With our luck, the Nautilus would take us back to save the last of the Neanderthals, so we can create a new species that wipes out early Homo sapiens. How do you feel about high foreheads?"

Tony continued to stare into the mirror. "The same way I felt when Franklin sold me on the idea of becoming the Taíno god. How long have you been standing there?"

Alicia laughed at the idea of her dear Tony as a god. "Just long enough for me to hear you say that we share the same odd propensity for lame analogies, Captain Nemo."

For the first time in years, Tony responded with laughter. "We are quite the pair. After a lifetime of playing lone wolfs, when the universe finally sends us the ones we want to spend all of our time with, mine dies, and yours is in charge of all the craziness."

"I never did get to share with you how much I missed you and how sorry I am for your loss. I can tell you that Sean feels the same, though he rarely talks about it."

Saddened by the mention of Renée, Tony slumped down onto the couch. "You don't know the half of it. After the Enterprise disappeared and the war ended, with Carl and Rebecca handling diplomacy, there wasn't anything left for me to do. I checked out long before I got stuck here."

Alicia sat down next to Tony. "All things considered, I would have rather been here, than the last four years back home. We fought the good fight. However, between big money and the pervasive surveillance of anyone with a voice, it didn't take long before we realized leaders of the opposition would be purged. George Orwell just got the year wrong."

"Loath as I am to admit it, regardless of whatever ulterior motives Franklin has floating around that big head of his, my last two years here have played out like an almost perfect world in the imagination of an average 10-year-old."

"Almost?"

"No pirates to swashbuckle with."

"Amen to that. However, if there were pirates to deal with, you do know they would probably be in spaceships and not frigates." Alicia gave her friend a quick kiss on the cheek. "Unfortunately, as much as I would love to catch up with your perspective on this round of craziness, I need to bring Sean up to date about what Rebecca is working on."

"I've missed our little chats, though I have no idea how Sean didn't screw things up with you without me around to interpret." Tony picked up the phone and connected to the CIC. "Yeah, you better come before I do unmentionable things to your beautiful wife." Tony winked at Alicia as he put the phone down. "So what's she got?"

"Trust me; it will be difficult enough to explain once coherently what Rebecca shared, what with all the manic filler she threw in for good measure. For some reason I seem to ramp up the crazy in that girl."

Tony knew exactly why. "You should know Rebecca had to put all of her crazy away once you and Sean disappeared. This is probably her way of exorcizing those demons and returning them to where they belong, on you."

Alicia punched Tony hard on his shoulder. "So now I'm the Devil and you are a god? What's next, Sean morphing into the Creator? Rebecca as the New-Age Madonna? Now that would be scary."

"So the usual?" Tony started for the bottle of JD, when Alicia waved him off.

"Better make mine a cup of coffee."

When he entered the room and found them relaxed on the couch, it brought a sense of normalcy to Sean. "Like we never left port." When he saw looks of confusion on both of their faces, he added, "You know, the day we left San Diego all those years ago. Anyway, unimportant. What pearls of wisdom did Rebecca share with you?"

For a split second, all Alicia wanted to do was boot Tony out of the room, drag Sean to the floor, and tear his clothes off. "Unfortunately, business first," she thought.

"First off, she is driving herself to exhaustion. It seems that though Rebecca has one of the finest minds I've ever seen, she believes sleep, and most likely food have no place in her world. I will keep an eye on that. Now on to the mixed bag that was her report." Alicia proceeded to update Sean on Rebecca's preliminary findings and concerns.

Tony interrupted before she could finish. "Wait. Did you say the Missouri is with us?"

It had not occurred to Sean that Tony didn't know. "That's right. Apparently, it is important for the original task force to be back together again for this adventure. You had disappeared from the Missouri bridge only moments before Rebecca jumped aboard from Washington, DC. Then after a brief conversation with Carl before he too faded away, your ships jumped into 2018 right after Alicia and I jumped to the Enterprise bridge from our honeymoon suite in Cambria. After the two groups formed up we all jumped into 1492."

"So everything I left behind is still in my cabin aboard the

Missouri?"

"Not only that," Alicia added, "as far as anyone on the Missouri is concerned, you have only been gone less than 24 hours, not two years."

While Tony tried to wrap his head around this bizarre timeline manipulation, Alicia continued her report on Specter. Minus all the hyperbole and without interruption, she arrived at her understanding of the evidence in about seven minutes. "Rebecca absolutely believes that Specter is under the control of a superior entity, and because it is Rebecca, I am inclined to agree. Franklin and Bowie are operating on a scale way above us, so why not? If taken solely on the face of things, you would think 1492 and 1942 have something that connects those years to us. Unfortunately there isn't enough information to determine much of anything as fact. Then there is the idea that this could all be happening in a lab somewhere in the Mojave Desert for all we know."

Alicia finished with a yawn, and realized she needed to take some of her own advice. "No offense to either of you, but it is 4 AM and I think we all would be better served if we got some shut-eye."

"I can't remember the last time I slept," Tony acknowledged with a yawn. "It's time for this kid to return to the Missouri."

Sean needed to make sure Tony understood their predicament. "Don't get too comfortable over there. The way the Big MO uses up fuel, our only option is to park her in Guantanamo and use her as a centerpiece for our on shore settlement. Also, before you go, I think we should all agree to keep what we know about Franklin, Bowie, and the spook in Specter to a select few. No one other than Osaka, Daily, and Rebecca need to know about them for now."

"Rebecca already knows. After you *leave*, I will inform Osaka and Captain Daily," an impatient Alicia offered before she added in her best motherly manner, "Now, say goodnight, Tony."

"I will check on the Missouri XO in the morning after I get some sleep." Then, before Tony headed out the door, he added quietly to Alicia, "Don't ride Sean too hard. He has a big day tomorrow." As the door closed, he smiled as he heard general chaos break out inside the room.

Fifteen minutes later, Tony landed on the stern deck of the Missouri and made his way to his berth. "No sense in waking anyone up," he thought. After numerous confused looks from the sailors he crossed paths with, he arrived at his quarters. "Yep, everything in my cabin is exactly as I left it over two years ago, or is that only last night while we were in the Mediterranean in 1951?" The impact of all of this conflicting information exploded like a bomb in his head. "How can any of this be possible?"

Back in the Admirals Ready Room, as the door had closed behind Tony, Alicia launched her suddenly naked body at him, her momentum knocking Sean backward onto the couch.

"How did you do that so fast?"

"We are going to finish our honeymoon, so shut up and do me," she demanded as she savagely ripped open the last of his buttons and smothered his chest with kisses.

Sean quickly found himself on the floor and naked before the last of his curiosity fled, replaced by his wife's passionate needs. The energy they expended over the next two hours meant they needed another four to rest. Thankfully, no one interrupted them for the entire six hours.

When they did wake up, both felt as if they fought a round with Mike Tyson. As lifeless as he felt, Sean's tired mind managed to dial in on what should be their next step. "I've decided that it is necessary to visit the Taíno settlement with Tony."

"Really? No cuddles, no talking with me over a cup of coffee, then a quick shower?" Alicia gave Sean a playful slap as she climbed out from under the covers. She then turned her back and thrust out her naked behind to wiggle it seductively back and forth in front of him. "Can't touch this, Mister *no time to cuddle.*"

Sean jumped out of the bed to grab her, but she eluded his grasp. He fell back into the bed as she disappeared into the bathroom. "Seriously lover, we have to try to get ahead of what may be coming our way, and the one thing we do know is the Taíno are important to the story."

Though she wasn't happy with Sean going on an away mission, Alicia trusted Sean's instincts. "What do you want me to do while you're gone?"

"Monitor the situation from the CIC," Sean answered, as he silently climbed out of bed and stealthily made his way toward the bathroom.

"And if something goes wrong?" Alicia's voice carried from the bathroom, so she didn't hear him coming.

He pounced on her as she buried her face in a washcloth. His fingers made their way down her slender frame and began to caress her thighs while she struggled unsuccessfully to fight him off.

"Stop it you pervert. You need to be visible for the crew, not locked away trying to hump your poor tired wife."

Ignoring her half-hearted pleas, Sean's hands roamed up and down her body, while the grin on his face made him look like a small child who just got a new favorite toy. "*Captain* Daniel Osaka is a big boy. He is more than capable of handling whatever comes up."

Giving in to the inevitable, Alicia grabbed his head hard and pushed his face into her chest. Thirty minutes later, Alicia was in the shower, as Sean lay collapsed on the bed.

Ten minutes later, as she toweled dried her hair Alicia playfully admonished Sean. "You better get up, lazy boy. You and Tony need to get going if you want to visit the Taíno while there is still light. I'm shocked he hasn't battered our door down by now."

"Could be he got zapped into the Revolutionary War as John

Paul Jones right before sighting the Serapis."

Alicia pulled a shirt from the closet and threw it at him. "Really, the Serapis, like how many people do you know who would get that reference. Get in the shower, Professor."

"I will agree to get up, if you promise more of the same action when I get back."

"No promises. But if you behave yourself, I might be willing to try that little something, something you brought up in Cambria."

"You make it sound like it won't be any fun." Sean pouted, as he stuck his thumb in his mouth mimicking the action of a baby boy.

Alicia shook her head in mock disappointment, before she said with a sigh, "I guess I have to lead by example. While you shower, I will inform Daniel and Captain Daily about our weird friends and then head to the CIC to get updated on anything we missed," Alicia added as she gathered the rest of her things and headed out the door.

"What, no clever come back?"

"This is me ignoring you," Alicia taunted, as the door closed behind her.

⸻ ❖ ⸻

Adonis liked the new digs. Actually, he loved everything that happened since meeting Sean Anthony in the hood. "This cat has some serious mojo. This is the second time I've been hustled off to a different location that for all I know could be somewhere on the moon."

When he looked around, the unmistakable tool marks on the towering walls identified his new surroundings as a cave, a cave Batman would have killed for. "Where's the Batmobile. Hello – Anyone else here?"

As he walked further into the cave, he could see the light intensifying. When he reached a turn, the cave opened up to reveal banks of computer servers lining both sides of the cave. Somehow

Sean Anthony had managed to increase the number of servers at their disposal to a total Adonis was sure rivaled the best the rest of the world had to offer.

"What are you staring at, dufus?"

Adonis turned to face a young girl no older than 15, though on closer inspection revealed a mind much tougher than her years. "Awfully cold for such a young thang. Didn't your mama teach you any respect for your elders?"

"One of the *thangs* my mother taught me was to never be afraid to state the patently obvious, therefore what were you staring at, dufus?"

"The handle is Adonis, sweatcakes." Something about the droll manner of the girl sparked his interest. "So what's a homely little slip of a girl like you doing mixed up with all of this?"

"So you're Adonis? Some of your code is okay. I actually have used bits of it now and again. I'm Phoenix." She boldly thrust out her hand for him to shake.

"Still my beating heart that such a little girl would find any value in a lowlife like me." In fact Adonis was thrilled Phoenix took notice of his skills, because she is a legend in the hacker world. She had crashed all the major social networks at the same time, an incredible feat, though not close to what their small group was attempting now. "Crazy shit all of this. Any ideas about where Mr. Voodoo Man stashed us this time?"

Phoenix did her own sweep of the cavern and in a matter-of-fact tone proclaimed to Adonis, "Shaanxi Province, somewhere on the Loess Plateau in China." Before Adonis could voice his disbelief, she added, "The rock material is unique."

Adonis' macho sensibilities were getting tired of being one upped by this little schoolgirl. "Shouldn't you be working on your assignment?"

"It is finished and waiting for him to tell me to execute." Phoenix walked away and headed to the nook that held the perfect hackers' kitchen. Cases of Red Bull with every microwavable product known to man and woman filled the large room, along with a case of cheap Vodka for Adonis.

"Bitch," he whispered under his breath, followed by a slight smile. "Cool kid."

On cue, Sean Anthony popped into the cave in the middle of the workstations. "Greetings fellow warriors against the status quo. Are you all ready to rip a new hole in your oppressors?" The cave reverberated with hell yeahs, fist bumps, and all around frat worthy exaltations. Through it all, having returned from the kitchen with a Dr Pepper, Phoenix stayed transfixed to her monitor, and only spoke up when the fanfare subsided. "I think you need to see this."

Sean Anthony walked over to look over her shoulder. "What is it?"

"They are announcing the arrest of families and friends of everyone in this room." She pointed to one. "That is a picture of my mom and dad."

The girl's dry delivery surprised Adonis, but that didn't stop him from punching up the site to see about those in his hood. Then he remembered they were already dead.

The rest of the hackers did the same, and it wasn't long before the exuberance turned to desperate questions directed at Sean Anthony.

As he walked down the row, he motioned for the room to calm down before he hit them squarely between the eyes. "Viktor, Vladimir has sent your family and anyone remotely involved with you to a gulag in Siberia. Sue Lin, in China they arrested your entire family, including your 12-year-old brother for treason. They face the death penalty. And you, Mr. Mean and Nasty, they didn't bother arresting anyone, they just blew the block to shit. Two hundred sixty men, women, and children are dead. This message is for all of you. What you must understand is there was nothing you could have done to change the outcome, except to have died along with them. They were coming for you when I gathered you up. This is the face of your enemy. They are real, and they are cold blooded.

"Now I am going to get a cup of coffee to give you all the space to decide if you want to continue." Sen Anthony started toward the kitchen, but turned back. "I cannot stress enough that the only way to save those still alive is to finish the job."

After Sean Anthony disappeared into the kitchen, the group of hackers came together in a huddle. After only five minutes of debate, Phoenix split from the group and walked into the kitchen. "We all understood from the day we hacked into a government file that the system would do everything in their power to destroy us. After they arrested me three years ago, it was because of their threats to ruin my family that I swore to hurt them for having the power to do so. Theirs is the old world. We want something better."

Sean Anthony smiled and handed her a remote. "Then go ahead and push the button."

When Phoenix did so, all the monitors in the cave began to scroll code rapidly across their screens.

❦

After eight hours of sleep, Tony checked in with the Missouri XO before he boarded the Seahawk to chopper over to the Enterprise, where he met Admiral Phillips and Captain Osaka on the bridge.

"It's good to see you again, Captain Knox. I hear I missed the Robinson Caruso look. Don't worry, Alicia filled me in on your exploits. Did you bring us any coconuts?"

"Knowing you like I do, Daniel, don't you mean beautiful native girls for your twisted pleasure?"

"Hey, I'm still single."

"Okay, enough of the frat boys crap. Neither of you would talk like this if Alicia were here." Sean needed them to focus on the immediate situation. "Tell me about what we will run into when we enter Nipe Bay."

Tony looked at the map of the bay and the surrounding area, and pointed to where he knew settlements existed. "Our best bet would be if only you and I take a launch in."

Osaka shook his head no. "I don't like it Admiral. With all the uncertainty, to have both of you alone and exposed is dangerous. At least add a SEAL squad to the boat crew."

Tony laughed. "If you knew the Taíno like I do Captain, you would know it took me two years to make them understand there were people out there who wouldn't think twice about slaughtering every last one of them. All adding the SEALs to the shore party would accomplish at best is confusion, and at worst, somebody getting hurt. Unfortunately, it would be one of them, so we'll do it my way."

Sean knew what he wanted. "Why don't we have the best of both worlds, Captain Osaka? Since it can travel independently while cloaked, Captain Knox and I can transfer to the Decatur for the trip. If it makes you happy, we can make sure Commander Barrish has a SEAL squad on board should the need arise. While the task force continues to Guantanamo, the Decatur will enter Nipe Bay cloaked. Tony and I will then take a launch to shore."

"Aye Admiral," Osaka agreed.

"You ready to go back to playing God?"

Tony decided to have a little fun with it when he noticed the bridge personnel's reaction to Sean's question. "What's the matter with all of you? Seriously, you didn't know I am the Supreme Being?"

"Yeah, and I'm Taylor Swift," Sean shot back as he reached for the phone to contact his Chief of Staff in the CIC.

"Alicia, Tony, and I will take the Decatur into Nipe Bay cloaked, and then take a launch to the beach. *Father* Osaka is concerned about our security, so have a SEAL squad and Knighthawk ready to go in one hour. Then meet me in the Admirals Ready Room, I need some breakfast before we go."

"Aye Aye *Admiral*," Alicia answered in her sexy voice.

The next morning, Sean and Tony stood on the bridge of the destroyer USS Decatur with Commander Logan Barrish as they made their way through the narrow channel into Nipe Bay. "Commander Barrish, drop anchor in the center of the bay and remain cloaked. We'll take the launch in from there."

"Aye Aye Admiral." After relaying the orders, Barrish stood smiling at Sean and Tony.

His smile irked Tony. "What do find so amusing, Commander?"

"Oh, I don't know, Sir. It could be that after reliving a part of history, things got a little boring when we returned to 2014. It may sound strange to you, but I missed the weirdness of it all." When he noticed Sean and Tony's look of disapproval, Barrish abruptly changed course. "Obviously, not the part where we lose ships and lives."

"Amen to that Commander, though you might have a point that this is the best place to be right now. As you know, oppression was the order of the day when we left. I always believed the public would re-engage when the government finally took away something they thought was important enough to fight for. Alicia and I were shocked that the only issue society found worthy was the right to splash the most intimate details of their lives all over the internet." Sean realized he was going off on a rant, and quickly shut it down.

Commander Barrish turned to Tony for his take on Sean's comments, but noticed a definitive lack of interest in his body language. "You have any thoughts, Captain Knox?"

"Well Logan, first off, I would have to say you definitely could use some form of therapy if you are enjoying any of this. Second, the Taíno have it right, and if what we are here for is to preserve their culture, I'll take what I can get if we can play any part to see that happen."

"That wasn't the question Tony." Sean was curious about what Tony really thought.

"Oh, you mean back home? What I think, if you must know, is that only a few people care enough to do even the most basic homework when it comes to civic responsibilities. Unfortunately, this makes those who are paying attention sound like Chicken Little screaming that the sky is falling. If history has taught me anything, it's that those who stick their neck out are the first to get it cut off."

Contrary to all the facts, Commander Barrish still tried to hang on to the optimism of youth. "That's certainly a bleak assessment. There are always exceptions that stand out to force change. History always seems to come up with the right people when things are at their bleakest; the Founding Fathers, Einstein, and Martin Luther King, as a few examples."

Tony shook his head as if to say you poor sucker. "Bite me. That you can name the few examples in a couple of seconds where freedom of thought went unpunished, when the list of deviants would take all day, only makes my point. People as individuals are mostly harmless if given the right enticements. It is when you put them in a group that they all lose their minds. The government hacks prey on this knowledge by stuffing tons of red meat and Kool-Aid down the public's throat, sprinkled with a daily dose of Dr. Feelgood's 'I've got a drug for every imagined neurosis you have, and, oh by the way, did you see the latest Modern Family, that Phil is such a riot.'"

Tony's verbal barrage was more than Logan could handle, so he quickly dropped out and picked up his binoculars to scan the area.

Sean leaned close to Tony. "So who stole your ball, Sunshine?" Sean chuckled as he too put binoculars to his eyes.

As the Decatur dropped anchor in the middle of the bay, Sean ordered Commander Barrish to prepare the launch.

"How long do you think you will be, Admiral?"

"I guess that depends on Tony, Commander. I will report every half hour, and let me know the minute you receive any unusual reports."

"You ready Tony?" He turned to see Tony already halfway out the door. "I guess you're ready," Sean muttered as he rushed to catch up.

Twenty minutes later, they were out from under Specter's cloak and racing toward the shore in the launch. Tony skippered the helm while Sean scanned the area ahead with binoculars. When they were within a few hundred yards of the beach, Sean could not believe what he saw. The Taíno were in the midst of one of the largest celebrations the island had ever known. It looked as if all of the island's inhabitants were there to greet them. As they closed on the beach, he focused the lenses on individual faces and got another shock when he identified a man who stood out from all the rest. A half-naked man with scraggly hair and beard was waving in their direction.

"Tony you are not going to believe who is on that beach." Sean handed the binoculars to Tony who turned the wheel over to Sean.

After scanning the shore for a moment, Tony yelled over the roar of the boat. "What is he doing there?" He looked again, and to his further amazement, the figure vanished. "He disappeared. I can't wait to see what trouble he's stirred up to get everyone here."

Another thing bugged Tony. "How did they all get here? There are only a few small fishing boats lying on the shore, not nearly enough for those assembled."

"Well, we are about to find out." As the launch approached the beach, Sean slowed it down and handed the wheel back to Tony. "So – grand entrance?"

"Why not," Tony answered with a grin as he gunned the engine.

Sean grabbed tightly to the railing as the launch violently took off and made a beeline for the shore. Tony timed his entrance through the surf so they caught a wave as it broke. At the same time, he cut power to the engine, allowing their momentum to ride the wave all the way to the shore. His rapid fire maneuvering brought the launch smoothly onto the sandy beach, coming to a rest on an even keel.

"Show off."

Tony turned to Sean, a broad smile plastered all on his face. "You're just jealous." In one swift motion, he jumped out of the boat and was happily surprised at who stood right in front of him when he landed. It was Yacahuey.

Contrary to Tony's theatrics, Sean cautiously exited the launch and stood next to Tony. All was silent around them, uncomfortably so considering they had no idea what Franklin had been telling them. Fortunately, Yacahuey rescued the moment, though the question he asked, confused both Sean and Tony.

He faced Sean and in a language foreign to him, stated in a formal tone, "Welcome to our home Jefferson." He reached for a basket of food from his mother and handed it to *Jefferson*. After Sean took it, the 300 or so Taíno all bowed down.

Tony raised his arms and in the same language delivered a quick speech, at least to Sean's ears what sounded like a speech. When he finished the mass rose as one and let out a great cheer.

Sean leaned close to Tony. "What was that all about?"

Tony laughed. "It would seem Franklin prepared them for the appearance of the god Jefferson. In addition, they want to know when the great ships of the gods will appear. Apparently, everyone is here to witness the miracle. We better show them the Decatur or this party is going to fall flat really quick."

"I'll be right back. I'm sure you can keep everyone entertained while I contact Barrish." Sean jumped back into the launch, and once out of view, contacted the ship on his radio. Moments later the sky lit up as the ship fired off a volley of florescent flares. Sean looked up to witness what amounted to a pre-Columbian version of a Rave, as wild dancing overtook the crowd. "You can disengage

Specter now Commander Barrish."

While the Admiral and Tony visited the Taíno, Rebecca continued her education on the upgraded Specter. She was in the middle of experimenting with how the central computer relayed commands, when a black and white skull and crossbones flag began to flutter across the monitor. "Skull and crossbones? What, are we back in high school hacking grades?"

"My bad." The Skull and crossbones disappeared, replaced with a picture of Hello Kitty. "Though more current and hip I fail to see how it would strike fear in anyone."

"And sarcastic too. How about we stick with what I had before." Though loath to admit it, Rebecca knew this AI [Artificial Intelligence] version of Specter didn't lack in wit.

"As much as it would enliven my day to continue, in all fairness, I should report that there is a significant energy surge fifty miles to the northeast of our present location." This switch to a matter-of-fact manner in how the automated voice communicated this news unnerved Rebecca. She thought there was something eerily familiar in the dialect. "Put it up on the…" Before she could finish her request, the region in question showed up on her monitor, and the view stopped her cold.

Specter stated the obvious conclusion. "The energy output is constant and covers five square miles of ocean. We are now sharing the same quadrant of the ocean with another task force. I relayed the coordinates to the CIC."

"That can only mean one thing." It didn't take Rebecca's genius to figure out that this was the threat they knew was coming. Unfortunately, she took her attention off the monitor to call Alicia in the CIC as two smaller signals separated from the main contact on a heading that would put them directly over the Decatur and the celebrating Taíno.

In the CIC, the Communications Officer handed the phone to Alicia. "Dr. Cutler says it's urgent that she speak to you Admiral Calhoun."

Alicia knew from experience that a warning of urgency from Rebecca always led to an eminent threat. "What is it, Doctor? You're sure? How far off?" She slammed the phone down and yelled out to the CIC Officer, "Get the fleet to General Quarters and cloak the task force, now!"

At the same time Alicia issued the order to General Quarters, Specter uploaded its interpretation of the energy spike to the CIC and Alpha Whiskey.

"Ma'am, two bogies are headed for Nipe Bay with four in trail. We have notified the Decatur and the Hampton of the threat, and Alpha Whiskey has dispatched a flight of six F-35s to Nipe Bay," the CIC Officer reported.

Alicia continued to calmly issue orders. "Task two cloaked F-35s to intercept and identify the initial contact. Send the Seawolf the coordinates with orders to close and report. Also, make sure we have a Hawkeye on standby. We may have to extend our CAP [Combat Air Patrol] and I don't want to be caught flat-footed." Alicia's rise to the rank of Admiral in the male-dominated service, and later Secretary of Defense wasn't because of her good looks. Her ability to see in the three-dimensional battlefield of the 21st Century and more importantly the nuances that decided success was second to none.

"Reposition the Indiana forward, and get me the CAG [Air Wing Commander, Captain *Dash* Nelson]."

After five minutes of organized chaos throughout the CIC the room suddenly became quiet, until the Communications Officer reported to Alicia. "I have the CAG, Ma'am."

Alicia grabbed the phone. "This is Admiral Calhoun. Captain Nelson, I know you want to be in the air but tough luck this time. I need you here in case we have to launch a counterattack. Any questions Captain? —Good, Calhoun out."

Alicia continued to deliver her orders without emotion, or any indication of stress regarding the potential crisis at all. This air of professionalism began to permeate throughout the task force, as news of the contacts spread through the ranks. On every warship, purpose overtook any anxiety the sailors had over their displacement as the strength of their senior officers rippled down the ranks.

From the bridge of the Enterprise Osaka watched as the dangerous choreography began to work its magic on the massive carrier's flight deck. Red, yellow, green, and blue shirted crew rushed to achieve the single purpose the United States designed and built the 1,000 foot long behemoth for, putting warplanes in the air.

Back on the beach, Tony watched the Taíno gather enough driftwood and stack it in preparation to create a massive bonfire on the beach. He glanced over to see Yacahuey pointing out to the bay. "Yúcahu, where did your great canoe go?"

Tony's adrenaline kicked into overdrive when his eyes confirmed the Decatur's disappearance. "Sean, the Decatur cloaked."

Sean realized he had left the radio hidden in the launch. He raced the short distance from the loud celebration to the launch, grabbed it, and keyed the mic. "What's the threat Commander?"

While still receiving Barrish's report, Sean ran back to the fire and grabbed Tony. "We have to get these people off the beach, now!"

Before either of them could move to do so, a loud explosion lifted a column of seawater 100 feet in the air in the direction where they last saw the Decatur. Sean ran back to the launch and grabbed his binoculars while Tony scrambled to move the Taíno off the beach.

When the frightened villagers had finally dispersed into the surrounding jungle, Tony sprinted back over to Sean. "Where the hell did that come from? Do you see anything?"

Before Sean could respond, from out of nowhere two sleek black fighter jets suddenly appeared overhead, and then just as suddenly disappeared. "Did you see the markings on those jets?"

"Kind of hard to miss a Nazi swastika on a flying wing." Tony grabbed his binoculars and focused them out on the bay. I don't see any sign in the water that they hit the Decatur."

Sean quickly weighed their options, and realized that for them there was only one. "We can't contact the Decatur without whoever is up there being able to track our signal, so let's do the smart thing and get off the beach and join your friends under cover."

As they were about to sprint over the open beach to the tree line, the ground shook as the flying wings roared past only a couple of hundred feet above their heads. "They're lining up for a bombing run on the Decatur!" Sean yelled over the noise.

Before Tony could reply, or the Nazi flying wings could release their bombs, the cloaked Decatur released its deadly combination of close in defense weapons. To both Sean and Tony time stood still as they watched this surreal battle play out. In real time, it wasn't much of a battle, as both the Decatur's radar controlled 5" and Phalanx Gatling guns slammed into the jets shredding both of the flying wings and their pilots well short of their target.

So mesmerized by the brutality of the quick action were Sean and Tony that it took more time than either would like to admit to rip their eyes from the falling debris and move to contact the Decatur. "Damage report, Commander Barrish." After listening for a minute, Sean gave him his orders. "Get underway to clear the bay at 5 knots. We can reach you in ten minutes at that speed, but order flank speed immediately if attacked again. We'll make our way back to shore if this occurs. Your only responsibility is to your ship and crew."

Then to Tony, "Tell your little buddy that we have to leave for now, but be back to get them as soon as we can. Whatever you do, make sure they understand that they can't leave by their canoes, and that they need to stay hidden for now."

Obviously conflicted by this plan, Tony argued for another plan. "I have a better idea. You head back to the ship, and I will stay here to make sure. Besides, if Franklin doesn't get his ass back and tell us what the hell is going on, I might turn in my god status. Keep in touch so I know what's going on, and when you're coming back."

Sean knew to argue was pointless. "Fine. At least help me get the launch back in the water."

Tony took the other side, and with all the energy they could muster slowly edged the launch into the surf. Sean jumped in, and once Tony was clear gunned the engine. With the throttle rammed to the stops, the waves bounced Sean around like a rag doll for the next ten minutes. When the cloaked Decatur contacted him, he found it extremely demanding to communicate and keep control of the rolling craft.

"Admiral, come 30 degrees to port. Good. Maintain that heading."

When he finally entered the outer limits of Specters cloak, he found the instructions had put him on a perfect parallel course, twenty meters off the Decatur's port stern. Sean only had to adjust his course slightly to come up on the port side of the destroyer. He waited until the last second to slam the throttle to a stop. Without a thought to the danger of the spinning propellers directly behind, he let go of the wheel and lunged for the third rung of the ladder as the launch slammed against the side of the ship.

Sean struggled with his grip as the launch veered off, leaving him hanging in the air above the water. A knotted rope dropped down next to him moments before his tenuous hold began to slip.

Moments later on the bridge, Barrish received confirmation. "The Admiral is safely aboard, Sir."

"Thank God, one less thing to worry about," Commander Barrish thought. Though the bombs had missed his ship, he had his hands full as they exploded close enough to cause minor damage that emergency crews now worked feverishly to repair.

Then more bad news came from the bridge radio operator. "Commander, the Enterprise CIC reports four more bogies headed our way. F-35s from the Enterprise are about to engage."

"Put it on the speakers." Then to his First Officer he ordered, "Prepare countermeasures."

However, before the XO could carry out the order, two of the approaching bogies suddenly came into view as exploding fireballs. A Sidewinder missile fired from the approaching F-35s had flown right up one of the flying wing's jet engine exhaust, while another missile struck the second enemy jet dead center.

Sean reached the bridge as the Enterprise CIC report shot out from the speakers. "Submerged contact five miles out from the bay entrance."

Sean took over tactical command. However, before he could issue his orders there was another loud explosion, this one from one of the four arriving flying wings that had blindly bombed the bay in an attempt to locate the cloaked Decatur.

Once again, fortune smiled on the Decatur as the bomb exploded 100 yards forward of the ship. Still, it created enough of a blast to raise the bow of the ship out of the water, giving everyone quite the ride when it slammed down hard on the water. Explosion after explosion continued over the next thirty seconds, though to those aboard it seemed more like a lifetime.

"Flank speed, Commander. Get us out of this bay."

Commander Barrish looked unsure. "What about the other contact, Admiral? Our course will take us directly in its path."

To Barrish's surprise, Sean smiled. "I have someone on it, Commander. Carry out your orders."

From the beach, Tony nervously watched the action take place over the middle of the bay as the F-35s destroyed the last of the Nazi jets, and he was not alone. Three hundred sets of eyes peered out from their jungle hiding places, stunned at the show the gods were putting on. Yacahuey was one of the few not impressed at the power thrown across the sky.

"Maybe our gods are not as wise as we thought," he mused. "If they were, why are they trying to kill each other?" The Taíno people had witnessed more violence in one day than they had seen in the last 400 years. Most of them understood that their lives had forever changed, and not for the better, though none understood why.

Positioned outside of the approaches to the bay sat the silent assassin. The German Captain had brought his attack submarine to a full stop only a minute earlier, and now listened intently to the acoustic signals the Decatur put in the water. With her jet engines powered up for flank speed, the German sonar operators could have heard the ship all the way to The Bahamas.

"Get me a firing solution. I want torpedoes in the water as soon as they clear the channel." The Captain gave his commands as if ordering a beer on the beach. He didn't know how they got here anymore than those in the Enterprise group, all he knew was his Admiral's orders were clear. It was them or us. He didn't have the luxury of thinking about the family he might never see again. This was the first time either he or any of the crew serving under him had ever been in an armed conflict, so he kept his focus on the impending battle. That his adversaries had quickly dispatched six of their most advanced fighters showed him that they were more than capable foes.

The sonar operator interrupted the Captain's musings. "Forty five seconds Captain. Targeting information loaded and torpedoes ready for launch."

"Open outer doors. As soon as we launch the torpedoes change course back to the group at flank speed."

"Yes Sir."

On the Decatur's bridge, everyone felt the stress from the attack. Racing along at close to 40 knots, their sonar was worthless with all the noise they were sending out from the thrashing propellers. "Admiral, do you care to share with us why you are so confidently reckless? Because it sure looks like we are going to take some torpedoes directly up the throat."

"I sure hope I do Commander. We should know within the next few minutes."

On the German submarine, the Captain counted down the seconds, and was about to order the attack when his sonar operator yelled out, "Torpedoes in the water Captain. Three thousand yards out and have acquired us!"

Still half a minute from launching his own torpedoes, he had run out of time to get within range of the Decatur. In desperation, he ordered his weapons officer, "Fire one, two, and three."

With his ship and crew now no more than sitting ducks, the Captain smiled at his folly. Another attack submarine had crept up on their port side, also masked by the loud thrashing sound of the Decatur. Every eye was on their Captain aware they would be dead in seconds. Not one of them flinched. As they awaited the impact, most turned and saluted the man who over their naval careers had become like a second father to them.

Though the Hampton had fired a spread of two torpedoes at the German sub, the first was more than sufficient to accomplish the job. It exploded one-third of the way up the starboard side, blowing the side of the sub into the engineering spaces that held the nuclear reactor. This led to a chain reaction that quickly reached the stored torpedoes in the stern and blew the submarine in two. Only those in the forward torpedo room survived the initial blast, but they too quickly expired as the submarine sunk to the depths and imploded.

As the Decatur cleared the channel, Sean witnessed through his binoculars the upthrust of water that announced the subs destruction, but he was more concerned about the torpedoes he knew were on the way. "Hard about to starboard." The risk of this maneuver was it exposed the entire length of the ship, so after ten seconds on the new course Sean ordered. "Bring us back to our original heading, *now.*"

He and anyone who could grab a pair of binoculars stared out the bridge windows trying to pick up any signs of the torpedo tracks.

One of the sailors pointed and yelled out, "Torpedo tracks to port, 500 yards out!"

All eyes swung to this bearing. Sean breathed a sigh of relief when he quickly calculated their course and realized they were going to pass a good 200 yards to port. Thirty seconds later, three loud explosions announced they had slammed into the beach.

In a heavy voice Sean observed, "It looks like they had to launch too soon. Another half a minute and we would have joined them."

The rest of those on the bridge let out a collective yell of relief, and to Sean's dismay, too much celebration. "Enough! We destroyed a submarine and its crew without any idea whether they deserved it or not. Those who gave up their lives for their beliefs probably had as much understanding of why they were here as us, so show a little humility, because it just as easily could have been us."

As the celebration on the bridge fell into an embarrassed silence, Sean ordered the radio operator, "Get me Captain Turner on the Hampton."

With the bridge personnel still silent, Sean took the phone from her after contact was established. "Many thanks from all of us aboard the Decatur. Maintain screening the bay entrance until further notice. Out."

Sean felt it was a perfect time to cement the *it's us against the world* mentality the crew would need to stay alive. Sadly, he understood perfectly well that it was a blatant manipulation of their emotional state, but theater has forever been one of the greatest assets in a commander's arsenal and Sean's timing was always pitch-perfect.

"Commander, let the crew know their actions went well beyond the call of duty. Job well done by everyone."

"Thank you, Admiral."

Sean wanted to collapse in a heap as the adrenaline drained from his body, but no one around him had a clue, as outwardly he remained unfazed. "Commander Barrish, you have the helm. I'm going to grab a cup of coffee in the mess."

"Admiral is off the bridge."

Amid the network of tunnels that crisscrossed under Vatican City lay an array of servers the Catholic Church used to tie the finances of its dioceses to the seat of power, and absolute power is exactly what the church represented to the modern world. It was ironic that a religious order supposedly dedicated to the messages of humility spoken by their savior, owned more wealth than many of the world's nations. With assets estimated in the hundreds of billions, the church operated as any other Fortune 500 company when it came to the bottom line. However, none of this hypocrisy penetrated the grey matter of the Cardinal responsible for the security of the church's internal computer networks.

Cardinal Sciner lived his life under the constant reality that any of the vast array of servers that tracked all the church's assets could crash. Those who served under him all grew to dread the moments when he focused these concerns in their direction. To say he could be an unpleasant man would be an understatement.

Today was one of the few days he was actually in a good mood, because they had finished the annual audit and profits were up twelve percent from the previous year. As he was about to leave his office, a priest he recognized as one of his top coders ran up to him in an obvious state of panic. The priest pleaded, "You have to come, Your Holiness."

Known for his sky is falling reputation, Cardinal Sciner cautioned the emotional priest, "Whatever it is can wait until I return in two days, Father O'Malley."

As much as O'Malley wished he could, he feared a greater wraith if he didn't stand his ground. "All of the church's assets are gone," he blurted out.

The Cardinal's blood ran cold. "What do you mean gone?"

When Sciner reached the main server room, he was horrified to see it shrouded in smoke from several small fires that were burning up millions of dollars of server racks. The Vatican's fire service worked frantically to save the servers not yet damaged. Outside of the room, the computer programmers stood around unsure of what they should do. Cardinal Sciner went immediately to the man who led the unit. "What happened?"

"It started five minutes ago when all the cooling systems abruptly shut down. The computers were supposed to do a dump and shut down, but when they didn't, we tried a manual crash that also failed. Right before the fires started, the monitors not yet affected ran this message."

The lead operator turned Sciner's attention to a 24-inch monitor connected to the only computer still running. Sciner observed a computer-generated avatar that stood alone on the screen dressed in a white summer suit. With perfect blonde hair that framed a face full of sparkling white teeth and a perfect smile that said, *don't you wish you were as gorgeous as I am,* the avatar mocked, "This is not a drill. I repeat, this is not a drill, you have been successfully hacked, and if you wish to regain control of your booty, you must perform two miracles for me. The first is to proclaim that God has found the actions of the current world leaders to be naughty and that your congregations have a duty to protest their displeasure in the most vigorous manner.

"Second, and more importantly, you will send representatives of the church to visit every person, including family members and friends, falsely imprisoned in retaliation for the cyberattacks on the US Government. No one less than a Bishop will suffice. When these demands are satisfied…" Someone off screen interrupted the avatar. "One second please.

"Okay, I'm back with one more request. Let women join your little fraternity as they have every right to be as miserable as you, and no more diddling little boys. Oh, and tell everyone God says it is okay to put a hood over it.

"Now in case you think we have it out for only your merry band of condemners we didn't single out the Catholics when we decided to redistribute your ill-gotten gains. All the major sects of Islam, Mormons, those horrible whack job Pentecostals, and Scientologists have become unwilling partners in our goal to level the playing field. Thank you in advance for joining the cause. God is great."

Cardinal Sciner's blood pressure skyrocketed to dangerous levels as he left the room to report the egregious news to His Holiness.

Seated in his private study with a glass of wine in his hand, Pope Leo XVI couldn't be more pleased as he read from a stack of documents detailing the reactions from many of the Bishops around the world. In fact, the reason the Pontiff made his trip to the United States three months previously was to give his blessing to the President's current course of action. This is why the majority of communications merely congratulated Leo for preparing the church against the current turmoil.

Yawning, he rose from his chair to return to his quarters for a quick nap before supper, but a knock on the door interrupted his attempt. "If you must Cardinal Rosch."

Elaborately decked out in the finely crafted scarlet red cassock, in strode a tall, rail-thin man who wore a scowl that would have terrified any sensible child. The scowl on his pockmarked face foretold the end of the Pontiff's good day. "What's the matter Rosch, nobody to flay today?"

Leo's dig didn't slow the Cardinal down. "The church's firewalls have been breached Your Holiness. All of our outside means of communication are down, which means we have lost touch with all of our dioceses throughout the world. Worse still, all of our accounts here in the Vatican have disappeared."

The blood drained from Leo's face. "What do you mean disappeared? Disappeared as in the assets are still there and you can't see them, or disappeared and may be gone?"

"Cardinal Sciner reported that we have suffered a massive cyberattack that may or may not have been able to transfer vast sums out of the church's accounts immediately before crashing." Cardinal Rosch then went on to tell of the demands the hackers made, which brought out a wicked tick on the Pope's temples. Rosch half expected the Pope to have a full-blown heart attack any second.

━━◆━━

The Decatur's cruise back to the task force went without incident, and by the next morning, the Decatur had rejoined the group as it approached the entrance to Guantanamo Bay. "Well, it certainly wasn't boring, Commander Barrish. Once again, I want you and your crew to know you conducted yourselves well."

"Always a pleasure to serve with you, Admiral. Your ride is ready to take you back to the Enterprise. Will there be anything else?"

"Thank you, and no Commander, I'm good. See you soon."

"Admiral is off the bridge."

Fifteen minutes later, Sean set foot on the flight deck of the aircraft carrier where he headed straight for the bridge.

The Officer of the Watch was quick to announce Sean's return. "Admiral's on the bridge."

Osaka was there to greet him. "Good morning, Admiral."

"Good morning to you, Daniel," Sean replied as he gave Alicia, who stood off to the side, a quick kiss on her cheek.

Though relieved he returned safely, Alicia went straight into her report on what had happened on the Enterprise while he was gone. "Our fighters have returned from Nipe Bay, except for two that are still flying CAP there, while the Hampton remains stationed off the bay entrance. We have two cloaked F-35s and the Seawolf monitoring the Nazi fleet we discovered heading west along the southern edge of the Dominican Republic."

Alicia's professional response as his Chief of Staff amused Sean. "Thank you, *Admiral*. It appears they are coming back for round two.

"Let's get the Missouri, Amelia Earhart, and Laramie into the bay, and send in the John Paul Jones and the Princeton for Specter upgrades. Inform Captain Lincoln that he has full responsibility for air and sea defenses of the Guantanamo Bay area, and to keep the bay cloaked at all times. He can use his MH-60R Seahawks to patrol the entrance to the bay.

"Station the Decatur forward of the task force and the Shiloh to port. Inform Captain Jackson to take over the Princeton's Alpha Whiskey shift. As for the rest of the task force, set a course southwest away from the bay, and remain cloaked until we resolve the Nazis threat."

"Aye Aye Admiral," Alicia acknowledged, still maintaining her professional stance. "Lt. Layworth, get me the CIC."

"Yes, ma'am…, CIC Officer on the line ma'am."

Sean's orders left Captain Osaka confused. "Excuse me, Sir, but why aren't we sending out a response to their attack? Defeating the threat takes care of the danger they pose to the natives."

During his overnight trip back on the Decatur, Sean's mind had cleared, and with it a better understanding of what they could, and could not do with the limited information they possessed. "As we were in 1941, the Nazis are most likely confused about where and when they are and what mysterious hidden force took out their planes and submarine. Our first concern is cause and effect, Daniel, and if you follow this train of thought our only concern will be to protect the region's inhabitants. That's all for now." Sean did not want a debate on the bridge so he gave Osaka his *we are through discussing this* look.

"Aye Admiral."

"Lt. Layworth, locate Dr. Cutler and have her meet us in the Specter operations room."

"Aye Aye Admiral."

When Alicia completed relaying Sean's orders to the CIC, she asked Sean, "What do you have in mind?"

"I'll explain later. Let's go see Rebecca."

"The Admirals are off the bridge."

When Sean and Alicia arrived, Rebecca was there with Dr. Forrest Phelps. After the greetings and prerequisite hugs mercifully ended, Sean began the conversation. "It looks like we are paying for the sins of our past actions. The planes that attacked were certainly 21st Century technology, and based upon our experiences in the 1942 alternate reality, apparently there was a 1940s reality where Hitler won WWII.

"The aircraft that attacked Nipe Bay were high tech flying wing fighters with swastikas, which might mean they may have experienced their own alternate reality adventure where they went back in their time and defeated us to end WWII. Based on what we've seen so far Rebecca, what's your read?"

"Admiral, I can't say with 100% certainty, but the fighters that attacked the Taíno certainly point to that scenario. Specter picked up the energy surge as an anomaly, as if it popped up out of nowhere, similar to how I think we would have appeared when we arrived."

Sean tried hard to come to terms with the implications. "Apparently, this was Bowie's big surprise, only a day earlier than he promised. How was Specter able to pick up the energy surge? Is this part of the programing?"

Rebecca was little help. "Well, yes and – maybe no."

Sean threw up his hands in frustration. "You're not helping Dr. Cutler. Could you please give me a straight answer?"

Rebecca didn't have the words. "I'm just saying…"

Alicia could see Sean's frustration growing and decided to take a different tack. "Why don't we leave Rebecca and Forrest alone so they can focus on the problem without the need to make you understand what they are doing before they are ready? This can't be easy for either one of them."

Alicia didn't wait for Sean to agree with her and grabbed his arm to guide him to the door. "Thanks Rebecca, call as soon as either of you discover anything new."

Without Sean in her face, Rebecca thought of something else. "I can tell you based on your description of the fighters, they may be advanced versions of the Horten Ho 229. If they won the war in their reality, they would have been able to continue to develop all the advanced technology the Soviets and the United States took from them. And if Hitler did conquer the world, they would not have had to deal with the Cold War or the race to the moon. They also would not have had a need to be overly concerned about advancing and perfecting their technology."

"Thank you, Rebecca," Alicia acknowledged again, as she pushed Sean the rest of the way out of the room.

Once they were alone in the corridor, Alicia admonished Sean. "When did you turn into such a bully? You seem to be channeling Tony's reactive *punch it if you don't like it* attitude. Sometimes charming for him, rather childish coming from you. Lighten up."

Sean didn't want to admit the attack from out of nowhere and the repercussions that followed rattled him; however, he realized that was no excuse. "Let's go back to our quarters so we can talk about it in private."

By the time they were back in the Admirals Ready Room with a cup of coffee in hand, Sean had figured out what had set him off. "It finally hit me today."

"Well that explains your behavior. I guess that covers it, moving on now."

Sean ignored Alicia's sarcasm while he searched for the right words. "This isn't easy you know. Who knew that merely the act of becoming your husband would lead to an obsessive need to keep you protected?"

Alicia's first reaction was to burst out laughing at the absurdity that after all the years they had spent in harm's way, suddenly now of all times Sean would go retro. Fortunately, she managed to keep a straight face. "And who knew you were such a softy." Then in a more serious tone, Alicia set him straight. "I understand how it feels to wait so long for something, only to realize when you finally get it that it is a virtual certainty it would not last."

Alicia smiled as she leaned forward to kiss him tenderly. "Let's face it, that is the story of you and me. Maybe what is bothering you is you feel guilty for wasting so many years and now all of a sudden you need redemption. Now don't you feel better?"

Her logical assessment of his mental state only made Sean feel worse. "It was weird. One minute I was trying to calculate which evasive course Barrish had put the Decatur on as the Nazis were on their bomb run, the next there you were on the bridge. My mind froze for a second, and that has never happened to me before."

"You've also never gone off on Rebecca before either. I get it. You don't want to be here and neither do I, or Tony, or all of those serving under you.. Though it probably did more good than harm for everyone to witness you lose it. We wouldn't want you to start getting the impression that you are infallible."

Alicia's subtle sarcasm made Sean noticeably relax. "I knew there was a good reason I married you. I also now know that it isn't fair to go off and play cowboy anymore. You were right to say I shouldn't have gone. It was selfish and childish of me, because if anything should happen to either of us, it would lower the chance that everyone else gets out in one piece."

"Wouldn't it have been much easier to tell me that you love me and couldn't live without me instead?"

Though Sean was willing for Alicia to have in the last word, it turned out she wasn't finished yet. "Anyway, moving on to something else that has me curious. Why is our priority the onshore settlement? I'm with Daniel. Shouldn't we be trying to figure out the Nazis' objective, and why they feel so strongly about trying to blow everything they come into contact to smithereens?"

On the other hand, this line of questioning was right in Sean's wheelhouse. "Think about it. One side sends Tony in advance to prepare the Taíno. Then shortly after the attack on Columbus, an advanced Nazi task force attacks the Taíno. Action – counteraction."

Alicia thought for a moment before she responded. "If that's the case, then how did the Nazis know to attack the Taíno at Nipe Bay?"

"Maybe they have a surrogate like we have Bowie. Also, there could be a Tony counterpart who has spent two years advancing those within their sphere of influence like, let's say for the sake of argument, a more violent pre-Columbian society such as the Aztecs?"

Sean poured them both another cup of coffee. "Or better yet, they are trying to maintain European encroachment into the Western Hemisphere. Remember, *there's gold in them thar hills.*"

Alicia chuckled. "The thought of a Nazi version of our Tony would be something to see in action. Then on the other hand, Tony under an authoritarian government, they'd kill him in a minute."

"I don't know. He survived ours."

Alicia countered. "Did he? Remember, he only came back in the Navy because you and I made it happen."

They simultaneously realized that they needed to return to the business of the task force.

"Enough of…"

"Don't you…"

Sean motioned for Alicia to go ahead.

"I wanted to let you know that everyone handled their jobs exceptionally well during the defense of Nipe Bay. Your idea to put personnel who were in 1942 onto the new ships helped to integrate them quickly into fighting shape. We didn't have a single major problem, or thankfully any losses."

"Sounds good lover. Where to next?"

"I'm headed to the bridge to check our progress."

"You could just as easily do that with me in the CIC. Why the bridge?" Then it hit her. "Because the most difficult thing either you or Tony will ever do is admit it's time for younger warriors to do all the things you are supposed to have outgrown by now. Remember, you promised me no more cowboy."

"Yippee ki-yay, Mother…"

"Sean!"

As retribution for her sarcasm, when they stood up to leave, he pinched her so hard on the ass she jumped.

"More and more like Tony is all I can say."

Sean smiled deviously and gave her a kiss as they headed out.

Alicia spent the next two hours in the CIC gathering battle readiness reports. Though satisfied with the positive news, she made a point to press upon the ship Captains their luck could turn just as quickly if any of their crew lost focus. Alicia spent twice as long with the ship Captains she was unfamiliar with, adding her experiences from 1942 to help build their confidence.

When finished, she decided a quick walk around the flight deck to stretch her legs would help recharge her batteries, and prepared to leave. When she stepped through the door to the corridor, she found herself back in the Admirals Ready Room starring straight at Bowie. "And here I thought you were Sean's play thing."

"Sticks and stones luv. Ch-ch-ch-changes, and time takes a cigarette and puts it in your mouth," Bowie sang as a lit cigarette floated from his lips. "Or in your case, time could not be more relative."

Thoroughly disgusted, Alicia turned and headed for the liquor cabinet, poured herself a tumbler of Jack, and sat down on the couch. "If you were the real Bowie, I would ask for your autograph, but clearly you are not him, just a poser."

Much to her irritation, he followed her footsteps to the Jack, and perfectly mimicking her previous movements poured himself one, walked over to the couch, and sat down next to her.

"Don't tell me you came to visit only to act like a child and irritate the hell out of me. Oh wait, that's what you are." Alicia regretted it, as soon as she said it.

"Oh dearie, dearie me, you have no idea what childish is." As Bowie said these words, the room around them rapidly faded into darkness, and then quickly lit up. Instead of on the couch in the Admirals Ready Room, they were now in the middle of a raucous nightclub. On the wall in front of the astonished Alicia lit in neon was Studio 54. To complete the nightmare, a man she should have known by name was snorting cocaine off a beautiful blonde girl's naked breast.

"I was just telling my little girlie girl here that if you had to be seen, we simply had to come here Andy."

Blonde shoulder length hair, nerdy glasses on a nerdy narcissistic face, of course. "Andy Warhol, really?" Alicia exclaimed.

Bowie took the offered diamond encrusted gold tube from Andy and leaned over to finish off the white powder, sucking off the residual from both breasts to complete the show. "Now that's what I call childish." This brought both men to laughter.

Thoroughly disgusted, Alicia knew when to throw in the towel. "Okay, I get it. You made your point. What do you want?"

"Merely a simple dialogue, that's all." As he talked the nightclub faded, and they returned to her quarters on the Enterprise.

Fine, dialogue you want – dialogue you get," Alicia fumed. "Were you and your friend Franklin responsible for siccing the Nazis on us, or are they pawns like us in this stupid game you're forcing us to play. What's next, George Jetson flying in on the back of The Flying Nun flinging Astro's shit at us?"

Feigning insult Bowie countered her sarcasm. "Would you be the one wearing the habit, because if you did, I could definitely see making that happen?"

"All right, no more sarcasm. Tell me what possible motive would you, or anyone else for that matter, expend what I can only imagine is an incredible amount of energy to put us here. If it's a game, the stakes have got to be ridiculously high."

This response from Alicia brought a clap, clap of approval from Bowie. "You have done nothing but question our motives since you got here. All in all, you have not been very gracious guests. However, since Franklin has worked so hard to save one of one of the greatest societies your species ever produced, I think I can cut you some slack."

This explanation didn't sit right with Alicia. "It seems to me that Tony and the Taíno had the situation well in hand without the additional need of a United States Navy battle group."

"Look at you trying so hard to figure out a strategy put together by a consciousness billions of times more evolved than yours. How quaint."

"Quaint my ass you pompous fool," was what Alicia wanted to say, but instead decided to move on. "So is this your alien version of Survivors? Only in this version people are supposed to die?"

"Au contrair, mon ami. Even Franklin and I have skin in what you refer to as a game. Why don't you offer me some more of your fine Whiskey, and I will spin you a yarn of old."

Bowie's change in tactics surprised Alicia. After she refilled his tumbler, she decided, against her better judgment, to play along. "Okay, I'm all ears."

"As you might have noticed by now, not everything under heaven and the stars is as it seems. Contrary to your belief that there is one great answer, in reality there are many. Now don't think that I or any other force of nature is any more powerful or magical than any other living creature. It is more a question of accumulated knowledge, which, if you don't mind me saying so, is closer to the holodeck on another famous Enterprise than to the idea of the one Great Creator. Think of it more like many creators instead."

Alicia wasn't in any mood to listen to metaphysical hubris coming from Bowie. "You sure throw around the word reality a lot. Considering from where I stand that is something in short supply around you. You seem to make it up as you go."

"Moi?" Bowie's empty glass refilled with the amber liquor as he lifted it to his lips to drink. "Down through time, Sun Tzu, Alexander the Great, da Vinci, Copernicus, Newton, Einstein, and yes, Franklin and David Bowie, stood out from the flock because of their revolutionary ideas. Now you must ask yourself one simple question, where did those ideas come from."

"I knew it. You just admitted you are not the real David Bowie."

Ignoring the obvious, Bowie continued. "You are the type of thinking person who has more in common with the aforementioned geniuses than you can possibly know right now. You must have spent hours trying to understand how all of their ideas fit together to provide a real purpose. You know, the whole enchilada, the why you are here and what happens when it all ends and you're all worm food."

Alicia started to get up to refill her drink, but fell back on the couch when her glass suddenly filled. "Cute. So this is all about resolving a midlife spiritual crisis?" Then more to herself, she added, "I know one ending I'd like to see."

Her comment elicited a smile from Bowie. "Not exactly, but you're close. Take you and your merry band of hopeless romantics. You have spent most of your lives convinced the corruption around you was driving your species right off a steep cliff, yet you persevered. To tell you the truth, humanity fell off the cliff a long time ago and it is only a question of if it survives the fall.

"It is shear folly for anyone to believe the speed of your species' advancements in technological development occurred organically. Let's just say that there are others of a higher calling who are pushing things along."

Alicia cut him off. "Wait! If I am reading you correctly this also means those of a higher calling created our shift into 1941 and by inference put us here now?"

"Not really germane to my story, dear. Besides the how you arrive where you do is irrelevant to the why."

"Which of course you have absolutely no intention of telling me." Once again, Alicia wouldn't take anything away from the conversation that she didn't already know.

"You're catching on." Bowie enjoyed watching the frustration in Alicia rise. "Pay attention now because this is important. As I was saying, what you accomplish will dictate not only the outcome here, but also actions in places you cannot imagine. You have more power to manipulate outcomes than you realize. Though Franklin and I will be able to do much to aid you, there are those who do believe you have the ability to survive what is ahead. Think of it as a multidimensional game of chess, because all the pieces are on the boards, and of course you and your hubby are the King and Queen on this board level."

"You mean, more like rats in a maze," Alicia countered as she rose from the couch. "To tell you the truth, if what you say is true about our ability to influence future events for the better, then I would have to reconsider the disgust I currently view you with. However, if you're jacking us around to feed your own sense of superiority, I would rather scuttle every last ship than continue to play your game."

Alicia leaned down to Bowie and added, "As you so succinctly stated, wham, bam, thank you *man*."

"You are quite the delightful creature. It is too bad you are married, or I would certainly make a run at you. Suck, baby, suck."

The look of disgust returned to Alicia's face. "Really, you went there?"

"You started it."

Bowie then reached down deep to build up a sense of foreboding in his voice. "Trust me when I tell you that this is about more than what is happening in your normal place and time. You would be hard-pressed to wrap your tiny little head around a fraction of the implications of what has been set in motion and your part in it."

Bowie gave her a quick wink, and before Alicia could say another word, he was gone.

"I really, *really* hate it when he does that."

⸻ ❖ ⸻

Seated in the White House Situation Room with enough top rank military brass to start a war, Aaron Fletcher leaned over to whisper in President Susan Harrison's ear. "You look like you just ate a plate of peas. Get tough. Your military leaders need to see you confident and sure right now." He needed her to stop acting as if someone had propped her up in her seat like a Raggedy Anne doll.

She struggled to put on the right mask, though it did nothing for the queasiness she felt for what they were about to do in her name. Eighteen hours earlier, she had ordered B-2 Spirit stealth bombers loaded with both tactical and strategic nuclear weapons to annihilate the rogue nation of North Korea.

The President understood much could go wrong when you release the nuclear genie over another sovereign nation, especially when the true reason for doing so led directly back to the criminal actions at the White House. Though Aaron had silenced most of those who knew about the administration's involvement in the destruction of San Francisco, the President knew it would surely come back on her. "The Japanese Prime Minister isn't going to like any of this."

Aaron smiled at her stupidity in thinking the tiny island nation any longer held any strategic importance. "Japan has no more power to influence international policy than the man on the moon. Someone has to pay for San Francisco, and North Korea fits the bill. Besides the Chinese have my, I mean our," he quickly corrected, "personal assurances that when the smoke clears, we will not object to their reunification with Taiwan." The President's Chief of Staff then checked the time on his phone and nodded to Susan.

"General Favors, it is a go."

"Yes, Madam President." The look on the face of the Chief of Staff of the Air Force betrayed that he obviously did not agree with this course of action. However, without a word of dissension he entered his authorization code, which when followed by the President's codes unleashed the dogs of the Nuclear World War.

"Madam President, it is time to make the calls to our allies and nuclear capable adversaries that this is a single strike targeting only North Korea. We don't want anyone getting any more nervous than necessary."

Not one of the B-2 crews could believe the President sent the go code. Stunned silence pervaded in the interiors of the six aircraft as they took the final steps to arm their nuclear weapons, and then head to their individual designated targets. Fifteen minutes later the first, and most important target, the capital city of Pyongyang became the fourth city destroyed by a nuclear explosion. Wonsan,

Sariwon, Kaesong, Kimchaek, Hamhung, and Kanggye followed in rapid fashion. A flight of F/A-18F Super Hornets from the USS Ronald Reagan stationed in the Sea of Japan hit the bunkers and missile silos identified by satellite imagery and information from spies and defectors.

The nuclear strikes immediately incinerated forty percent of North Korea's entire population, and those who lingered, suffered excruciating pain without any hope of rescue. Fallout from the numerous blasts blew northeast over Japan and the Russian Kamchatka Peninsula bringing misery to their remote populations.

Unfortunately for the US President and South Korea, two nuclear tipped rockets made it out of their North Korean silos unscathed. The first only needed to travel one hundred fifty miles to Seoul, while the second headed to Busan, the nation's second largest city. These had equivalent yields to the bombs dropped on Nagasaki and Hiroshima, so over 50 percent of the affected populations survived the immediate blast. The collateral damage actually fell under the Pentagon's risk assessment predictions.

After the real time video from the bomber group and satellite imagery arrived, a satisfied Aaron nudged President Harrison. "You have some make up sex to perform with the Japanese and South Koreans. Remember, as sorry as you are for giving the order, it was righteous retribution for San Francisco. I don't see any of the major players offering any more than a vote of condemnation at the UN, and we both know how meaningless that is."

Aaron felt his phone vibrate and knew he needed to take the call in private. "Excuse me, but while you smooth ruffled feathers I need to check in with some of my rather more shadowy contacts."

"Don't be gone long. I will definitely need your advice." President Harrison remembered his warning about giving him orders. "I mean there might be those who are not as happy as you about what we did."

Aaron looked like he was about to scold her, but then became somewhat perplexed. "Is she showing a little backbone and directing it at me?" he wondered. He shook it off and exited the White House Situation Room as happy as any psychopath who had just murdered millions could be.

When he got some distance from the Situation Room, he hit callback on his cell phone. "What is so damn important that it couldn't wait? You knew we were in the middle of a nuclear strike." Aaron listened for a moment, and found humor in his adversary's latest challenge. "Went after the Vatican did he? That's okay, I have it covered. I know what he is going to do next, and have a nice little surprise planned for him."

As the 300 or so Taíno gathered again on the beach, they all cast a wary eye at Tony. Yacahuey explained, "They fear the gods that challenged you with those flying monsters are more powerful than you, and that you will run away to save yourself rather than fight off the evil you brought to us."

Hoping they were still in range, Tony grabbed his magic talk box. "Captain Anthony Knox calling the USS Decatur CIC. Over."

"Go ahead, Captain."

"Inform Admiral Phillips that now would be a good time to orchestrate an uncloaked pass over the bay for show."

"We will pass your request on Captain and get back to you. Out."

"Make it quick."

Upon receiving the request, Sean quickly complied, as four uncloaked F-35s buzzed the bay in formation with a deafening roar. The Taíno reacted with quiet trepidation, not sure which gods they belonged to.

Through Yacahuey, Tony spoke to the Taíno as he pointed to the sky. "My flying brothers destroyed the demons that attacked you, and as you can see they are still in the sky protecting you. Your defeat of the Spanish today insured your immediate survival. Over the next year, you will need to prepare for the return of those from across the great sea. For now, enjoy your celebration, and then I promise you can return safely to your villages."

With this reassurance, Yacahuey let out a giant whoop, which got the rest of the villagers to once again dance around the great fire in celebration of their hard won victory.

For an unknown reason the unrealistic thought of wolfing down a giant New York thin-crust pizza overwhelmed Tony's senses, which brought out a twisted laughter from the Taíno god. "It is too bad none of you will ever enjoy the decadence of a great slice of pie."

Yacahuey pointed behind Tony and asked, "Yúcahu, is that what those are?"

Tony whipped around to the sight of fifty pizza boxes and ten cases of soda sitting in the sand.

"Very funny Franklin," was the last thing Tony thought before he found himself seated back in the living room of his home across from him. "So did you send everyone back home, or should I go see for myself?"

"They are all where they should be and unfortunately so is the Nazi task force that attacked the Taíno. However, before we get to that, I thought now would be a good time to fulfill my part of our contract."

Before Tony could react, a desperate need for sleep overwhelmed him and he collapsed to the floor unconscious.

Franklin stood over him with a smile. "I am a man of my word, Captain Anthony Knox. Pleasant dreams."

When Tony woke up, he wasn't surprised to find himself back in his bed. What did surprise him was the body he bumped up against when he turned onto his side.

"Stop moving around. Can't you see I am trying to sleep?"

Fearing that Franklin had put one of the Taíno women next to him, he ripped the covers back.

The naked body he exposed was not Taíno. "What's wrong with you? It's never enough for you." The white hands grabbed the covers and threw them back all the way over her head. "And if you ever expect to get another piece of this, you better leave me alone."

This time he slowly lifted enough of the cover to see her face. "Renée? I've had some extremely vivid dreams since I got here, but this one takes the cake."

She smiled, though her eyes remained closed. "You are really beginning to annoy the hell out of me."

Since that awful day he lost her over a decade ago, Tony thought of Renée every night before he fell asleep. All of his previous dreams combined didn't compare to the reality of this one. Then, the horror of how all of those other dreams ended in her brutal death forced him to jump out of the bed.

The suddenness of his action brought about an equal response from the now very irritated Renée. She threw the covers off and sat up glaring at him. "What is wrong with you?" She sat for a moment pouting before she shook her head in frustration and laid back down in mock surrender. "Fine, if the only way you're going to leave me alone is to let you maul me, make it quick so I can get back to sleep."

Stunned, all Tony could do was sit on the edge of the bed and stare at her.

Renée grabbed his arm and pulled him back into bed. She wrapped her arms around his neck to pull him on top of her and into a passionate kiss.

It only took a couple of seconds for Tony to push his concerns out of his mind and allow himself to surrender to her passion. He gave himself fully to the ensuing frenetic lovemaking. The usual descriptions of such a reunion paled in comparison to what occurred over the next hour. Upon conclusion, Renée rolled away and threw the cover back over her body. "Now let me sleep in peace."

Tony propped himself on his side and stared down at her, trying desperately to forestall the usual depressing ending. As hard as he tried to stay awake, he slowly lost the battle as the memory slowly faded away.

The next morning Tony woke up extremely depressed, which did not surprise him as this always followed a night dreaming about Renée, though now that he thought about it, she hadn't died. As he lay in bed mulling the meaning of this new twist on the old dream, a hand suddenly grabbed his arm.

"A penny for your thoughts, studly."

Tony whipped around to see her just as he had left her in the dream.

Renée could see the confusion written all over his face. "You look like hell. Did you have some kind of scary-ass nightmare last night?"

At a complete loss for words, he threw his arms around her and squeezed her so tight she had to pull away.

"Take a breath Tarzan. What's the matter with you? You're acting like we haven't seen each other in years."

As the portal above their bed let in the morning light, a now fully awake Renée slowly became aware of her surroundings. Now the one confused, she bolted upright. "This isn't our cabin aboard the Missouri. How did we get here, and where is here?"

When she turned for answers from Tony, confusion turned to concern at the sight of him looking like he was about to cry. "What has happened now?"

Tony tried to pull himself together to explain, but waved her off. "You are going to have to give me a minute."

"How exactly does one explain to their loved one that for the last eleven years they were dead?" he thought. Tony decided it was best to stall until he figured that one out.

"We definitely need a pot of coffee first." Without waiting for a reply, he jumped out of bed and headed for the kitchen.

Fortunately for Tony, Renée's last memories had not caught up to her yet, so she figured that this was another weird reaction from their meddling in 1942. Based on Tony's state of mind, obviously she wasn't going to like what he was hiding, but considering how relaxed the night's activities made her, she wasn't in any hurry to hear bad news. Instead, Renée began to take in the strange house she now found herself in as she followed him to the kitchen. "Since when did we go in for suburbia chic?"

When they reached the kitchen, Tony wasn't surprised to find freshly brewed coffee already made, and to top that a full breakfast spread covered the kitchen table. "Franklin?"

"Okay, when he starts talking to himself it's time to find out what he knows that I don't," Renée thought. "Franklin? Who the hell is Franklin? Okay, this is starting to freak me out." Renée tried to control the queasy feeling that rose from the pit of her stomach. "Either we had the mother of all drunken binges, or you need to explain yourself."

Tony grabbed her hand and steered her to one of the chairs. "You are going to need to sit down."

"That bad?"

"What is the last thing you remember?"

His question triggered the memory of where they were. "I remember leaving the Capitol Building, and then people shooting at us." She winced at her next memory. "I got shot!" She frantically reached for the spot on her chest where the bullet had entered and rubbed it. "I got shot in the chest, and it hurt like hell. I also remember you holding me while we flew back to the Enterprise. Then I was in Sickbay, and then…"

"You passed." Tony couldn't find any other words to soften the news.

Renée took a moment to absorb the news, before asking in disbelief. "How can I be dead? How long was I dead? A minute, an hour, how long!"

Tony took a deep breath and tried to explain. "This may take a minute to become clear, so please be patient." Tony sat down across from her and silently cursed Franklin for not making this part easier on him.

With everything to lose he bit his lip and dove in. "You are in my house in the jungles of Cuba before it was called Cuba, on the day after Columbus was to land in 1492. Franklin is Benjamin Franklin, yes, *the* Founding Father Franklin. He put me up here two years ago, and it stayed that way until yesterday when the Taíno and I ambushed Columbus, and the Enterprise Task Force showed up with…"

Renée interrupted him. "I need something stronger than coffee."

Tony didn't hesitate. He rushed out of the kitchen and came back with a bottle of champagne and a bottle of Scotch.

Renée grabbed the Scotch from his hand as he sat down. "Lose the champagne, big boy." Renée stated in a terse voice. "If there *is* a reason to celebrate, it won't be for a while." She poured a double shot and quickly downed it, poured another and downed that one as well. She wiped her mouth and steeled herself. "Okay. Could you at least start with me getting dead, and going from there?"

Despite the knot growing in his stomach at the thought of having to recall that difficult day, Tony swallowed hard and obliged. "We got you back to the Enterprise, but not before you had lost too much blood. The doctors couldn't save you.

"After discovering on the bodies of the rednecks who shot you information about who ordered the attack, Sean moved the task force south to bring them to justice. That was eleven years ago for me."

This news shocked Renée. "Dead? I have been dead for eleven years? How can that be?"

Before Tony could answer, Renée pushed herself away from the table and stood up. She then began to pace the room. "You expect me to believe I have been dead for eleven years? What about my family? Do they have any idea about what happened to me, or has anyone returned home to let them know?"

Renée sat back down at the kitchen table, put her hands over her face, and began to cry. "How can this be?"

Tony moved around the table to sit next to her and took one of her hands in his. "I am truly sorry I was not able to return and inform your family myself, but I'm sure Sean and Alicia explained to them what happened. You can ask when we see them.

"For all I know you being dead for eleven years, seems completely irrelevant to what has happened since that day. To you it could have only been minutes."

This only made Renée more upset. "What difference does it make whether I was dead for years or minutes? Dead is dead."

This led to another thought, one that she instinctively knew to be true. "You had something to do with this, didn't you? Who did you promise what to?"

Tony tried franticly to save the situation. "If you would be patient, I can fill you in on everything that has happened since that day." Tony needed to get her mind off what they could not control, and proceeded to narrate the bizarre series of events that led up to the present. "Like I said, it has been eleven years since I lost you, but only for me. It only got worse when we were on our way back to Cuba after a second trip to Europe when Sean and Alicia disappeared with half of the task force. That left me alone to command the Missouri, John Paul Jones, Princeton, Hampton, and the two supply ships. When we returned to our homeport in Guantanamo Bay, I tasked Dr. Cutler to take over Alicia's diplomatic duties, and Captain Carl Eddington as her military adjunct. We were in the 1940s reality for almost a decade in total, during which Rebecca and Carl married and had a son.

"I was a wreck for years after losing you. Lost in self-pity, I wasn't much good to anyone, and to be honest, I was close to joining you when I disappeared while on maneuvers in 1951. That's when I turned up here in 1490. Franklin appeared and convinced me to become the Taíno god Yúcahu to prepare them for the attack on Columbus. It took a while for me to stop dwelling on the life you and I should have shared, but over time, I replaced the pain of losing you with the joy of helping these wonderful people."

"So what happened to Sean and Alicia?"

Tony could see that Renée was calming down so he slowed down his narrative. "Their half of the task force returned to 2014 only minutes after they had left 2014. Then according to what they told me yesterday, four years later in 2018 while on their honeymoon in California they jumped to the reconstituted Enterprise Task Force on duty in the Atlantic. Then my ships from 1951 joined them, and they all jumped into 1492 the day before yesterday. So for Sean and Alicia and the half that returned to 2014 from 1942 it has been four years since we lost you, for Rebecca and the Missouri half it has been nine years, and for me it has been that nine years plus the two years I have been here."

After four tumblers of Scotch Renée was quite numb. "So what's next? Are you going to keep playing god, or is it back to the Enterprise to figure out what we need to do to get out of *this* mess?"

"I wanted to stick around until the Taíno were safe, but that was before you showed up. Instead, I think it is as important to let Sean and Alicia know that you are back as soon as possible. As fantastic as it is to have you back, there has to be something on the immediate horizon we will all absolutely hate." Tony understood that Renée's return came with a price, and this one would most definitely be a doozy.

Tony leaned over to hug Renée, and this time she relented. While still in their embrace, the monitor on the counter suddenly came to life with the cheery faced Franklin coming into focus on the screen.

"She is certainly quite the looker. I can see why you were so lost and cranky without her."

Renée walked over to the monitor and put her face inches from the screen. "So Tony isn't crazy, there is a Benjamin Franklin Gollum." She poked the screen where his forehead was. "So are you the one responsible for all of this?"

"I would rather only admit to bolstering the power of your love to shatter the barriers nature constructed to hold you back from your one true love."

Franklin's poor attempt at a poetic response only caused Renée to shake her head in disgust. "I guess it could be worse," she stated sadly. "I could still be dead." With that, Renée walked out the back door.

"One would think she could show a little gratitude. I can see why you two are such a match for one another."

Franklin's sarcasm was lost on Tony. "And I can see why you are clueless when it comes to women. You could have done a better job of laying the groundwork, as opposed to dropping her into my bed unannounced."

Franklin chuckled at the idea that anyone would ever accuse the raconteur who seduced all of Paris of ignorance when it came to the fairer sex. "You have no idea how difficult it was to pull this off. Trust me when I say that might be the only sex you are going to see for the foreseeable future regardless of how I handled it. I just figured you might appreciate starting with, as opposed to without. Oh, and by the way, you're welcome."

Tony found little to argue with Franklin's rational thinking about what his priorities would be if he had just returned to the land of the living. "I've got to go make sure she is all right." As the door closed behind him, he added, "Thank you."

Tony found her sitting by the Koi pond and sat down next to her. "So what can I do to help?"

"How about send us back home before we disappeared in that

storm off San Francisco in 2014 and forget this ever happened."

"I can't say I would be opposed to that idea, except the only way we got back together was because of that little trip."

"It's not that. You know I've always had a good handle on things, but seriously, how do you get over being dead for eleven years?" Renée put her head on his shoulder. "And better yet, why me?"

"Good question. I have been asking for a straight answer to the same question from Franklin for the better part of two years, why me. Maybe now that you're back we will both find out what makes us so special to those pulling the damn strings?"

"Is he still on your monitor?" She peeked behind Tony to see if they were alone.

They got up to go find out, but before they could take a step, Franklin appeared in front of them.

"You couldn't be more mistaken than to assume I want something in return. I promised her return if you complied, and I am a man of honor." He pushed his glasses lower on the bridge of his nose and winked. "Of course none of this agreement impacts your fellow travelers, so you might consider it wise to limit your contact."

"And there it is." Tony picked up a rock and threw it angrily into the pond scattering the fish. "What else?"

"It's complicated."

Tony started toward Franklin in a menacing manner. "So is warping mind and matter, but here we are."

Franklin figured, "What the hell," and threw Tony a bone. "I can let you know that you will need to decide what you need to do to protect the Taíno, and more germane to the situation, what it is that you can't do. Obviously, this concerns your friends as well. You all have so much to do, so I suggest you get started."

Before either could ask what this cryptic message meant, Franklin began to fade away with his hand covering his mouth as if hiding a secret.

"Cheeky bastard."

"You have no idea, Renée." Tony absently skipped another stone into the pond. "You have no idea."

No sooner had Franklin vanished, than the green mist rapidly swirled around both Tony and Renée prompting them to cling to each other desperately. When it cleared, they stood side by side alone in the Admirals Ready Room on the Enterprise. Before they could react, the ship's klaxons began wailing its call to General Quarters.

Pope Leo XVI had exhausted all of his options to unlock the stranglehold computer hackers had placed on the church's massive computer networks. His conversation with President Harrison did little to reassure the Pontiff.

"What do you mean you know who did it? If you knew, why didn't you stop them? Your government spent hundreds of billions of dollars to collect every last piece of personal information on your citizens and you can't find the ones the technology was built to find in the first place?"

Pope Leo paused to let the sarcasm sink in. "Makes one wonder if you may have overreached your ambitions, Madam President."

Seated off camera, Aaron seethed. The plan was to produce evidence that North Korea delivered the nuclear attack on San Francisco, not listen to the Pope whine about lost wealth. Further frustrating his plans, the Vatican was supposed to be the target of his next big surprise, but now that would have to wait.

Instead, Aaron focused on President Harrison's response. "On behalf of the millions of American Catholics, all I can offer Your Holiness is that we have identified those responsible and Homeland Security has promised they will find the location of their operations shortly."

"And in the meantime? How are we going to continue to aid the millions of impoverished souls who depend on the church for their salvation?"

Aaron had enough of the pompous asshole. "Bullshit. More like how are the select few of you going to continue to gorge yourselves without them filling the collection baskets every Sunday?"

Suddenly another voice entered the conversation. "I hate to interrupt, Your Eminence, but I believe it's in your best interest to wrap it up."

Stunned, Pope Leo spun around and looked up to see Sean Anthony perched high on the top of the head of the resurrected Jesus that is the centerpiece of the giant sculpture La Resurrezione. "Who are you, and how did you get past my guards?" The Pope didn't wait for an answer. Instead, in an amazing act of alacrity for such an old man, he launched himself from his papal chair while loudly screaming for his guards.

In the Oval Office, President Harrison chimed in with her own disbelief. "How could someone be able to do that?"

Aaron immediately put the teleconference audio feed on mute and admonished his boss. "Could you shut up for a minute?" Aaron stood up and paced the Oval Office as he considered his options.

A challenge from Sean Anthony interrupted his thoughts. "Unless you believe the voices of a billion pissed off Catholics won't put a crimp in your plans, now might be a good time for you to join us."

By now, the sound of guards pounding furiously on the massive double doors was an obstacle to their conversation.

Aaron cursed silently before he turned to warn the President. "Don't do anything stupid while I'm gone."

The President's frayed nerves took another hit when Aaron simply disappeared in a puff of green mist.

Thinking Sean Anthony wasn't paying attention to him, Pope Leo made a dash for the doors, but ran head first instead into an invisible wall before he could take a second step.

From his perch from high above Sean Anthony warned him. "Be patient for a moment. I'll get back to you." He then turned to face the doors the guards were finding impossible to open. He smiled as he could hear momentum building, then judging the ebb and flow of their efforts, waved his hand with a flourish and without warning, the force holding them shut abruptly gave way.

The suddenness of the doors flying open sent the guards and their weapons crashing out of control to the floor. They picked themselves up just in time to see a second intruder introduce himself through a curtain of green mist. At the same time, Sean Anthony came down from his perch above the throne. Now being the one closest, Sean Anthony received the brunt of the attack from the twenty-strong contingent of the Papal Swiss Guard. With the fear of striking the Pope if they opened fire, they opted instead to attempt to tackle Sean Anthony, but succeeded only to pass right through his form as if he were but a ghost.

"Don't you just love modern technology?" Sean Anthony observed to Aaron. "I bet you didn't know how easy it is to send a holographic projection halfway around the world."

Off camera, in a cave somewhere in China came a quick rebuttal from a slighted Adonis. "You damn well know it wasn't that easy, right? Why can't a brother get a little love?"

No sooner had Adonis registered his complaint, than a life-sized doll replica of him appeared in the adjacent empty seat. "Bitch, bitch, whine, whine, when will I ever be loved?" The cave full of hackers burst out in laughter.

"Very funny." The chagrined Adonis sank deep as he could into his chair.

Back at the Vatican, the Keystone Cops disappeared in a swirl of green mist as the grand doors slammed shut again.

Sean Anthony's theatrics did not amuse Aaron. "Nice touch, though I can't see what you hope to gain with this pitiful magic show."

"I'm here to see if the old man in the funny costume has made up his mind yet." Sean Anthony walked over to where the Pope had gone to hide behind the giant sculpture. "You know it wasn't only the money we managed to liberate." He leaned in to whisper in Pope Leo's ear. "Only half of what we now know will make the pedophile scandal look like grade school gossip."

This refocused the Pope's attention. "You're the one who hacked the church."

"Well, me and a few of my closest friends," Sean Anthony replied.

Aaron watched with an evil glee as the blood drained from the face of the man in the funny suit. Oddly enough, the two agreed that some actions went too far to stomach. "So here we are again, Sean Anthony. All of this going through intermediaries is a pain in the ass. How they manage to put one foot in front of the other without tripping is truly a miracle."

Aaron then addressed the visibly shaken Leo. "What's the matter, Your Holiness? Not exactly the image of God you were prepared for?"

Too stunned to respond, the Pope could only stare blankly at the strangers.

"Isn't it funny how popping in unexpected can throw a pontiff off his game? Why don't we give him a minute Aaron? I can wait."

Pope Leo at last found his voice, shaky as it was. "What do you want from the church?"

"He speaks," Sean Anthony exclaimed. "Didn't you get my message? I thought we made ourselves perfectly clear about our demands. You know the whole part where you denounce President Harrison, help the poor, etc."

Aaron decided this was an opportune time to interject. "By the way, his name is Sean Anthony Eddington." Aaron turned to face his brother to confirm. "That is your nom de plume these days, isn't it?'

"I'm cool."

Aaron turned his attention back to the Pope. "Sean Anthony and I are competitors in matters your narrow little mind could not begin to comprehend; yet, ironically enough, we share a common loathing of cults such as yours. The sheer audacity to place yourself as the one voice to interpret the will of your one God for the masses takes one huge set of cojones. And if that isn't bad enough, add in your obsessions with personal aggrandizement and ostentatious greed, and even I am offended. This role is solely reserved for ones such as myself."

"And that's saying something," Sean Anthony interjected.

"You mind?"

"No, go right ahead."

Pope Leo shrunk further into his hiding place.

"Anyway, if either Sean Anthony or I wanted to celebrate our greatness with inferiors licking our feet..." Aaron snapped his fingers and three gorgeous women wearing nothing but a smile appeared out of nowhere and seductively danced in circles around Sean Anthony.

Though he enjoyed the show, Sean Anthony knew better than to let it continue for too long. "You do know that what we are doing here will not go unnoticed, so you might want to dial it down a little."

Aaron shrugged. "That's always been your problem Sean Anthony. You need to learn to live a little. Besides, your bit with the guards gave me the leeway. But if you insist..." The women disappeared with another snap of the fingers, and he returned his attention on the Pope.

"In fact, if either of us had our way, you and your shriveled up brethren would be transformed into minimum wage fast food workers at Burger Queen. Anyway, once again, I digress."

"You are prone to that, and it is one of the precious few endearing qualities you possess." Sean couldn't resist the dig.

"*Annnyway*, as I was trying to say." Then in a voice of equal parts John Wayne and a broadcast news anchor, Aaron addressed Leo. "My guess is that my brother is here to offer you the deal of a lifetime, but I must warn you to consider deeply whom you sell your soul to pilgrim."

Sean Anthony laughed at Aaron's opening volley. "Seems like not much of a choice at all when you consider the precarious position the man who heads up the world's wealthiest private entity."

Sean Anthony took his turn to belittle the Pope. "Do you want it back, or do you wish for a more chastened life?" Sean Anthony then replaced the Pope's robes with the tattered uniform of the homeless, complete with the soiled stench from weeks of unwashed wear.

Aaron watched as the Pope scratched vigorously at the parasites that now inhabited his scalp. "I can understand how living among the lepers doesn't fit your idea of a good time, but it could be worse. Consider how unhappy I will be with you after I destroy my dear brother, if you agree to anything that delays that inevitable outcome. Within the next two days I will render him as useless as a matzah ball at a Palestinian dinner table."

Pope Leo stared at the two men now knowing how it feels to be a slab of meat placed between two starving lions. He stepped out from his hiding place and took a deep breath before he declared to Aaron, "The church does not have two days. Though I appreciate your government's concern, I must respectfully reject your warnings."

Then with a surge of confidence he didn't feel, the Pontiff aggressively announced, "I must also raise serious concerns about the reckless actions that led to so many innocent deaths in both North and South Korea. Later today, the church will issue a proclamation to the members of the Catholic Church to reject your legal interpretation on the suspension of human rights. The Vatican will cut off all formal ties to your government unless you restore the rule of law to your citizens."

Sean Anthony chuckled at the Pope's predictability. "Unfortunately for you Aaron, he is after all a man after your own heart, always on the make for expedience over substance."

"No matter. It isn't as if the church's support is critical." Aaron changed Leo back to his formal attire before he swooped over to grab the frail man by his neck. "You have ensured your institution's demise, little man. Though it is in my power to crush the life out of you at this moment, instead I look forward to the moment your church lies in ruins for your lack of foresight." Aaron released his grip and the Pope dropped like a sack of potatoes to the floor.

Aaron then turned to Sean Anthony and with a smile added before he disappeared in a green flash, "It looks like everything has to get bigger."

Sean Anthony added his own threat after he left. "I don't envy your lot, *Mister* Leo. Then again, I don't give a rats ass as long as you follow through with your declaration. Remember, not only will I take it all away again, but trust me when I say the last thing you want is to have both of our attentions directed toward making your life the living Hell you promise to all the nonbelievers." With that, Sean Anthony's holographic projection shimmered and disappeared.

Alone and lost in the turmoil, it took Pope Leo five minutes before all the qualities that elected him Bishop of Rome returned. He picked up the phone and called Cardinal Sciner. "I have worked out a deal for the return of the church's funds, but first you need to inform the press that I have a major announcement to make concerning the attack on North Korea by the United States."

President Harrison received the next shock of the day when Aaron returned, seated exactly where he was moments earlier.

"What the hell are you?"

"Your worst nightmare is all I am. We have lost the support of the Catholic Church, but this shouldn't be much of a problem. You will need to make an announcement…"

This is as far as Aaron got in updating the President before she went over the edge and exploded, "I thought the idea was for you to keep a low profile? How can we maintain control over the population if one of the world's most influential spiritual leaders comes out against us?"

Aaron ignored that she was coming apart. "Actually, I believe this will work out quite well for *me*."

President Harrison looked at Aaron as if he was the one who had lost his mind. "You must be delusional if you think the Catholic Church is not an important part of keeping millions of Americans pacified."

"I have a plan in place to give the church plenty to deal with. So if you will excuse me, I must see to it."

"What plan?" Though her voice had steadied and the shaking had subsided, President Harrison still appeared vulnerable.

Aaron made sure to keep her that way. "It doesn't matter if you know or not, and remember what I said about questioning my actions. The thought of my fingers around your frail neck does excite me so." With a wicked smile, Aaron disappeared again.

In his office, Aaron opened his bottom desk drawer, took out an untraceable cell phone, and sent a text message before returning it to the drawer. "It's good to be the king."

⚜

Rebecca was well into her third hour of deep sleep after thirty-six hours of nonstop work poring over Specter's schematics with Dr. Phelps. The flutter of her eyelids suggested a very active dream state.

She found herself walking hand in hand with her husband along an idyllic mountain stream. In all of her years, Rebecca had never felt the overwhelming sense of peace and tranquility as she did in this moment. Fine moss covered the ground they strolled through, tickling her bare feet, which reminded her of long ago days when as a child she believed all was possible. All at once, every epiphany Rebecca experienced in her lifetime and the emotional exhilarations that came along for the ride, ignited down to the very core of her soul.

In rapid succession, a series of firsts flooded her memories: the thrill of the first ride in a car; peddling a bike, then falling down and skinning a knee; the sheer height of a 60-story skyscraper; and pounding a screwdriver into a battery-powered radio because the holes seemed too small to let all the music out. Hundreds of them, from the most mundane to the most defining moments drove home the point that Rebecca wouldn't change a single one of these memories great and small – well maybe one. She now wished chocolates had never crossed her path since she discovered the run on the ship's galley had emptied the shelves when it occurred to most there wasn't a Hershey's factory available to resupply. "It figures that the one place I could get it, South America, wasn't on our list to visit," she lamented. "What an odd thing to dream about."

Once this strange observation passed, Rebecca found herself back in the moment she became aware that Sean Anthony had sprung to life in her womb. Never before had Rebecca felt so connected to her own existence. Unfortunately, this memory turned her euphoric state to one of darkness as the pain of her son's absence changed her mood to such a melancholy state the vibrant colors faded into shades of grey.

Carl gathered his wife in his arms and consoled her. "I am truly sorry that events have precluded your rightful role in raising our son, and me from being by your side. I give you my word that in a short time we will be together to experience all the joys that are your birthright."

Though his words pierced Rebecca's melancholy state, they unleashed a mother's anger instead of providing comfort. "You do realize of course the longer you keep me away from our son, the more likely it is I will make some mistake that could conceivably put all of us at risk. You can't expect my concern for our son's safety to not cloud my judgment."

Instead of satisfying his wife's blatant attempt to manipulate his emotions, Carl shifted the landscape into one so alien in its beauty that Rebecca didn't have a choice about whether to stay mad or not.

The air included not only the oxygen needed for life, but with each breath she took, a mixture of scents assaulted her senses in waves that released a torrent of energy throughout her body. Sight, sound, and hearing began to meld into one, which amplified her awareness of her surroundings to such a fine point Rebecca could sense life right down to the molecular level. In other words, it became the young scientist's perfect dream, which set off alarms. "Perfect?"

With a bit of frustration, Carl pleaded with her. "Do you have to question everything? Will you please be the woman I married and simply enjoy the thrill of it all?"

Between Carl's pleading and the wonderment surrounding her, the scientist in Rebecca caved. "Don't you think this means I am finished with you," she admonished before giving in to the wonderment around her.

Immediately she became aware that regardless of the entirely alien feel there was a somewhat familiar memory just out of reach of her consciousness. This familiarity gave Rebecca a measure of comfort. Then, without warning or any grand explosion of adrenaline one would associate with an epiphany of such scale, a lifetime of assumptions about how the universe worked shredded into confetti.

Thoroughly immersed in its glow, she didn't feel herself lift off the ground. "This is what being a god must feel like," were the only words her mind could come up with to describe the moment. However, the same doubts remained. "As mind-blowing as all of this is, everything you are showing me only makes it more difficult to understand why our son isn't here to share it. In giving me these wondrous insights, it only makes it more difficult to understand why I can't get a straight answer from you to such a simple question?"

"There is nothing simple about it, or what I am attempting to do. From the moment I fell in love with you, I knew the time would come when I would literally have to move Heaven and Earth to save you. Unfortunately, that requires Sean Anthony, who embodies everything you and I represent, to operate in the center of it all in your home reality. His role in the outcome is every bit as critical as the decisions and actions you and your friends take." To Carl's way of thinking, this clearly answered Rebecca's concern. Once again, he was mistaken.

"Who do you think you're talking to, June Cleaver? You say his role, his role in what?" Rebecca fumed. "And what does that have to do with us stuck in the middle of a 15th Century muck up? For such a supposedly advanced entity, you can be unbelievably clueless."

Throughout the centuries, Carl still had not figured out the most basic differences between his species and humans. If one did not like the answer given, regardless of its merits, there wasn't a single explanation, however pragmatic that would satisfy them. Out of options, he did the most human of things by simply changing the subject as only he could.

Suddenly, Rebecca found herself lying on a massage table on the most beautiful beach she could have imagined. She quickly realized she wasn't alone as two hands began to massage her naked back in a manner that made it impossible not to get lost in ecstasy. The abrupt switch from the overly hyped surreal sensibilities to the more subliminal, oddly enough intensified the experience. Rebecca managed to shunt all concerns to the back of her mind except one. "Leave me alone to enjoy this, thank you very much, however, when these hands are…"

Before she could finish the warning, Rebecca's eyes closed and her mind went numb as she felt herself carried away into the space where only personal pleasure mattered. Time stood still as the hands softly turned her onto her back and began to work their magic. Slowly they explored in detail every erogenous zone, some of which she never knew existed, and when it seemed as if she was about to explode, the hands flipped her onto her stomach and started the journey all over again.

Rebecca slowly drifted into a dream state. "How strange to be in a dream within a dream, but what the hell, roll with it," she chuckled. Two hands kneaded her body, as another set of hands massaged her temples immediately suppressing every bit of stress right out of her mind. All in all, everything one could ask for in a dream.

Twenty minutes later, when she realized the hands were gone, she sat up to see Carl sitting on a nearby lounge chair smiling at what he had witnessed. As much as she tried to show her disapproval of his latest blatant manipulation, the afterglow of her experience betrayed her. "Obviously it is more important to you to keep things from me out of either a real or imagined threat, so for now I'll ignore your obfuscations."

That might have been that, except a subtle grin of self-satisfaction proved to Rebecca that Carl still didn't get it.

Rebecca gracefully slid off the massage table and strutted enticingly over to her husband to give him a loving kiss. Instead of the kiss he expected, she grabbed his balls and slowly began to add pressure, which forced him backward off the lounge chair.

"You didn't mean any of that, did you?" was all the highly distressed Carl could eke out.

"For such a superior entity, you sure are gullible. Now, *where—is—my—son?*"

At the sight of his father's predicament, an amused Sean Anthony entered their thoughts. "Now might be a good time to give dad a break mom."

Upon hearing her son's voice, Rebecca released her hold on her husband. "Sean Anthony? Where are you?" she pleaded, but Carl had cut him off.

Without Rebecca's knowledge, Carl responded to Sean Anthony. "Thanks for the save, but allowing you two to reunite would be like waving a red flag in front of Durius. No can do."

"Wouldn't you rather have mom working with us instead of always having to challenge everything you bring up. Rather chauvinistic if you ask me."

The sarcasm Carl heard in his son's voice reminded him of his stubborn wife. However, he reconsidered the risks of reuniting the two before he acquiesced and allowed Sean Anthony's thoughts to enter Rebecca's mind.

"Hi mom."

With another shock to her sense of reality, Rebecca now viewed the world through the eyes of her son.

"Though dad thinks it is not a good idea to share a little of my current reality with you, I can't see how it would hurt. Besides, with a little help from you I think he is finally coming to the conclusion to do otherwise is a fool's errand."

Rebecca looked around the room her son was in, and immediately recognized the ornate trappings of St. Peter's Basilica in Vatican City. She sat, or Sean Anthony sat high above the altar on the Chair of St. Peter. Rebecca had to admit the view was inspiring. She also could not believe how all the frustration of missing him dissipated to the point of irrelevance so quickly. "Why are we up here kiddo?"

"Well, Dad caught me in the middle of something important, and with all you have already experienced in your dream, I felt this part should be simplified. Needless to say, I am about to put a major cramp in the side of those who wish to see it all end."

Unfortunately, this only further confused his mother. "End of what?"

Sean Anthony didn't sugarcoat it. "All life as we know it."

All of a sudden, the dream abruptly ended with Rebecca back in her bunk on the Enterprise, the whole experience still firmly rooted in her mind. As she gathered her wits, she could hear the blaring call to General Quarters reverberating through her head.

"Take a closer look at what Specter is picking up lover," was Carl's last message before he left her consciousness.

"What a crazy-ass dream. Wait, that was too real to be a dream." She closed her eyes, and every moment of the dream stared right back at her. "Okay, not a dream," she exclaimed as she bolted upright and scrambled out of bed with only one thought. "I have *got* to get some chocolate."

When Rebecca arrived in the room that housed Specter's control systems, Forrest was frantically fumbling for the phone. When he saw her, in a near panic he blurted out, "Take a look at the data stream over the last twenty minutes."

She only needed a second to see what had Forrest so flustered before she calmly picked up the phone and contacted the bridge. "Is Admiral Phillips there?"

"Admiral, Dr. Cutler for you."

"We are in the middle of something Dr. Cutler, so please be quick."

"Admiral, initially Specter picked up multiple energy signals about two hundred miles east southeast of our position on a vector to Nipe Bay. Then ten minutes ago a field of interference one hundred miles around the contacts appeared and we can't distinguish the energy signals from the clutter."

Sean quickly updated Rebecca. "Yes Dr. Cutler, our recon flight witnessed a flight of fighters launch from their carrier and head for the Taíno. Coincidentally, after they formed up exactly ten minutes ago, the entire flight cloaked. So we are obviously reading from the same page. Both the Hawkeye's and our intercept F-35s are also experiencing the same interference. We are working on it, but our Aegis systems can't track them, and we are running out of time before they reach the Taíno."

Rebecca closed her eyes and rapidly scrolled through the mass of new information she knew about the upgraded Specter and in a stroke of genius furiously began to type commands into Specter. "I think I can use the data Specter collected to isolate the attackers out of the clutter and send the tracking data over to the Aegis systems. Is there any way you can give me twenty-five minutes?"

"We haven't got that much time, Doctor."

While Sean and Rebecca talked, Alicia had looked at the chart to see that based on speed and distance the hostiles would be over the village in fifteen minutes. Then she had a stroke of genius. Looking at the position of the task force, as the tip of a triangle in relationship to Nipe Bay and the Nazi flight, a dangerous gambit formed. "Our only course of action to save the Taíno is to uncloak and use the task force as a decoy. That should give us maybe twenty minutes, and that is only if my assumptions about their speed and weapons range are accurate."

"Hold on Rebecca." Sean turned to Alicia and in a calm voice asked, "Do you think putting this entire task force out as bait is worth it? We could be making some rather presumptive assumptions about their capabilities when you consider we just found out they can cloak."

Alicia smiled and shrugged her shoulders. "Do we have a choice?"

"Do it."

Alicia relayed the order to the CIC Officer as Sean addressed Rebecca. "We are counting on you."

"I'm on it." Rebecca set down the phone and furiously continued to type in code to have Specter isolate the targets and to create the link to the task force Aegis systems. While working through the problems, she noticed something different in how her mind attacked the problem. It seemed as if the commands she entered were coming from outside of her consciousness, and the more she separated her conscious actions from what she witnessed on the screen, something extremely bizarre occurred. The link she was attempting should have taken hours, not minutes. "Oh well better not look a gift horse in the mouth." Rebecca laughed at the absurdity of the cliché. "Still, something isn't right." Goose bumps rose from her arms at the thought.

While Rebecca generated code, on the bridge Sean and Alicia listened as the loudspeakers crackled with the calculated countdown to when they would have to cloak and change direction at flank speed. Thirty seconds from zero, Sean had enough. "Cloak the fleet."

Immediately after giving the order, Rebecca called. "You are good to go! We have range and speed. Wait, Admiral I think…"

An alert from Alpha Whiskey rang out from the speakers. "Missiles launched, thirty-five miles out and closing."

Unfortunately, they were too late. As the task force cloaked and turned west, a giant explosion on the port side of the Enterprise rattled the windows. Sean grabbed his binoculars to see the forward section of the destroyer the USS Winston S. Churchill lift out of the water and break off at the bridge. Not more than two seconds later, he watched as another missile struck amidships creating a fireball that obscured the embattled destroyer. When the smoke cleared, the ship had disappeared under the turbulent waters of the Caribbean.

Sean and Alicia looked out from the bridge of the Enterprise to see the Aegis cruiser directed task force defensive systems suddenly come alive. Though there were no visual sightings, surface to air missiles filled the air from every quadrant of the Enterprise Task Force. The ensuing battle lasted only minutes, yet the volume of Phalanx 20 mm Gatling gun fire and missile launches that filled the air gave the moment a surreal quality, something no one who witnessed it would ever forget.

The silence that ensued after the task force defensive systems went quiet highlighted an eerily spectacular fireworks display that filled the sky as fragments of the exploded missiles and their targets spiraled slowly into the ocean. The Specter enhanced Aegis systems managed to down the rest of the incoming missiles and most of the attacking warplanes before the others turned away.

When the battle ended, the loudspeakers on the bridge came to life with another alert from Alpha Whiskey. "Two submerged contacts approaching from the east. The Indiana has engaged."

More followed. "Torpedo through the water tracking forward contact – thirty seconds to contact. Torpedo fired at aft contact – correction, two. Five seconds, 4, 3, 2, 1, forward contact hit. Ten seconds to aft contact – contact destroyed."

Over the next twenty minutes, responsibility for the safety of the task force continued to consume Sean's thoughts. Preliminary battle assessments throughout the group confirmed that the only fatalities were on the destroyer USS Winston S. Churchill, and Seahawk helicopters were in the air to pick up all survivors – friend or foe.

Again, the bridge speakers crackled. "The enemy force has reversed course to the east."

If all of this wasn't enough, as Sean turned to Alicia, his wife's expression of shock stopped him cold. "What is it?"

Without saying a word, she pointed behind Sean. Standing in the bridge doorway was the newly reborn Renée, with Tony right behind her.

Without skipping a beat, Sean quipped, "If we were not up to our necks in it at the moment I would have you slapped in irons for being absent without leave for the last four years."

Sean looked around the bridge to see those who were aware of Renée's death transfixed on the apparent apparition. "If you don't mind Captain Aslan, I think now would be a good time for you and Admiral Calhoun to retire to the Admirals Quarters."

He then nodded his head to the door to prompt Alicia. "Would you mind Alicia?"

"Not at all. Come on Renée, you can tell me all about what it is like to be dead. Considering our current situation, it might prove useful." She followed Renée off the bridge, leaving Sean and the rest of the bridge staff zeroed in on Tony.

"What? I didn't have anything to do with it." Then to shift the focus off him, he suggested, "You know it might not be such a bad idea to find out what the commander of this Nazi force knows, or doesn't know, or more importantly wants to know."

A parley was the last thing on Sean's mind. "Let's worry about that when we are not under attack. Before you arrived, we lost the Churchill, and based on how fast she went down, most of her crew."

Tony immediately changed tack. "Where do you need me?"

"Come with me."

"Admiral is off the bridge."

In a small office inside a hangar that stood alongside one of the runways at King Abdulaziz International Airport in Jeddah, Saudi Arabia, sat a diminutive man of European descent. Slightly rotund, with thinning hair, and a pockmarked face only a mother could love, he fingered the phone he felt vibrating in his pocket. Upon retrieving it and checking the text, he smiled. "So it has come to that after all," he thought with a touch of finality.

At last, he would have his revenge for the friends he lost in a terrorist attack while deployed in Afghanistan. For once, he didn't mind the blistering Arabian heat as he calmly changed into the vestments of a Catholic Monsignor, took a small bag from one of the lockers that lined the wall, and strode outside.

Fifteen minutes later, Father Duvall took off in his Gulfstream 4 en route to Riyadh. Within minutes, his target came into view. He turned off the autopilot and banked the jet sharply to the right.

Air traffic control picked up the course change and attempted to make contact to see if the pilot had lost control and needed to declare an emergency. After several failed attempts to communicate and with the jet on course toward restricted airspace, the controller hit the emergency button that alerted the Saudi Air Defense into action. Though two F-15 Eagle fighters were airborne in minutes, they were nowhere quick enough to divert the jet registered to the Catholic Church from its current course.

"One last thing to do," Monsignor Duvall calmly thought as he switched his mike on. "This is Monsignor Michael Duvall from the Holy Trinity Parish in Tipperary, Ireland. For far too long, those of the Islamic faith have perpetrated atrocities against those of the Christian faith with impunity. With the blessing of the Vatican, today marks one man's attempt to show the world what an eye for an eye looks like. God bless the righteous."

As he signed off, he put the twin-engine jet into a steep dive. One pair of twin spires of Islam's most sacred mosque, Al-Masjid al-Haram in Mecca, acted as goal posts to guide him to the object of his attack. The thousands of pilgrims had only enough time to witness their imminent demise as the jet filled with C4 plastic explosive hit the central courtyard at over six hundred miles an hour. The resulting detonation obliterated the cubical Ka'Ba, the Islamic version of the Hebrew Holy of Holies, and everything else within 200 yards. As the blast wave hit the outer walls, six of the nine 292 feet tall minarets swayed and then toppled.

The effect of this one man's fanatical act did more damage to the world's teetering stability than the nuclear detonations in Korea had on the politics of Asia. Holy War VI went into hyperdrive across the Middle Eastern world as mindless violence spread like wildfire in its wake.

The Coptic Christians of Egypt were the first to feel the backlash with ninety percent of their numbers brutally murdered within the first twelve hours after the attack. All across the Middle East Shia and Sunni Muslims put aside their mutual hatred and turned it on the Christians. The enemy of my enemy.

From Africa to Southeast Asia roving bands of armed Muslim civilian militia, often joined by their nation's soldiers, stormed the American and European embassies. Hundreds of embassy personnel were brutally murdered, their mutilated corpses dragged behind cars through the streets to the cheers of those lining the sidewalks.

Before any of the European nations under attack could coordinate their response, violent protests erupted in their own backyards. Armies that had mobilized when the nuclear genie erupted from the bottle now had to confront tens of thousands of raging Muslims bent on destroying everything in their path. A complete breakdown of civil law occurred when members of the forces sent to quell the violence found themselves dealing with suicide attacks within their ranks.

In the United States, the intelligence networks showed off their full potential as government troops swooped in to empty every Muslim neighborhood. Entire families simply disappeared into the confines of the nation's largest sports stadiums, now requisitioned to imprison anyone associated with Islam.

In the White House Situation Room, Aaron delivered the news. "The President has received word from the Israeli ambassador that it had no other choice but to launch tactical nuclear weapon strikes on Riyadh, Cairo, Damascus, and Tehran." Though solemn in his delivery, underneath this mask of compassion Aaron was absolutely giddy.

Another Fine Mess

No one questioned why the President was missing. An unspoken agreement existed among the military leadership that Aaron's brutality was preferable over her less strident policies.

"Per the President's orders, we have rounded up the most vocal Clerics and given the order to close down every mosque throughout the nation. We will meet all attempts to defy this Executive Order with lethal force. " The head of Homeland Security refused to disguise the satisfaction in his voice that the gloves had come off, civil rights be damned.

The sheer volume of brutality released in the name of their god fascinated Adonis. "There goes another Gothic Church in southern Spain." He looked up from his monitor and to his surprise found that no one else appeared interested in the news. Since the attack on Ka'Ba over a week ago, the mood in the cave in China had remained solemn.

Phoenix walked over to his chair. "What do you think he is waiting for? We've had several options for a response ready for a week. All he has to do is set us loose." Phoenix crossed her arms and turned to see Sean Anthony engrossed in his laptop. "All he's done since the attack is sit there and look at old historical documentaries on his computer." She lowered her head closer to Adonis. "I've had nothing to do..."

"Give it a rest girl. He knows what he is doing. Obviously he is waiting for something else to happen."

"I'm not stupid. Of course he is waiting for something. I want to know why he hasn't told us exactly what that something is."

"Because, I won't know what that *something* is until that *something* happens." Sean Anthony had quietly walked up behind the two wearing a big smile. "There has never been a doubt that anarchy would be a major component of the changes we are in the middle of bringing about. Don't worry; I'll let you know when it reaches the point where it is necessary for us to intervene."

Sean Anthony walked back over to his computer, and continued to scan through old documentaries, leaving their imaginations to run wild.

❖

Neither men spoke a word on the short walk down to the Admirals Ready Room. Sean headed straight to the bottle of Jack Daniels Single Barrel, poured out four healthy portions, and handed them out. After a quick toast where everyone down their Whiskey, he spoke. "First off, may I say welcome back to the living, Renée."

Instead of immediately replying, Renée got up and poured herself another drink, drained it, and quickly refilled the glass. "Considering I never knew I was dead, and then again how would anyone know they were dead. Anyway, all I can say is where does this leave me now?"

"The same place as everyone else, trying to figure out how to stay alive." Alicia leaned over and gave Renée a hug. "Let's face it, since the War Game to test Specter off the coast of San Francisco in 2014, there is a chance none of what has happened since is real, especially since Benjamin Franklin and David Bowie were thrown into the blender. Regardless of the how, I'm so happy that you made it back."

Sean felt less willing to accept her reincarnation on face value. "Were you aware of this possibility Tony?"

"To be honest, Franklin promised as much the day I showed up in 1490, though I never believed he could bring it about."

Sean's anger over the unprovoked Nazi attack erupted and he took it out on Tony. "Okay, spill it. How much have you not told me about what is going on? Make it good, because we just lost over 300 good men and women and I need you to assure me there wasn't anything you could have shared to prevent it."

Tony replied defensively. "Franklin never stated anything to account for you or the Nazis being here. The only thing he shared with me had to do with the Taíno and Columbus. I am as in the dark as you, so the only issue is how do we respond, not for you to get all pissy with me."

Alicia jumped in to calm the two warriors down. "Really Sean, how much could Tony know half-naked, drinking coconut milk, and throwing pointed sticks at fish for two years? It wasn't like he could build his own Specter." As she knew would happen, the image of Tony trying to work with even the most basic electronics made everyone laugh.

Tony calmed down and repeated his earlier idea. "What do we have to lose if we contact the Nazis? Who knows, maybe from where and when they came, they were the good guys. It worked for us with Admiral Halsey at the Panama Canal, why not here." Tony was unusually pragmatic. This of course put three sets of eyes squarely on him.

Even Renée was puzzled. "Who are you, and what have you done with my Anthony?"

"Oddly enough, he makes a good point." Sean begrudgingly stated, still convinced Tony was still holding something back. "That Renée is here with us right now calls into question how vulnerable we are. Who is to say that we lost the sailors from the Churchill, or the Nazis lost those in the jets or submarines? Maybe Renée exists in hundreds of other realities and Franklin plucked her out of one of them. Who is to say that Renée is our Renée when she has no memory of being dead?"

"I don't think there is any way for us to know, Sean," Alicia responded. "Renée, for all intents and purposes is our Renée, and to question why any further than that would accomplish nothing more than give all of us one massive headache. I for one am getting tired of trying to resolve questions more suited for Einstein."

Sean brightened up a bit. "Then here is what we are going to do. If we have learned anything, it is that death doesn't necessarily mean forever in this gladiator ring of a reality. So let's change the rules and not play. I intend to cruise right up to the Nazis and uncloak our task force. Let's see what happens when we change the game."

Alicia warmed to this radical idea. "I'm open to any option, other than going mano a mano until inevitably we become food for the sharks."

Tony was opposed to the plan. "How do you propose selling the idea to over 10,000 sailors that they will be essentially standing in front of a firing squad and everything will work out just fine? Sounds a little too much like Jim Jones ordering his people to drink the Kool-Aid to me. Besides, what makes you think those pulling the strings will allow that to happen?"

"Who says I will give anyone the choice?" Sean was adamant about trying.

A knock on the door interrupted their conversation. "Enter," Sean ordered.

Rebecca strode forcefully into the center of the room and announced to all, "Carl came to me in a dream and let me tell you, you are not going to believe what he showed me."

She then noticed Renée seated next to Tony, and without the slightest pause to consider the insanity, walked over and gave her a big hug. "Now we have the dead coming back to life as well? How cool is that?" she exclaimed after she let Renée go. "Any ideas about how?"

Tony shook his head. "It's a long story Rebecca. So is your news more incredible than this?"

"Well, if telling you that Carl and our son Sean Anthony are responsible for everything is bigger news than raising the dead, then yes." She proceeded to explain in detail everything that Carl showed her and the experience in the Vatican with her son. In conclusion, she added, "He made it seem as though we are more responsible for what is happening than we know. When I think about all of those people from the past, and for all I know the future that scrolled through my mind, I felt each of their lives as if they were my own. To tell you the truth, it helped me make better sense of who I am."

None of this was going down well for Sean. "If what you say is reality, and not some fantastic dream, then none of it changes our situation in the here and now. Real people are firing real missiles in an era where they should be shooting arrows. On top of all of that, I am supposed to entrust those I am responsible for to some power's altruistic attempt at – oh, wait, I'm sorry, we don't even know what, and all the while dangling like marionettes under the strings."

Alicia had a different take. "On the bright side though, you do have to admit that at least the strings offer more options than President Harrison's reality offered when we skipped out. Also, without 1941 where would you and I, Tony and Renée, or as strange as it sounds to say after what Rebecca said, she and Carl be? Personally, I prefer the company I am keeping now to the jail cell that was the best we could have hoped for back home."

Rebecca jumped back in. "I got the distinct impression that cutting the strings is exactly what Carl and my son are trying to do. I may be reading more into what they could not share with me, but our struggle is their struggle, and that is why they picked us. Human or not, Carl has a good and kind heart and I know he would tell us more if he could."

Sean agreed with their assessment, but going along with grandiose ideas that could lead to the sacrifice of others was not in his blood. "If what you both say is true, none of it matters in that the safety of the crews comes first, and we just lost a destroyer's worth."

In case they didn't have enough to digest, green mist announced Bowie's arrival. This time he was plainly attired, similar to when he fronted the obscure band Tin Machine in the 90s. "They will blow you out of the water if you pull up and ask to share tea." He lit a fag, sat down, and crossed his legs. "Oh, and yes, you will be dead. Do not believe for a second that because your dear friend has returned that anyone else will. Dead is still dead, at least as who you are at the moment."

At the sight of the Glam Rock icon, Rebecca began to laugh as she pointed her finger in his direction. "My parents were totally into you. I can't believe you're standing right in front of me."

Rebecca walked up and tried to pinch his arm, but Bowie quickly moved off. "What is wrong with this one?"

In between fits of laughter, Rebecca answered, "Wrong with me? I'm not the one who is impersonating one of the weirdest entertainers of the 20th Century."

Bowie put on his most menacing look. "You do know that I can do perfectly awful things to you, don't you?"

"What are you going to do, turn me into a Unicorn if I don't stop laughing?" This of course got her laughter rolling again.

As amusing as this was to Sean, he had enough. "Not now Rebecca," he demanded as he turned to the apparition.

"So what if we do attack and defeat them. What do you have to offer that makes sense for us to do so?"

"Well, Admiral Phillips, if you choose not to engage you all will have a front row seat to observe the massacre of the lovely Taíno."

Bowie then turned to address Tony. "Franklin told you that you had the choice to rejoin your former friends or stay with the Taíno. He also told you if you rejoined your friends you would suffer the same consequences as them. It appears you have already made the choice."

Alicia wanted to scratch his eyes out. "You bastard."

Bowie threw up his arms in mock defense. "Hey, I am only the messenger." With that joyful bit of news, he once again disappeared in the green mist.

This left Sean to make the decision.

After taking a moment to mull it over, he asked the others, "We can't stand by, can we?"

The look from Tony, Alicia, and Renée was the only response Sean needed.

⎯⬥⎯

As much as he would have liked to continue to revel in the sheer magnitude of the violence he had set off, Aaron needed to ratchet up the rhetoric. He had made sure the audio recording of the Catholic terrorist's declaration hit the world media within minutes of the attack. Aaron now had to add fuel to the fire he had unleashed.

With most of the social media centers controlled by the oligarchs, it no longer mattered where the news originated. All news became world news with a single sensationalized picture or tweet. In the West, Aaron called in favors from every talking head, vacuous celebrity, financial CEO, and of course the evangelical firebrands in America to raise the pressure on those citizens who still had an independent voice.

Aaron's response to these attacks on Christians was to vilify all Muslims. It only took an hour for the reports of assaults on those of Middle Eastern ancestry broke out across the nation. In a nod to America's whitewashed history, and egged on by the media's constant dire warnings of Muslim reprisals, gangs of armed citizens vented decades of frustration over the never ending War on Terrorism.

Under strict orders not to engage, the military units enforcing martial law stood down throughout the onslaught. This allowed mobs to set the closed Mosques ablaze as a backdrop to the carnage. America's Night of the Long Knives wiped out ninety percent of the US Muslim community.

The President was exhausted. "I have been on the phone all day with leaders from around the world lying my ass off that everything will be fine, as their Muslim and Christian citizens find ever more creative ways to brutally murder each other. I swear to

God, I'm seeing more headless bodies on the news than those with their heads still attached."

Aaron had managed to avoid the President while he consolidated his power with the generals, but he still needed to keep up the charade for a little longer. He sat on the couch across from her in the Oval Office and calmly began to read the numerous dispatches from an imploding world. "Both the Chinese and the Russians wish to formalize a hands off approach with us regarding our respective regions. Sounds good to me.

"China is about to move on Taiwan, which is why I'm surprised we haven't heard from the Japanese ambassador about it yet. It seems they got our message when we pulled the Seventh Fleet back to Pearl Harbor that they were on their own."

The further he got through the dispatches, the more excited he became.

President Harrison's expression conveyed an altogether different reaction. She once again spiraled into a panic. "How can you be so calm? You can't think this is what we had in mind. What good is it for us to take control of a world that is economically and environmentally useless? The only reason I let you convince me to go along with your crazy plan was to end all terrorism, not have the world swimming in it."

Without looking up Aaron shot back. "No, the only reason you let me convince you is because like most politicians you are a greedy, power-hungry despot who wanted to go down in history with all the other great sociopaths."

Without any regard to her personal health, she violently shook the papers she held in his face. "In these pages are urgent requests from NATO and the United Nations demanding clarification of our intentions. So far I've counted ten different instances where we are in direct breach of existing treaties, six of which we authored." She threw the papers in the air, and fell wearily back into her chair as they floated down around her.

"None of that includes the pressure I am receiving from Congress about keeping them in the dark. Add to this that you convinced me to pull back all of our military assets around the world over the last year, so now we can't influence events in Europe and Asia if we wanted to."

"As usual, you can't see the big picture." Aaron rose and motioned for the President to follow. "If you will come with me to the Situation Room, all will be revealed."

When they arrived in the protected bunker under the White House that served as the military command center, President Harrison immediately noticed something missing – people. "Why did you bring me down here?"

Aaron walked up to one of the screens that showed a battle underway in the desert of what looked like a Middle Eastern country, complete with all the carnage. "Because I wanted to show you why all of our forces are safely in the Western Hemisphere and not getting chewed up while spread paper thin around the globe. By the end of next week, the only countries of consequence not caught up in total war will be in North and South America and Australia. The only thing we will have to fear is the nuclear fallout blown in from Asia and the Middle East. According to the models, we will see a rise of seventy-five percent in cancer cases over the next twenty years. All in all, a small price to pay to end the chaos."

President Harrison pointed to one of the displays that showed a number counter as it passed the thirty million mark. "What do those numbers represent?"

"Duh."

⎯⎯⎯✦⎯⎯⎯

In the Admirals Ready Room, Sean turned to Rebecca. "I'm sure no one here has to remind you how important it is that we can continue to feed the Nazi positions and maintain communication with our command and control. Are you up to it Rebecca?"

Rebecca had remained unusually silent since Bowie's visit, but perked up with the mention of her name. "Once again into the breach boys and girls. Could you please have the galley send over some food, and keep the coffee coming? I am famished, and I'm sure Forrest is too." Without another word, she headed down to the Specter control room.

In war-planning overdrive, Sean didn't give her another thought. "Alicia, get an update on the Nazi force and how long it will take to resupply for battle."

"I'm on it," Alicia responded as she reached for a phone. "Might as well order in some lunch for us as well. Might be the last meal we get for a while."

Sean noticed Renée looked edgy and thought, "I bet she doesn't know what role she has in all this, and we can't afford to waste a valuable asset."

"Renée, could you please assist Alicia with whatever she needs?"

Renée's memories took her back to the hours they pored over documents together to supply Sean with the necessary strategic picture in 1942. "Of course Admiral. Just like old times."

"Tony, I need you to work with the CAG and Alpha Whiskey on an attack plan."

"Yes Sir." With a simple half-ass salute, Tony got to work.

Without skipping a beat, Alicia reported. "CIC reports the Nazi fleet headed due west along the south coast of Haiti. Their best guess is that they will turn north as soon as they clear the island."

Sean took a moment to study the map Tony had pulled up of the Caribbean. "Then we will change course to head northeast to Guantanamo Bay. I want to be in range in case we need to lend them our support."

Alicia continued. "At our present speed, if they do turn north, that should have us within the launch window in about 90 minutes. As presently configured our task force is equal in numbers to theirs."

"We should also add some firepower from Guantanamo Bay and recall the Hampton." Tony never executed an attack plan until he knew he had utilized every resource at his disposal to possess numerical superiority.

Alicia had a thought and grabbed the phone. "By now Rebecca should have an idea about how long the Specter upgrades are going to take."

"Good. When you're done, have the CIC patch Captain Daily through the next time he checks in." Sean needed a one on one with his third in command.

Renée with a phone cradled in the nook of her neck reported next. "Staff reports supplies to be squared away within two hours, but with our reduced speed it will extend us to 3 to 4 hours to come within a launch window and be close enough to Guantanamo."

Sean then countered Tony's earlier suggestion. "We have to leave the Hampton on patrol outside of Nipe Bay until we know for sure if there are any other forces the Nazis have deployed."

"Rodger that." Alicia said as she hung up the phone. "Unfortunately, Rebecca can't promise any of the Specter upgrades will be completed in time to do us any good."

With Sean's refusal to redeploy the Hampton, Tony's sense of urgency increased to find whatever advantage, no matter how small, to improve their chances. He shook his head while contemplating the unknowns of their foe. Then it struck him. "I have the plan I used in the naval exercise in 2014. Expect a mirror of us, plan accordingly."

"What's that Tony?" Sean only heard bits of Tony obviously thinking aloud.

A knock at the door interrupted Tony's reply. Lunch had arrived.

Planning and dispersal of orders took only a momentary break to pass out the meals, but quickly resumed as first the CIC called for Sean with Captain Daily on the line. The Seawolf, which Alicia had dispatched earlier, was now shadowing fifteen miles aft of the Nazis.

"Mark?"

"Let me guess Admiral. You need me to blaze a path to glory for you again. The silent service my ass. More like the out of sight, out of mind service, until you surface pukes find your ass in a sling."

"At least you make a smaller target, and let's not forget you have meters of water protecting you from what would sink us." Sean smiled as he looked at his watch. "Seriously Mark, we will launch our counter attack at 1700. Your targets will be the flattop and the attack sub. We will take care of the rest."

Then on a more serious note, he added, "If they do manage to take us out, you are to assume command of whatever units survive. If the worst happens and you don't have the resources to continue the fight, try to get the survivors ashore. Beyond that, use your best judgment about how to proceed."

When Daily didn't immediately respond, Sean thought they lost contact.

"Sorry about the delay Admiral, but we are tracking one of their attack subs, and it's a shock how much noise we are hearing from their propeller cavitation. Apparently, silence isn't a priority, lucky us. Anyway, I got it. Take care of your command in the unlikely event of your premature demise."

"Rodger that, Captain. I have to get back to work. Good hunting."

"Daily, out."

As they spent the next two hours planning, reports and orders flowed back and forth. "CIC reports the Hampton has cleared the area outside of Nipe Bay and has picked up faint signals of an underwater contact one hundred fifty miles north northeast of the bay. Captain Turner has changed course to investigate," Alicia reported as she put down the phone to move on to the next task.

Tony was unhappy with what he still didn't know. "Here's hoping that this isn't a game of whack-a-mole where every time we take one of them out, two show up. Considering how loud they are, it would make sense that their goal might be for us to expend our ordinance until we become defenseless."

A call came in for Renée. "Resupply is complete and we will be within the launch window in 30 minutes."

"That should do it. Let's head for the CIC," Sean concluded as he got up to leave but stopped short of the hatch. "I'm sorry Renée, but until I know more about all the psychobabble that is flying around like monkey shit, you are going to have to sit this one out. Stay here in our quarters until we get through the attack." It was one thing to have her assist Alicia, but quite another to be an unknown in the middle of a battle.

Tony didn't hesitate. "After the attack we will be close enough to Guantanamo Bay for us to chopper over to the Missouri. If it is all right with you, that is."

Relieved that Tony accepted his order for Renée to stay behind, Sean replied, "Works for me."

Tony grabbed Renée by the shoulders. "This will be over soon and I'll see you right after we kick their ass."

"I understand, go get 'em lover. Good luck."

Tony gave her a quick but passionate kiss and a confident smile. "Luck has never had anything to do with it." He gave Renée one more quick kiss before he followed Sean and Alicia out the door.

⚫

Sean Anthony sat with his legs stretched out on the table as he stared out at the young hackers. He always knew the game would reach this obvious stage, except he envisioned it would occur after more foreplay. Apparently, Aaron wants a quick resolution. "Too bad."

Sean Anthony had argued with his father about the timing of this particular stunt, but with the current state of affairs, it was now or never. He sprang out of his chair to address his cohorts. "Can I get your attention?" His voice reverberated throughout the cave.

He looked directly at Phoenix as he spoke. "You asked when we would reply, well here it is. Time to clue you all in on a little secret no mere mortal has had the pleasure of knowing. You are aware that slaughter is the rule of the day, and it may appear that we have lost any chance of containing it, but we do indeed have cards to play."

This elicited stares of confusion from most, but nothing registered on the face of Phoenix. This caught Sean Anthony's attention. "I suppose you think you already know."

"Of course I do. I'm a genius. You want to tell us why we were picked for this sick adventure, and why now is our time."

Sean Anthony bowed down and waved his hand for her to continue. "Enlighten us, Master."

"Everyone in this room is related somewhere in the past, and you and whoever you are involved with know exactly how. Now you are going to tell us." Phoenix folded her arms and waited.

Thoroughly amused by her mental acuity, Sean Anthony could only laugh. "Out of the mouth of babes. The bottom line is Phoenix is partially correct, only you're not just related, you all come from the same seed."

Sean Anthony pushed a button on the remote he was holding and a holographic image appeared along the cave wall. The video that played had a strange quality about it as if you could walk right in and be a part of it. "What you are viewing is real, only real in the sense that all of what you are seeing happened long ago. This is where humanity stood during the hunter-gatherer times. See the young man in the middle of the screen? Let's call him Number 6, and the time is approximately twenty-seven thousand years ago."

The video centered on a hunched over man-child about 15 years old staring into a fire, surrounded by his tribe. There were women working animal skins, men sharpening stone tools, and children suckling at their mother's breasts. Suddenly a bright light from above lit up the group. The light slowly played over each individual until it focused on the 15-year-old. Except for the young man stuck in the light's glare, the rest of the group slumped to the ground unconscious. The light then gained in intensity, exposing the boy's body down to his atoms. Then just as suddenly, the light disappeared. The image slowly tightened on the young man until the entire frame showed only one of his eyes that reflected an image of the Milky Way Galaxy.

"There were six Imprinters who shared their DNA with six humans, three males and three females. Number 6 is the one each of you sprung from, your own personal Adam. Your particular lineage led to Hemiunu, the architect of the Great Pyramid, Pythagoras, Newton, Darwin, Plank, Fermi, and all the way to Steve Jobs. Yes children, your evolutionary lineage is Number 6."

Before any of those in the room could react to the shock of such a revelation, or challenge it, they all went unconscious. All of their deepest thoughts and memories, along with the experiences of millions of others began to spiral in, all while Sean Anthony focused his efforts to keep the influx of energy from overloading the electronics in the cave.

Time lost meaning as this played out with the collective recovering millennia of lost memories that connected to every drama this line of humanity had created from the day the consciousness awoke in that fifteen year old boy. When the explosion of information revealed all, Sean Anthony stood in the room with a very awake Phoenix, whose sky blue eyes now emitted an intelligence never seen before in human history.

"Why did you wait so long to bring me in?"

Knowing there wasn't a right answer, Sean Anthony meekly shrugged his shoulders.

"You've got to be shitting me!"

"Nag, nag, nag. You know, if you don't learn to show more respect, I will make you relive that dreadful little bitch you were in 1870." He barely paused to acknowledge her look of feigned indifference. "You remember don't you dear? The flaming red hair and all of that talent tied up in ill-conceived machinations that invariably led to the same disasters?"

This got her attention. "You wouldn't dare. Besides, it was your fault that she did all of those terrible things."

To Sean Anthony's amazement, her expression instantly morphed into a coy sultry seductress. Phoenix slowly scanned the unconscious hackers as she put her hand on his leg and slowly worked it up his thigh. "You never had any complaints," she purred, as she drew her lips closer to his.

Sean Anthony gently removed Phoenix's hand from his inner thigh. "So now you're going to give me shit about waiting too long to bring you back? Correct me if I'm wrong, but wasn't it you who suggested it would be safer to keep your association with me a secret until I deemed it safe, and it was me who argued against taking the chance."

Phoenix rolled her eyes, cocked her head, and put a finger to her lips in a Betty Boop pose. "You know it's always a woman's prerogative to change her mind."

Sean Anthony shook his head in disbelief. "That would be if you were any other woman, which you are most definitely not."

"Then there is that." Phoenix looked around the cave confused. "So what went wrong?"

"I didn't wake you up because something went wrong. It's that I needed someone who could reconnect with those of your heritage, and since I couldn't think of anyone who was available for the job with the necessary brilliance for what I have in mind, you're it."

"And here I thought it was because you missed me."

Sean Anthony gave his best impersonation of George Clooney rolling his eyes as he swept up Phoenix in his arms, bent her backward, and kissed her lovingly on her lips. "You know I only live to savor every moment I am in your presence."

Then to Phoenix's shock, he released his hold on her, and she fell hard to the ground as he straightened up with a look of total indifference. "Or was it savoring there wasn't anyone around who could bust my chops. I always get the two mixed up."

Instead of the anger most would feel at the painful prank, Phoenix laughed at the droll manner in which Sean Anthony pulled it off. "Help me up asshole."

When Sean Anthony bent down to comply, Phoenix used her leverage to drag him down to the floor next to her. For the next fifteen minutes, the two lovers wrestled for control over each other, neither willing to be the one to transfer this kinetic energy into what they both desperately wanted.

As usual, it was Sean Anthony who gave in to the inevitable by tearing her top down to her navel and burying his face into her chest. Another fifteen minutes later, a naked and sweaty Phoenix sat up. "So what's the job?"

Recognizing the moment as over, Sean Anthony grabbed what was left of his shirt and put it back on. "I need to find someone close to the President."

"I suppose I could do it if it is something important," Phoenix offered, as she gathered her panties and bra to get dressed.

"And?" Sean knew there was something she wanted as he pulled his pants on.

"No more partitioning my memories for one. We sink or swim as who we are, not hiding out in the mind of another me."

Sean Anthony playfully tweaked her left nipple. "I missed you too. Now can we get to why you're here?"

"Cool. What are you waiting for?"

"First, I need to wake the kids and get them back to work," Sean Anthony answered, as the hacker group began to stir.

As he became conscious, Adonis could see Sean Anthony and Phoenix making their way over to the awakening hackers. He got up and gave her a hug. "What a dope trip, man. Mind sharing is better than any drug I have taken. What a rush! Imagine that, me a little slip of a white girl. Though we got to get us some junk in that toothpick you call an ass."

Though Sean Anthony knew it was his way to lighten the mood, he motioned for Adonis to dial it down. Then to all of the group, "We need to get back to work, so man your stations ready to receive data." With that, Sean Anthony touched Phoenix's forehead with his finger.

Phoenix smiled as the memories of all of her past lives flooded her mind. Once connected, Phoenix reached out to the millions of other lives that shared her lineage and now walked the planet in this reality. For ten minutes, she remained silent as her consciousness narrowed the search to the eastern seaboard of the United States.

Bypassing anyone whose vacuous thoughts included idolization of the Kardashians, watched Faux Cable News, or believed man walked with the dinosaurs, she focused her attention on those closely associated with the ruling elite. As she typed in a search on her computer she announced to Sean Anthony. "We have several options available, though I think this one is what you are looking for."

Sean Anthony nodded in agreement. "How about that? You found one right in the Devil's den. Let's take her out for a spin."

⬥

Focused on the pending attack, Sean couldn't worry about the implications of Rebecca's briefing or of Bowie's warning as they made their way down to the Enterprise CIC. Fortunately, for those under his command, Sean found it easy to push aside one crisis when faced with an imminent threat.

Once they entered the CIC and settled in, Tony handed Sean the war plan he developed working with the Air and Sea Warfare Commander, Captain Frederick Johnson of the Aegis cruiser Chancellorsville, and the Air Wing Commander [CAG], Captain

Dash Nelson.

Sean tossed the report onto the console. "Lay it out for us Tony."

"Four F-35 Lightnings, two F/A-18F Super Hornets rigged with extra fuel, and one Advanced Capability EA-6B Prowler have joined the two F-35 Lightnings and one E2D Advanced Hawkeye assigned to cover Guantanamo and Nipe Bay and to aid the Hampton in its search for the unknown underwater contact to the northeast. Further, we tasked four MH-60R Seahawks to supplement the two on the Princeton for antisubmarine patrol of the areas in and outside of both bays while the Hampton is away."

Tony took a quick drink from his coffee cup and continued his briefing. "I assigned two additional F-35 Lightnings, two F/A-18F Super Hornets rigged with extra fuel, and one additional EA-6B Prowler, to the four F-35 Lightnings and E2D Advanced Hawkeye currently flying CAP for fleet protection. The Indiana will remain with the task force.

"For the counter attack, we have eighteen F-35 Lightnings, eight F/A-18F Super Hornets, two rigged with extra fuel, two EA-6B Prowlers, and one E2D Advanced Hawkeyes to join the two F-35 Lightnings and the one E2D Advanced Hawkeye currently on recon over the Nazi task force. This leaves us four F-35 Lightnings in ready reserve.

"At 1700 hours, the Seawolf will launch its torpedo attack on the Nazi carrier and their attack sub. At the same time, the two EA-6B Prowlers will jam the Nazis as the F-35 Lightnings led by the CAG, Captain *Dash* Nelson, take on the Nazi fighters sent to attack us.

"While the F-35s engage the Nazi fighters, the F/A-18F Super Hornets under the command of the DCAG [Deputy Air Wing Commander] Captain Tobias Harris will attack the two cruisers and two destroyers targeting their defense systems. As needed, a flight of Tomahawk cruise missiles will follow, guided by the E2D Advanced Hawkeyes to their destinations to finish the job. Any questions?"

Tony's plan pleased Sean. "As in 1941, your war plan employs overwhelming force with an eye to not wasting armament we can't replace. Well done."

"Alicia?" Tony asked.

"I agree with the Admiral that is if everything goes to plan and we do manage to inflict mortal damages. However, have you given any thought to search and rescue, because more than likely there will be hundreds of survivors in the water? Also, I think it wise that we commandeer their supply ships while we're at it."

Tony paused for a moment and made a face as if anxious that he had not thought of this before, and then he snapped his fingers and smiled. "Funny you should ask grasshopper. If you had looked at the last three pages of the report lying there, you would know we have SEAL squads and Marines preparing for such a contingency. That is if everything goes to plan.

"Regarding the survivors in the water, there will not be much we can do over the four hours it will take us to arrive on the scene, but fear not. What do you think their supply ships will be doing during this time? These ships will be overloaded with wounded, and because of this will need our assistance.

"Of course we will search for and rescue downed pilots along the way and any remaining sailors in the water once we get there. While we were busy planning, I made sure Renée sent out a request for all German-speaking members of our crew to be available once we take the ships. The biggest question after all of this is accomplished, is what are we going to do with them once we have them?"

"That all depends on if this is their first go around." Sean didn't have time to give this possibility his proper attention, but knew there was only one option. "Disarm them and put them ashore at Guantanamo under guard until we figure out what they know, and go from there."

"Or we could drop them off on the uninhabited tiny island of Navassa, where we can leave them with food and water for a few weeks. I'm sure after that, cooperating with us will be preferable to remaining there." Tony picked up the report, leafed to the back, and pointed the relevant page toward Sean. "Says that right here."

Sean struggled to maintain a straight face at Tony's take down of Alicia. When he looked over at his wife, he was glad he didn't smile, because the look on her face clearly stated Tony would pay. "Anything to add, Alicia?"

"Not at this *time*." Her icy reply, coupled with the darts her eyes were throwing at Tony confirmed this.

Tony gave her his most innocent look, then a quick wink. "Then it looks like we are good to go."

Sean looked around the CIC and noticed Tony's irreverent attitude had loosened the mood considerably. "Just like old times."

At 1530 hours, the flight deck of the Enterprise began to launch its arsenal at a rate of one shot every thirty seconds. To someone unfamiliar with the process, the noise and chaos looked like a disaster ready to happen at any second. One could consider the ability to launch the additional twenty-eight aircraft in under 15 minutes without mishap the definition of the word miracle, except the United States Navy of the 21st Century practices those miracles every day they are at sea.

Fifteen minutes after the first fighter piloted by Captain *Dash* Nelson catapulted off the deck, his group of 18 F-35 Lightnings formed up and headed toward the Nazi task force, with Captain Harris and his group of F/A-18F Super Hornets in trail.

Twenty-five miles ahead flew the two EA-6B Prowler jammers, as the E2D Advanced Hawkeye kept watch and relayed tracking data from the Specter enhanced Aegis systems on the Chancellorsville that now locked onto an incoming flight of bogies.

Captain *Dash* Nelson used this data to set up his strike force. "Let's get some altitude boys and girls, looks like the bad guys want a piece of big daddy. Split." With this command, they paired up in twos and spread out at different altitudes to pick their targets out of the radar blips supplied by Specter.

Less than five minutes later, all hell broke loose in the skies above the Caribbean Sea as over forty warplanes met head on. With a mix of short, medium, and long-range air-to-air missiles at his disposal, Captain Nelson radioed his flight. "I count twenty-six bogies at twenty-five thousand feet and closing to fifty miles. Cleared to launch Fox Threes."

Fifteen seconds later, 26 medium range Aim-120 air-to-air missiles filled the air with contrails as they sped to their targets. The integrated fire control systems homed in on the individual targets and fifteen seconds later, multiple targets disappeared as they violently blew apart and fell out of the sky.

Dash had no time for satisfaction as moments later his sensors began to wail a warning to him that one of the enemy missiles had locked onto him. "Looks like they have the same idea." He jerked the stick back and slammed the throttle into afterburner, which forced the F-35 into a rapid climb. With his heads up display following the motion of his helmet, he could see where his group's missiles had found their targets as explosions and smoke preceded the wreckage of multiple flying wings falling from the sky.

Unknown to the American fighters, their enemies lacked Specter's ability to see through their cloaking devices. This allowed the F-35 stealth capabilities to mask their heat signatures, so most of the barrage of missiles aimed at the F-35s flew harmlessly past. This played out the same as the range closed to short-range Sidewinder missiles, and then 25-millimeter cannon fire from their 4-barrel version of the GAU-12 Equalizer shredded the remaining Nazi warplanes.

The adrenaline high of combat quickly faded as the aerial combat turned into a turkey shoot, leaving *Dash* with only sympathy for the pilots of the doomed squadrons. He had to shake it off. "Reform at 30,000 feet. We have cleared the way to target. Captain Harris, time for you to earn your pay."

No more than ten seconds after his communication, *Dash* witnessed multiple missiles rising up from the sea fifty miles to the east. It appeared as if the Nazi task force had unleashed every one of their anti-ship missiles at once. "Enterprise, we have over fifty missiles headed your way." *Dash* followed the surrealistic sight of missile after missile falling harmlessly into the sea as the two EA-6B Prowler jammers interrupted their radar tracking abilities.

As the group of F/A-18Fs headed for the Nazi warships, Captain Mark Daily aboard the attack submarine Seawolf ordered, "Down periscope." He had taken the last range estimate to load into the Seawolf's torpedo guidance system before they could launch. On their way to their launch position the Seawolf's sonar picked up the location of the Nazi attack submarine that protected the carrier, and like *Dash*, Mark realized this too would be a turkey shoot with the Nazi attack sub in firing line with the Nazi carrier. One spread would get them both. He didn't hesitate. "Fire 1, Fire 2, Fire 3, Fire 4, Fire 5, Fire 6."

Everyone in the control room silently counted down the seconds it would take for the torpedoes to reach their targets, and forty-five seconds later the sounds of multiple explosions, two of which were clearly the attack sub imploding confirmed the kills.

"Sir, sonar confirms the destruction of the Nazi attack sub."

A cheer went up that Captain Daily quickly stifled. "We didn't do anything but kill fellow submariners who, like us, more than likely have no more idea why they were here than we do. Be grateful that our systems are more advanced. Now let's finish our part of the mission." To drive the point home, he ordered, "Up periscope."

Unlike the days of old, where the viewer glued his eyes to the periscope, this ship had a color monitor mounted to the bulkhead that bore witness to a series of explosions that cleared the decks of the stricken carrier. The next wave of internal explosions blew the island right into the sea, and more blasts tore the massive ship to pieces. As he watched, one final gigantic detonation literally lifted the ship up out of the ocean, breaking her into three pieces before sinking under the waves. As the stern section angled up before its final slide into the depths, the ship's name came into clear focus, startling the sub driver.

"Captain, surface ships headed our way – Torpedo in the water."

"Emergency dive, evasive action, flank speed. Prepare countermeasures."

Throughout the boat, the crew's focus and concentration zeroed in on their individual duties. Each one of the officers and crew knew that any minor slip-up or inattention to detail could prove catastrophic. Watching the silent flurry of activity around him made Captain Daily smile knowing his team was the best the Navy or any branch of the military had.

"Sonar, have they acquired us?"

"Negative, Captain. Still searching. Closest contact, 3,000 yards and closing. Wait—, torpedo has acquired us. Range now 2500 yards."

Since they were near the surface, Captain Daily knew their best option lay in utilizing the Seawolf's speed to outlast the torpedo's fuel. However, when he considered the chance it could detonate close enough to damage his submarine, he knew there was no way to repair the damage in 1492. "Crash dive the boat." It would be all or nothing.

The Seawolf immediately tilted downward at a 45-degree angle, and at their flank speed of 38 knots, she shot down into the depths at a dangerous rate. Anyone who had not braced themselves went stumbling forward to crash into unforgiving parts of the sub's interior.

"Read out our depth every two hundred feet."

"Eight hundred… one thousand…"

"Range to torpedo, two thousand feet," sonar reported.

"Eighteen hundred…, sixteen…, fourteen."

"Captain, our speed of descent is increasing."

"Maintain course and speed. Ready countermeasures, release on my command."

"Depth now two thousand…, twenty-two…, twenty-four."

"Emergency surface, blow all tubes." Daily now calculated how long it would take the dive planes and the added buoyancy from blowing the ballast tanks to arrest the forward momentum of the 12,000-ton runaway train the Seawolf had become on the crash dive to the bottom. For several tense moments it seemed as if this dangerous maneuver did little to slow the sub's descent.

"Torpedo closing to twelve hundred yards, Captain."

They were running out of time. Suddenly it seemed as if they were in zero gravity as they finally leveled out."

"Launch countermeasures."

No sooner had Daily issued the order than the Seawolf shot almost vertically straight up. "All stop!"

The boat immediately went quiet as she rapidly rose, the tension throughout the crew palpable. "Where is it?"

"Torpedo has reached countermeasures, lost acquisition."

Before Daily could question further an enormous explosion violently shook the Seawolf. Fortunately, because Daily ordered the shutdown of power to the propulsion systems the nuclear reactor did not scram. Outside of more than a few soiled shorts among the officers and crew, the Seawolf escaped with only minor internal damages from flying debris. However, they were not out of the woods yet, after all, they had all the control of a champagne cork suddenly released from its bottle. "Set dive planes to 45 degrees down." Daily's meager attempt to arrest the boat's upward speed did little to slow her rise.

One of the F/A-18F Super Hornet pilots loitering in the area got the shock of his life when the Seawolf shot high into the sky like a giant grey whale exposing a good two thirds of her length before crashing onto the surface of the ocean, for the moment completely vulnerable to attack.

All of Captain Daily's previous intensity and demanding focus dissipated, his manner now that of a country gentleman taking a quiet stroll through the countryside. "Get us moving. Once again boys and girls, emergency dive." This calmness immediately refocused the battle-hardened crew, and they went through their duties as if on an exercise.

While the Seawolf evaded the oncoming torpedo, F/A-18F Super Hornets attacked the pursuing destroyers from above mostly disabling their air defenses while other F/A-18Fs went after the cruisers with such ferocity that one of them blew up in a massive fireball that shot three hundred feet into the air . At this point, Captain Harris ordered in the coup de grâce. "The carrier is gone and the destroyers and cruisers are damaged, but not out of action. Send in the Tomahawks."

The Chancellorsville, Shiloh, and the Decatur unleashed twelve anti-ship missiles toward the four Nazi destroyers and cruisers. As the two E2D Advanced Hawkeyes guided them to their targets, the F/A-18Fs continued to harass what was left of the air defense systems on the Nazi warships.

After the Tomahawk missiles found their targets and the four warships went down, Captain Harris reported. "Admiral, confirmation that all combatant surface elements are neutralized. Waiting for reports on our casualties, but as far as I can tell everyone safe and sound." As the adrenaline drained from his body, his imagination turned to the carnage they had so effortlessly unleashed upon thousands of other men and women. It took every fiber of his being to return to his immediate responsibilities without losing it. "They never had a chance, Sir."

Sean could hear the grief in the Captain's voice. "Rodger that, Captain Harris. Have your squadron continue to monitor the area until further notice."

"Aye Aye Admiral."

With that, Sean turned to the CIC Officer. "Let's get the F-35s back on deck. No need to waste their fuel."

With the threat of the Nazi surface fleet gone and Captain Daily once again in control of his boat, he returned to periscope depth and reported in. "Admiral, a private line please."

Sean nodded to the Communications Officer who patched him through to Sean's phone. "What is it, Mark?"

"After the aircraft carrier broke up we got a good look at the name on the stern plate, and you are not going to like what it was."

"Like I have liked anything since we arrived here. Spit it out Captain."

"Sean Phillips bad, Sir." As Captain Daily dropped this bomb, a tracking officer yelled out a warning. "The northern air group reports multiple objects breaking the surface about one hundred fifty miles northeast of Nipe Bay, Sir. It looks like they have a boomer unloading its payload in our direction."

As the F-35s and the F/A-18Fs rushed to destroy the missiles in their boost phase, a massive ocean upheaval erupted immediately under where the missiles launched. A report from the northern air group's E2D Advanced Hawkeye quickly followed.

"The Hampton found its target. Scratch one boomer."

While the battle seemed a one-sided affair, Rebecca and Forrest closely monitored the data streaming through Specter's computers. With a violent jerk of her seat, Rebecca turned to face her fellow engineer. "Why is it that every time we move through time and space it has to be about kill or be killed? Is this the only thing we are good for?" Rebecca thought for a moment and slapped her forehead. "Why didn't I ask him when I had the chance?"

Used to Rebecca making abstract observations, Forrest shrugged his shoulders and gave his take. "Maybe the only reason we have been killing each other since time began is simple entertainment for some advanced version of the Roman Empire. We are simply the spoils of war waiting for the next Moses to free us. How else do you explain the collective stupidity of man?" Forrest looked up from the monitor when Rebecca did not reply to see her staring at him as if he had lost his mind.

"Why that is quite the cynical view of the cosmos for such an educated man Dr. Phelps."

Before the chagrined scientist could explain, Carl was in Rebecca's head laughing. "You had better get back to monitoring the situation love."

Rebecca jumped out of her seat at the sound of his voice. "Did you hear that?"

"Hear what?" Forrest immediately regretted further engaging Rebecca's train-off-the-tracks conversation.

She smiled and sat back down, then quickly jumped to her feet nervously scanning the room.

Forest knew from experience that Rebecca could go all-scattershot when hung up on a problem, but this was something new. Following her lead, he began to examine everything around him. "What are we looking for, and should I be worried?"

"It's nothing." When she turned around and to see Forest looking high and low, he reminded her of Jimmy Stewart deep in conversation with his friend Harvey. "Never mind Elmer Dodd. I've been a little jumpy lately. Could you keep an eye on things for a minute? I need to use the little girl's room."

"No problem. Are you sure you are all right?"

"I will only be a minute," was all she would say as she rushed out of the room.

After she was gone, Forest wondered aloud, "Who the hell is

Elmer Dodd?"

Immediately upon closing the bathroom door behind her, Rebecca demanded, "Now look here *Mister Captain Carl Eddington*, I am getting incredibly pissed off with this game of kill or be killed. We just destroyed thousands of lives and I am not happy."

"You have to trust that if I had any other choice, none of this would be happening."

Rebecca tried to calm down as she stared back at herself in the bathroom mirror, half expecting his face to replace hers. "Okay, I know I'm wide awake and this surely isn't a dream, so why have you returned, or did you ever leave? How in the hell are you doing this?"

He ignored the last question. "An unexpected emergency that needed your immediate attention, that's all."

Rebecca knew her husband well enough to notice a touch of urgency in his voice. "What is it now? I mean really, what possibly could follow up killing a few thousand 21st Century Nazis? Joe Cocker on the back of Gigantor firing disrupter rays from a flaming guitar?"

As urgent as Carl's message to Rebecca was, the image his wife painted forced him to enjoy the moment.

"Are you still there?"

Before Carl could respond, the sound of Forrest yelling through the bathroom door interrupted. "Dr. Cutler, you *have* to return to Specter. We have incoming ballistic missiles that are more than likely nuclear tipped."

"I'm coming." Then to Carl, "Nuclear tipped warheads?"

"That's what I've been trying to tell you, and no, Gigantor is not the one who fired them."

Rebecca was not amused. "This isn't finished. Now you need to get out of my head."

"Dr. Cutler, is there someone in there with you? Shall I call for help?"

"No Forest, I'm alone and fine." Then to Carl, "I have to go. Do I need to know anything else?"

"Go to work. Love you."

"One last thing *buster*. When this little drama cools down, you bring Sean Anthony back to me."

God or no god, Carl knew better than to argue with her. "As you wish," and he was gone.

Rebecca knocked Forest to the ground when she threw open the bathroom door. After she helped him up, they rushed back to Specter in time to see that a nuclear missile would be slamming into their immediate vicinity within minutes atomizing everything for miles around.

In the Enterprise CIC, the CIC Officer reported to Sean. "Sir, the F-35s from Nipe Bay downed all but one of the ballistic missiles the Nazi boomer launched."

Sean wished he had more time to decipher what his name was doing on the Nazi aircraft carrier. Unfortunately, he was too busy trying to save his task force. "It looks like our only hope is that it explodes far enough away the fallout doesn't fry us. Since they didn't have the ability to see through our cloaking system to locate us, they targeted their missiles to blanket the entire area."

Tony shook his head as he got up from his seat and walked to the door. "You're still talking about a bull's eye that is one hundred miles wide. If you don't mind, I would like to be with Renée just in case. Hope to still be around to see you guys in a few minutes."

"Give her my love," Alicia said in farewell. She then walked over and sat in Sean's lap. "Screw protocol. If this is it, I prefer to melt with you."

Sean laughed, though the rest of the personnel present thought they were crazy for remaining so calm. Sean noticed the panicked looks and tried to reassure them. "This shit happens all the time.

I don't believe our demise at this point would be worth all the trouble it took to put us here."

The CIC Officers immediately turned back to their screens and watched their lives play out. "Sir, the one that got through is headed straight for us – impact in two minutes. However, we still have the Aegis Ballistic Missile Defense System, but there is only a 30 second window to hit it, and a nuclear explosion is still a possibility."

"I guess that's it then." Sean leaned back and wrapped his arms around Alicia.

As the seconds ticked down, Alicia squeezed Sean with all of her strength. His last thought before impact, "She will squeeze the life out of me before the missile arrives."

Then—, nothing. Sean opened his eyes at the same time as Alicia to see David Bowie sitting at the tracking station, decked to the nines in his White Duke persona and everyone else gone. "Honky Dory – was that close? That was close. I was sure you were scrambled spam."

Ignoring the apparition, Sean picked up the phone and called the bridge. Silence was the only response.

"That whole battle was so predictable. You could see them, but they could not see you. I almost turned the telly to the Doctor, but then to see that nuclear warhead headed straight for you and then disappearing, bloody brilliant. How did you manage?"

Alicia exploded. "You arrogant little twit. What the hell was Sean's name doing on their carrier? Who were those people? Were they us?"

"So many questions and so little time." He took off the white fedora from his head, and after several twisting and flipping maneuvers sat it top up on the desk. "Honestly, I have nothing to do with any of the battle elements. Not in my job description. As to the rest of your questions, I think you will figure it out if you are as smart as advertised. I am only here now because of the cause and effect brought about by your victory over the evil forces of

Fascism."

Without saying a word, Sean stood up and walked over to him. Still silent he delivered a vicious punch to Bowie's face. "I think we are done. Do what you will, but that was the last battle we fight under your terms."

Without skipping a beat while he rubbed the spot where had Sean delivered his punch, Bowie responded to Sean's other complaints. "How bloody right you are. You have earned the right to set your own course. That is if Franklin agrees, and as I am sure you have discovered, he can sometimes be infuriatingly unpredictable."

"*Please*. Like you're the image of predictability?" Alicia, usually not one for violence enjoyed Sean's out of character moment. "More and more like Tony," she thought.

"If what you say is true and you truly had nothing to do with that missile simply disappearing before annihilating you and your merry band of sailors, someone much more aware than myself has decided to take an active role."

"You're wasting our time. If you're not here to tell us anything, why are you here?"

Bowie's clothing morphed into that of an old time telegraph operator, replete with armband and visor. He stood ramrod straight as he read from a piece of paper that had materialized. "To let you know that this world is yours to try to fix all the flaws you believe led to the mess you left behind in 2018. Everything you believe to be evil about your history, you can rectify in this one. Unlike your manipulations in 1942, you will quickly discover you can better control your destiny in this time and space, that is if you are correct in your assessments as to why your kind feel it necessary to beat each other over the head with their sense of self-importance.

The paper disappeared. "In a nutshell, if you make your way across the pond and change the entire socioeconomic structures, nasty people will stop showing up to kill you. If you choose to sit on your ass and let the world go by, you will become as extinct as every other society in the Americas."

"So you are telling us that we are supposed to enlighten the world of 1492 with our sense of self-importance? Boy, I can't see how anything could go wrong with unleashing over 10,000 armed to the teeth sailors from the 21st Century."

Alicia was just getting started. "I can see it now. Hello, Mr. and Mrs. King and Queen of name any country. We are here to not only dethrone you, but also to empower your ignorant peasants to think for themselves to build better lives, you know like the lives your former Kings and Queens lived. Then by the end of our lives, or when sanity prevails and whomever sent us on this ridiculous journey allows us to return home, some despot new to history takes our place and the cycle continues."

"I see why you keep her around Sean. She really is more than just a pretty face." Another lit fag appeared in Bowie's hand, which he proceeded to take a drag off and blow in her direction. "Maybe, maybe not. Only time will tell."

Green mist formed out of the cigarette smoke and covered Bowie as he announced his farewell. "Ta-ta for now."

Alicia waved the smoke out of her face. "I *really* hate it when he does that."

Sean shook his head. "I am not buying it. We have seen too much action, counteraction. We have another counterpunch coming."

At this point, the CIC came alive again. "Sir, before the Aegis Ballistic Missile Defense System could engage, the missile simply disappeared."

"Knowing how crazy this has become, I wouldn't be surprised if we wind up in the Aegean Sea with Poseidon himself attacking us with his laser beam trident," Sean quipped, only half kidding.

On the couch in the Admirals Ready Room, after they realized they were still very much alive and the adrenaline rush from such a narrow escape subsided, Tony and Renée shared their own moment of truth. His lips had just come off hers when he caught sight of Franklin sitting at the conference table.

"So much for a little afternoon delight," Renée quipped. "I was just getting started."

Franklin raised his eyebrows. "If only you had the time for me to come back later. Alas, you need to make a life-altering decision right now."

"What are you talking about? Tell me something that hasn't been a part of my daily life for the last two years." Then Tony must have channeled Sean, because he repeated Sean's question to Bowie. "So who controls who? Is Bowie the boss man, or crazy old you. Considering how long you have hung around, my money is on you."

Franklin cocked his head and raised his left eyebrow, as if to say, "Silly boy, why do you still bother to question me." He smiled and three cut crystal wine goblets materialized in their hands. "When wine enters, out comes the truth. Anyway, I must get to why I am here so soon after your miraculous escape. In the most simple of terms, you can stay here or go back to the world you were born to."

Burned too many times to count over the course of their relationship, Tony cut to the chase. "So Renée, I and everyone who came from my reality can all go home, or choose to stay? So who gets hurt if we decide to go, and what do you get out of it when your terms for leaving are unacceptable and we stay?"

"I had such a beautiful speech all prepared that went on and on..."

"Franklin." By now, even Renée knew better.

Franklin shrugged his shoulders. "If I must. If you stay, you help ensure the safety of these wonderful people of the Western Hemisphere and they have a chance. If you leave, they all die as before." Then, looking down and under his breath, he added the clincher. "And no, Renée can't leave with you, and all the others in your group have to agree to stay as well."

Tony liked it better before given the *choice*. "So you lied. There is no choice, and without the agreement of the over 10,000 personnel it would be only Renée and me against the world. When you said there wouldn't be any strings attached, this is what you meant by no strings?"

This question confused Renée. "When did he say that? Strings attached to what? Me?"

Tony quickly diverted the conversation. "By the way, what the hell was Sean's name doing on that Nazi ship? Did we just kill ourselves?"

"No harm in letting you know that they were your counterparts from a reality where Hitler conquered America, only two generations removed. Truthfully, as you know by the direction your government took, absolute power always leads to brutality, and bombastic hubris becomes the norm. You came to understand that for you to survive in the world you left behind, it demanded the same blind obedience to power.

"The difference is you and anyone else aware enough to see, came upon the reality far too late to change the oppressive state of affairs. Though, truth be told, you never had a chance to begin with. However, right here and right now you can create your own truths, and as an added bonus you will live a *very* long time if you and your friends decide to stay."

"That's a lot of truths." Tony didn't have a problem spending the rest of his life living among the Taíno, especially now that Renée was there to share the joy, but he turned to Renée for her take. "What do you think? I have to admit the lack of luxuries and the simplest of amenities suck, but the people and the environment more than make up for what you lose."

"Seriously Tony, if it wasn't for me, would you stay, or was that part of the deal that brought me back. Was I some kind of bargaining chip in all of this and you won the bet?" Not only did Franklin's terms upset Renée, the thought that she was part of some grand bargain made her want to kick both men in the balls.

Tony knew it was hopeless to avoid it, so he told her the whole story of when he first met Franklin, and when he finished, he apologized. "So it wasn't so much a struck deal, as a reminder of what I could have. You never left my mind from the day I lost you."

"I can vouch for that," Franklin offered in support.

"Thanks Benji." Tony put his arms around Renée's waist and continued. "I never believed you would return regardless of his promise, but if there was even a one percent chance I would have agreed to take on Columbus by myself." He tried to give her a kiss, but Renée turned her head.

"You're not off the hook yet mister." She turned her attention back to Franklin. "If I am real, why would going home end my life? What exactly am I?"

"If all goes to plan possibly a goddess and mother figure to hundreds of millions." Franklin then performed a perfect bow fit for King Louis the XIV. "However, the goddess part can only happen if, like I said, your merry band of brothers and sisters decide to remain as well. Otherwise, you get the usual fifty to 60-year lifespan." Then once again, under his breath, he added, "Followed by a constant stream of disease ridden Europeans landing on these shores with no one to stop them once you are dead.

"In other words, if you can't change the barbaric ways of the Old World Order, all you have done is delay the inevitable." Franklin paused for effect, tilted his head, shrugged his shoulders, and smiled. "On the other hand, if you managed to give the Old World something else to worry about without blowing them up to get their attention, maybe you could buy your beautiful subjects the one or two hundred extra years they require to prepare a proper defense against the heathens. Did I mention that you would live much, much longer in order to accomplish this?"

Tony saw issues as well with the idea. "You can't expect thousands of sailors to agree to that, and you can't expect me to try to convince them they should, especially if every time we turn around someone pops up to try to kill us. When you refuse to give the slightest hint what the endgame is, I get nervous. What constitutes victory?"

"As I stated, if you go to Europe, no boom, boom, no threat. It is all right in front of you to figure out. As you so succinctly stated the longer these people and weapons remain, it will be only a matter of time before attrition brings defeat. Once you make your decision, it is irrevocable, and I will disappear once again into the mists of time. One thing that could help you convince the meek among you, is to remind them that as long as they don't get themselves killed in battle their lives will endure tenfold."

Franklin bowed down low while removing his hat and sweeping it across his chest. With these final words, he began to fade. "The Queen awaits."

In the most desolate region of the Southern Pacific Ocean, one thousand miles from the nearest land, a ballistic missile suddenly appeared out of thin air 30,000 feet above the water. Seconds later, at an altitude of 500 feet above the ocean surface, its nuclear payload exploded, obliterating a few stray birds and a pod of dolphins minding their own business. As the missile descended, in her last act of defiance, one of the female dolphins admonished her mate. "You know this is your fault, don't you? I told you we should have migrated weeks ago."

Long ago tired of her sniping, he leaped high into the air enthusiastically greeting the blast with his final thought being, "Anything would be preferable over another minute with you."

⊶⊷

Darius [Carl Eddington] knew his decision to intercept the nuclear missile would bring a smile to his adversary's face, but nobody ever said that saving humanity would go flawlessly. "Not exactly what I wanted to do, but not the end of the world either. Besides, it was time to stir the pot again anyway," he mused.

"Why didn't you let their Aegis Ballistic Missile Defense System take it out?"

"I couldn't take the chance the nuke would explode when the missile hit it," Darius explained. "If I lose Rebecca this time, it's over."

Cromulus [Jesus] shook his head in agreement. "As much as I enjoy watching you wrestle with your objectives, Darius, I still don't see how any of it gains you an advantage. From what I've seen so far, this is still a family matter between you and Durius, and to tell you the truth, regardless of her caustic personality, she still has an equal say regarding the outcome of your pets."

Darius smiled as if he knew something Cromulus didn't. "I'm counting on it."

"You are also putting a lot of trust in people who lack even the most fundamental powers of observation. I mean really, Darius, I don't see an Einstein or Confucius in the bunch. I believe the saying goes something along the lines of bringing a knife to a gunfight."

This elicited a chuckle from Darius. "Coming from the King of Kings, I'd think you would favor my odds purely from the moral high ground, which by the way you know I happen to be holding. Considering the story of David defeating Goliath came from your overly imaginative mind, I would think with Sean Anthony's crew and their youthful optimism in the mix, you might show a little more faith in my judgment."

"Look at what faith did for me Darius. I was barely off the cross when my disciples began to twist everything I had preached to suit their contemporary audiences. Then I found it amazing how their successors changed the message to whatever suited their means. When did I ever say, 'Blessed are the sociopaths for they shall torture and enslave their way through the gates of heaven.'"

Darius sat with Cromulus in a modest home overlooking the

Mediterranean Ocean on one of the many Greek Islands that dotted the Aegean Sea. On the opposite end of the room stood a portal that allowed them to see right through to Bowie's conversation with Sean and Alicia, and then Franklin's with Tony and Renée that was about to begin.

"Knowing Durius, it shouldn't be long before she responds." Cromulus wanted to know what Darius had in mind when she did.

Darius waved off his concern. "You know as well as I do the most Durius can do is bring in a force relative to the one I saved, and I have every confidence my people will handle the challenge. Besides, I've made sure she has better things to do elsewhere than to hang around this little backwater for too long."

Cromulus disagreed with Darius's lack of concern. "As I recall, the last time anything similar occurred, she re-routed an asteroid twenty miles across, and used it to kill off almost every living thing on the planet. Like the nuclear explosion that went off over the Pacific, she will only need a moment. I could see her using one of the many off planet lowlifes to pull a "Take me to your leader moment, or better yet, building a zombie army."

"If she reanimates the dead Cromulus, then you can make good on your second coming promise by convincing them their Day of Judgment has arrived. Besides, when you've finished it would screw with all those still left behind who thought they would find their place in heaven."

"Thanks for reminding me of the lost opportunity for my big second coming of Jesus moment. Your dance with Durius put a kibosh on that ever happening. If I knew what you were up to sooner, I might have shown up as Jesus more often. Of course, if I had, it would have cheapened the grand finale. Think of it, Jesus walking on water right outside of Manhattan. Or better yet, Jesus going to Disneyland on Easter day."

Carl interjected. "How about Jesus as a guest on the Daily Show?"

"That would have been one hell of a show."

In truth, Darius counted on his ex to react impulsively. "That Durius had Rebecca in her sights and I interceded will lead her into a purely emotional act of violence, which will be painful, but not something I can't handle."

"Or she can appeal for a judgment against your actions, which could be far worse. Hell, even I would have to rule in her favor. Either way, you had better hope those who are ambivalent to your wishes remain so. With your success still far from certain, calling attention to yourself will come back to bite you in the ass, if it hasn't already."

"That is awfully cynical coming from the *Son of God*. Besides, I haven't given it a second thought, and do you know why?" Darius answered his own question before Cromulus could. "Because my shrew of an ex-wife has dulled the senses of anyone who cared to take a peek over the last 25,000 years. Nothing ever changes. Man rises, man falls, and it is always a man. You can count on one hand the times where a woman rises and falls. I should have done something much sooner, like you did 3,000 years earlier when the Pharaohs reigned supreme."

"You mean my little sit down with Akhenaten and Nefertiti?"

"You definitely played the long game when you introduced Aten, the first monotheistic god in history, to the Egyptians, which led to the Jewish god and ultimately to you as Jesus and Christianity. These days you have exactly fifteen minutes to impact millions before some vapid diva leaking her sex tape steals your thunder."

Jesus sighed. "They sure knew how to throw together a temple back then."

"You mean *you* knew how to. Who else but you would be so over the top to build the Great Pyramid so you could generate enough power for cold lemonade? If the archeologists only knew." Darius wanted to get back on message. "Anyway the main reason so much is at risk is…"

Cromulus finished Darius's thought. "Your pets are too easy to sway. That's what you get for overriding their survival instincts with a liberal dose of emotions." Cromulus shook his head in pity. "You wanted to evolve your pets, yet no matter how many attempts you made to push them along with bigger and better toys, it still came down to clubbing the girl over the head and dragging her back to the man cave.

"I performed miracles that were every bit as clever as yours have been; yet, here it is 2,000 years later and I am still the most popular kid in school while you sit in the shadows. Imagine if I had the use of an aircraft carrier back then." Cromulus picked up his glass of water, which turned into wine before reaching his lips.

Darius shook his head in agreement. "Can you imagine me trying to pull off the whole *offer my blood for their salvation* bit, and getting away with it?"

Cromulus laughed at the thought. "And that is why you used someone as suave and manipulative as me instead. It's too bad you didn't foresee how Durius would use it as a battle cry. Last I checked, it was about fifty-fifty on lives saved against lives taken in the name of Jesus, same old same old. You're a fool if you think you can ever change this equation, knowing as I do that only a small fraction of your pets can think past where their next meal is coming from, let alone survive the intellectual jump you have in mind."

"Exactly correct." Darius leaned back, closed his eyes, and smiled. "I can see why you would think my situation is hopeless with Durius holding all the cards, and me with only a few exceptional individuals. Truth be told the battle is mine to lose, and she doesn't have a clue."

"Good luck with that. Why don't we count how often the humble, noble of heart, or intellectually enlightened have held sway over the masses?" Cromulus countered sarcastically as he scrolled brutal images of thousands of people being tortured across the opening in the wall. "Most of these were the best and the brightest, who Durius kept feeding to those who only saw them as threats. Remind me again exactly how many Einsteins did she have tortured and killed before one finally slipped through the cracks."

"All you are doing is making my case," Darius replied confidently. "Better oblivion than another one thousand years of this shit." Darius changed the images to a Disneyesque flyover of an untouched landscape. Small settlements lay scattered throughout scenes of pastoral beauty.

"You are a hopeless romantic who is unable to see that when the Pied Piper pipes, the rats will follow. You can't remove the fear of a hungry tiger ripping them to shreds from their DNA any more than you can replace it with bliss and harmony. Look at us. We have had a billion years to evolve into many forms, and yet where are we in our understanding of the totality of existence?"

"Stuck in a conversation like this, is where." Darius was anxious to move on, so with a thought, the portal image changed to the Enterprise Admirals Ready Room. "This should interest you."

Cromulus took a seat on the couch next to Darius as bowls of buttered popcorn appeared on their laps. "Has it got subtitles? I love movies with subtitles."

Excerpt • Book IV

From the Judgment In Time Series
Another Side of Armageddon

"Yes Sir," Renée acknowledged. "It seems Commander Gable has a Taíno scholar under his command named Lt. Commander Maria Brizuela, and it turns out she had some interesting information to share."

"Brizuela, what an interesting name. Where does she hail from?" Sean asked.

"The name dates back to a Taíno cacique, or chief, named Brizuela of Baitiquirí, which is on the coast about twelve miles east of the entrance to Guantanamo Bay. According to history, he is ruling there now. She has studied the Taíno as well as the history of all the pre-Columbian peoples of the Western Hemisphere since she was 9 years old."

Sean shook his head in disbelief. "Correct me if I'm wrong, but isn't it an incredible stroke of good luck to have someone so versed in an almost completely lost culture right here in our midst?"

To Sean this sounded like something Bowie or Franklin would have dreamed up. "Are you sure she is for real?"